Yates fired at the enemy . . .

De Kuyper fired back with a plasma discharger.

Sam Yates dived out of the doorway in reaction to the first plasma bolt, though it was past him and crashing on the far wall before his brain told his body to move.

The fireball congealed, some of it across his back and shoulders. When he hit the floor beside the two women, the sheet of redeposited glass shivered off in flakes and shards as his muscles flexed.

They weren't going to win a slugfest against a plasma discharger in the hands of a man who knew how to use it.

"Come *on* and keep *low*!" Yates said . . .

Other books by Janet Morris

THE KERRION EMPIRE TRILOGY

DREAM DANCER
CRUISER DREAMS
EARTH DREAMS

THIEVES' WORLD™ NOVELS

BEYOND SANCTUARY™
BEYOND THE VEIL
BEYOND WIZARDWALL

Other books by David Drake

HAMMER'S SLAMMERS

JANET MORRIS
and DAVID DRAKE

KILL
RATIO

ACE BOOKS, NEW YORK

This book is an Ace original edition, and
has never been previously published.

KILL RATIO

An Ace Book / published by arrangement with
the authors

PRINTING HISTORY
Ace edition / October 1987

ISBN: 0-441-44116-5

Ace Books are published by
The Berkley Publishing Group,
200 Madison Avenue, New York, New York 10016.
The name "ACE" and the "A" logo
are trademarks belonging to Charter Communications, Inc.

PRINTED IN THE UNITED STATES OF AMERICA

10 9 8 7 6 5 4 3 2 1

PART ONE

Chapter 1

DINNER FOR ONE

If Sam Yates hadn't been so upset by the call he'd just gotten from his wife back on Earth, he might have paid more attention to his waiter before the fellow died.

Communicate through my lawyer, Cecile'd written in the note she sent after slamming the phone down a month ago. He'd called her then to say he was accepting the transfer to the headquarters to the UN Directorate of Security.

On the Moon.

Cecile'd said she wanted to talk about his feelings. More accurately, she'd wanted to tell him what his feelings were . . . and when he disagreed, she'd hung up on him. That was fine, since it absolved Yates of a duty he was otherwise going to feel no matter what.

But *why* in the name of all that's holy was Cecile calling him directly, now—at his office—to natter on in her usual fashion at Earth-Moon rates?

"Sit here, please," said the Arab waiter to another customer, a little man whose puffy, pasty features indicated that he had been away from Earth's sun and gravity much longer than Sam Yates.

Le Moulin Rouge served French cuisine, but it was owned and operated by what had been a family of Algerian diplomats accredited to the UN. They were Arabs, only two generations removed from their Egyptian roots. The Kabyle Revolution had deprived them of their diplomatic posts and probably gave them good reasons not to return to Algeria as well. The restaurant was an obvious source of livelihood for expatriates who chose to remain on the Moon.

The little man trying to insist on a separate table for himself obviously didn't understand the peculiar conditions

3

of the Moon. Yates wasn't a cop—not really: he nudged microchip files—but categories were his life, and the argument caused him to shift his tablemate from one slot to another. The fellow wasn't a Moon local, as he'd assumed, but rather a recent visitor from an orbital habitat.

It was a paradox of human psychology that space was at a premium on the Moon, a planet comparable to Mercury or Mars in size; but orbital habitats, built in hard vacuum, were under no such restraints. The first construction at a habitat site was the electromagnetic envelope which turned away the hard radiation of space. A habitat could be armored with slag to soak up radiation the way the Earth's atmosphere did, but that wasn't nearly as practical for an installation that was expected to grow over a period of years.

As soon as an electromagnetic shield was in place, it could be expanded simply by reeling out more wire and boosting the current flow. Habitats grew like coral reefs, accreting layers of aluminum beams and foamed-glass paneling on the outside. Often the habitat's rotation was slowed while progressive demolition turned the old core areas into low-gravity recreation areas.

But humans on the Moon lived in tunnels carven through rock, a laborious process complicated by the difficulties of getting from one point on the perimeter of a colony to another. Much of the volume created when teams tunneled outward had to be devoted to roadways. On an orbital habitat elevators crossed the center of the dome or sphere and reached the opposite perimeter with very little intrusion into the population's living area.

It would have been easy enough to build up from the lunar surface, creating structures similar to those of orbital habitats, except that they were stressed against the Moon's real gravity instead of the centrifugal force that mimicked gravity off-planet. The problem was that the mass of the Moon prevented electromagnetic shielding, and the faint lunar atmosphere and magnetic field did little to protect humans on the surface from the constant, omnidirectional sleet of cosmic rays. Even transportation across a colony was as difficult on the surface as it was beneath several meters of shielding rock.

But the most important reason lunar colonies were underground was that humans on the Moon clung to tunnels as the proper way to live, with the fervor of northerners refusing to give up their clothing in the tropics of Earth. The edge between survival and death for humans was so narrow everywhere off the planet on which they evolved, that customary uses quickly gained the stature of laws graven on stone.

So the dining area of Le Moulin Rouge was cramped into six double tables, and the likelihood of the little man from a habitat occupying a table alone was roughly equal to his chances of floating home without a ship to carry him. Yates tried to ignore the silly argument beside him by glancing at his fellow diners until his *truit amadine* arrived.

Only two of them were women—a consideration never far from the surface of Sam Yates' mind. A party of Indian diplomats filled the tables on the other side of the narrow aisle. In addition to the five men in severe suits and string ties, there was a woman wearing an orange sari and a caste mark on her forehead.

Yates' side of the restaurant had a more diverse clientele. Two men at the table behind him were talking volubly in low voices. The language sounded Slavic to Yates, but he couldn't be sure even of that.

The two people at the table closest to the kitchen door were not a couple. The man was craggy, severe, and wore a full black beard that added an apparent ten years to what was probably his real age of forty or so. Like Yates, he was waiting for his meal. The way his hand hovered over his ordinary goblet of water suggested that he, like the little man arguing with the waiter, was from an orbital habitat where the rims of tumblers were turned against the slosh induced by rotation. He did not speak, and his eyes focused inward with no attention on his immediate surroundings.

Part of those surroundings was the woman who shared his table. She was as well worth a man's attention as anybody Yates had met thus far on the Moon.

She had short black hair and a skin whose translucent white avoided the pastiness that drove many of the Moon's inhabitants to tanning lamps. The neutral colors of the woman's skin and hair made her a true exception, a person on whom kaleidoscopic contact lenses were attractive instead of being merely fashionable.

As she lifted a careful spoonful of onion soup from beneath its insulating blanket of cheese and crouton, those dazzling, prismatic eyes met Yates'. The woman looked away as her features hardened into something less attractive.

Yates looked away also, embarrassed in spite of himself. It wasn't a crime to look—wasn't a crime to *ask,* for God's sake, and he'd always been willing to take no for an answer.

He didn't get told no very often, of course.

The little man sat across from Yates, stiff with an emotion the security man assumed was anger. Yates nodded to him, a gesture calculated to lie between curt insult and a desire for conversation. The cultural assumptions behind the nod were those of central Pennsylvania, where Yates was born and raised; not those of the Moon, and certainly not those of the habitat from which this visitor came.

Which the categorical part of Sam Yates had decided was Sky Devon. It *might* be Sky Devon, the agricultural habitat funded by British "farmers"—most of whom were titled—with the aim of one day supplying the food requirements of all humans off-Earth. A self-sustaining orbital farming operation—foods that humans *liked* to eat, not simply algae to cleanse and reoxygenate the atmosphere—was the most expensive part of an orbital habitat, as well as being more difficult to set up and maintain than nonbiological construction processes.

Sky Devon was intended to replace self-sufficiency in the design parameters of future habitats. The low cost of orbit-to-orbit ballistic trajectories was combined with biological expertise in tailoring plants and animals to controlled levels of light and gravity. The biotechnicians and agronomists of Sky Devon were in every professional way the equals of the engineers employed on metallurgical and power satellites.

The little man's Yorkshire accent, coupled with a jacket of lightweight tweed, made Sky Devon his most likely provenance. That didn't matter to Yates, beyond the fact that it was a win in a game that he played with himself, and wins were pretty damn hard to come by, some days.

A dumb twat like Cecile shouldn't have been able to get to him. Not that she was that stupid. And not that the whole thing, the marriage and the reasons the marriage hadn't worked, weren't more the fault of Sam Yates than of any of the remaining five billion possibilities, give or take, in the human universe.

Yates raised his water glass. His tablemate was staring after the waiter and growling.

No, by God, he was subvocalizing, speaking in the back of his throat to trip what must have been an implanted microphone, because there was no mike pad visible above the collar of jacket. That was unusual enough to make the security man in Yates wonder—until his ice water bathed him, nostrils, eyes, and forehead to the line of his dark blond hair.

The Moon's gravity was sufficient to make Earth-standard tableware perfectly practical, but it demanded slight differences in technique. Mostly it demanded a little care, and Yates hadn't had enough time on the Moon to develop care at a reflexive level when his conscious mind was distracted.

Just now the Moon had reminded him that the water in his glass had as much inertia as it would on Earth, even though there was only a sixth as much gravity to hold it back when the container stopped at the level of the drinker's lips. Yates sputtered, the focus for everyone else in the restaurant. The waiter, returning from the kitchen with a pair of croissants and a ball of whipped butter, paused to snatch up a napkin to replace the one with which the embarrassed customer now mopped himself dry.

Out of the corner of his eye Yates could see the woman with prismatic lenses giggle, then look away demurely as she raised another spoonful of hot soup.

Well, it had been that sort of day, hadn't it?

Thinking of Cecile tossed Yates' mind back to the woman at the next table. She ought to smile more. Good humor turned features that could otherwise look sharp, almost jagged, into something close to real beauty.

The body wasn't bad either. He'd seen bigger tits than the pair beneath the dress of black fabric with a white stripe woven in with deliberate irregularity. Still, these breasts were the right pair for the ensemble—taut body, firm legs, and better muscle tone than Yates expected to claim himself after he'd been in low gravity as long as she'd been.

The way she moved proved she'd been on the Moon for

a while. Her motions were smooth as those of a gear train: without the fits and starts that would, for instance, have spilled soup from her spoon. There was also an underwater slowness about the arcs that her hands described. Faster movements, no matter how smooth, would spill fluid from an open-topped container—the way Yates had drenched himself with his water glass.

The Arab waiter set the dish of croissants down beside the tall, bearded man sharing a table with the woman. The fellow ignored the food—and the water—with a studiousness that would have constituted a deliberate snub under other circumstances. Was it some sort of cultural thing? Goodness knew where the bearded man came from.

Now that Yates thought about it, he realized that the fellow *hadn't* stared when Yates had made his newcomer's error with the water glass. That pair of eyes, set deep in a craggy face, remained turned toward—if not focused on—a wall during the impromptu comedy. The bearded man was either preoccupied, drugged to inertness, or—just possibly—scared out of his mind.

"Permit me, sir," said the waiter in French-accented English. He set down the fresh napkin and whisked the damp one out of Yates' hand before the security man recalled himself to the business of being a customer in a restaurant.

Yates wondered how many other languages the waiter spoke. English would be technically sufficient in a diplomatic enclave like this; but part of the ambiance of a restaurant was the degree to which it took the customer's personality into account.

The waiter coughed, spattering the security man and the table with fluids. Yate's tablemate flung himself backward into the wall—a load-bearing section of living rock which didn't quiver at the impact.

The waiter covered his mouth with the wet napkin. His eyes above the linen looked startled. Yates blinked at him in surprise, then glanced away in transferred enbarrassment. Didn't seem to be anybody's day. At least customers at other tables weren't staring at the waiter the way they had when Yates' water—

The spatters on the tablecloth were ruby, and the drop that the waiter had coughed into Yates' glass was swirling and dissolving in eddies of fresh blood.

Yates was a big man, six-two and, on Earth, a hundred ninety pounds, but he placed more stock in his quickness than he did in mere physical strength. He stood, his braced legs hurling the table in one direction and his chair in the other as he reached for the waiter.

The man coughed again, then threw himself away from the hands Yates was clamping about his shoulders to restrain him. The motion was convulsive, not a deliberate attempt to escape. The napkin flapped to the ceiling, then drifted down. It was soaked with blood of so bright a crimson that it looked orange.

Yates' chair had clattered against the table across the aisle, exciting the sextet of Indians into a flurry of motion and words in several non-English languages. They didn't know what was happening.

Neither did Sam Yates, except that the waiter was dead even as his body arched toward the table where the woman and the bearded man sat.

Yates had three years in the U.S. Army behind him, two of them spent in Central America while President Stewart tried to make the world safe for oligarchy by stationing an American soldier in every hut in Nicaragua. He'd seen men die like this before, an instant after an unstable bullet hit then on one side of the chest and keyholed through both lungs before blasting a hole out the other side as well.

He should have heard the shot. Damage like this was a velocity effect, and the ballistic crack of a multisonic bullet ought to have echoed like machine-gun fire in these narrow confines.

The waiter's body sent the French onion soup off in a lazy trajectory of its own as the table collapsed and the black-haired woman tried with partial success to avoid the corpse. Her mouth was open but she was not screaming, and the hand she raised toward Yates was an instinctive defense against the man whom she believed was responsible for the waiter's bloody collapse.

The bearded man rotated his head to watch the body thrashing on the overturned table. His attention was mechanical, a thing that his eyes were doing while the higher faculties of his mind remained dissociated.

Sam Yates had more pressing problems than the varied reactions of the diners between whom the corpse lay. No one from that direction had shot the waiter, so someone at the outside door must have—

Or maybe not.

The two Europeans who had been seated at the table nearest the door were in panicked flight. As the security man turned, one of the pair slammed the red emergency exit plate set into the center of the clear door panel. Alarms rang, audibly and at the nearest patrol substation.

The door, impeded by those waiting outside, did not open immediately. The customers in the corridor had become spectators. They pressed against the door for a better look, their faces suffused with interest rather than terror.

Nobody'd been shooting from the corridor. The sight and sound of the weapon would have scattered those people like bits of a dynamited tomato.

Yates almost grabbed the two Europeans, but the goblets and flatware they'd been using were scattered across their table. The men weren't escaping assassins, but just a pair of citizens terrified by gouts of pulmonary blood. They'd be needed for evidence, but the fingerprints they left all over the utensils made them easy to find. Hell, they'd probably contact Security themselves, once they'd talked to their home government and their panic had subsided.

Couldn't blame them for panic. Yates' hands were scarlet with the reminder of the waiter's dying hemorrhage.

No one ran from the kitchen in response to the alarm. Humans were too rare—and therefore expensive—on the Moon for service industries to be staffed at levels that would have been normal on Earth. One waiter, supplemented from the kitchen at need, handled all the dining-area fuctions, including those of maitre d' and cashier.

The door to the corridor kept diners in the restaurant until they had paid and would-be customers outside until there were tables to seat them. Because that was normal on the Moon, diplomats from UN Headquarters accepted Four Star food in an ambiance close to that of a Downside—Earth—lunch counter.

But there was additional staff in the kitchen. Yates banged through the swinging door and headed for the phone, half expecting to slam aside a cook running into the dining area to see why someone had pushed the alarm that unlocked the way to the corridor.

One of the four people in the kitchen was alive. She was a woman in her late teens, dark-haired but with blue Kabyle eyes. Instead of screaming, she huddled in the angle formed by a wall and the oven. Her knees were raised to her chest, and she had pressed the knuckles of both hands against her teeth.

The smell of burning flesh probably came from the middle-aged man who lay across the range top with a spatula in one charring hand. A refrigerator stood open, and a tray of salads had fallen across the woman who had collapsed in front of it. A second man, old enough to be the father of the first, was sprawled where the door had slid him as the security man entered.

It had been a long time since Sam Yates had seen that much human blood in one place. Not since he'd inspected a bunker after a heavy mortar shell had pierced the roof and exploded among seventeen Nicaraguan children.

There was a phone to the left side of the door. Yates' eyes were flat as he stepped toward it, wiping his bloody right palm on his shirt front so that he wouldn't ruin his jacket—or the evidence on-site.

The little man who had been at Yates' table was in the way, still muttering under his breath as he scanned the kitchen.

Sam Yates had been cool—not calm, just emotionless—to that moment, operating by reflexes that he hadn't needed since he left Central America. This one wasn't his job, he just happened to be here, and there was enough human emotion under those reflexes for Yates to grab the little ghoul by both lapels and slam him against the wall. "What the *hell* d'ye think you're doing, buddy?" the security man shouted in the other's face. "Get out or—"

Or what? the fellow from Sky Devon—assuming—was terrified, not a curiosity-seeker at all. He was saying, "The woman in the corner appears to be alive and unharmed, though deeply frightened. The man at our feet is not moving. The man—"

"*Jesus!*" Yates shouted, brushing himself free of the

little man whose flat "ays" made his cold voice sound like that of a machine running at too low a voltage. A would-be Good Samaritan, scared to death, and now with his clothing bloodied by a newcomer to Headquarters Security who'd rushed in where he had no business. Congratulations, Cecile, you'll be delighted to know that you've helped your husband fuck up his career on a whole new planet. . . .

Yates took his identification card from the case in his inner breast pocket and set it against the wall phone's speaker/microphone plate. Instead of keying his identification number into the card's minuscule pad, he poked the red triangle for Emergency.

Behind him the little man was walking stilt-legged around the kitchen, muttering to himself in a quietly demented fashion. He pinched the fabric of his jacket away from his chest in apparent fear that the bloody smudges Yates left on the tweed would soak through to his skin.

The fabric couldn't have been pure wool after all—there'd been a slick stiffness to the lapels. Maybe it wouldn't cost Yates a month's salary to replace—assuming that he had a salary after he'd manhandled a citizen that way.

"Emergency, Specialist Gomes," said the speaker plate in the voice of a woman whose first language was not English.

The wall niche in which the restaurant's phone was recessed was big enough for a view screen, but the instrument itself was voice only, like most of those in the UN colony. The designers had not figured on the influx—inevitable, nonarchitects would have said—of hangers-on who would follow transfer of the UN's formal headquarters to the Moon.

Space was at a premium, but more important, the lines that had been laid in bedrock and intended to handle the colony's communications needs into the twenty-second century, were overloaded seventy years before then—and nobody wanted to face the disruption their replacement would entail.

You could still get full audio-visual connections if you were willing to pay for them. The cost for that order-of-magnitude increase in line usage ensured that your screen would be blank unless you were calling a chief of mission—in which case you'd see a receptionist exceptional for beauty, as defined by the employing nation.

"This is Supervisor Samuel Yates, Entry Division," said the security man, bumping his knees against the wall as he bent to talk directly into the plate. The phone hadn't been installed for somebody of his height. *Nothing* much had been, except for the offices of people with too much rank to be Yates' business. "You've got an alarm call at Le Moulin Rouge, Central Sector, but I don't have the coordinates. You've got four dead here and a woman in shock, so don't . . ."

The fellow from Sky Devon slipped out the door, already open because the woman with kaleidoscope lenses was standing there, listening to Yates.

". . . just leave it for the next patrol, okay?"

"One moment, please," said the speaker plate while the dispatcher checked location and availability of personnel.

The woman's prismatic eyes were squarely on Yates as he waited for the dispatcher. That might have been a way to avoid looking at the bodies and the incredible quantity of gore elsewhere in the kitchen, but her chin was thrust out firmly in a triumph of will over emotion. It struck the security man that most people didn't have a past life that fitted them to function in carnage of this sort.

"There is a uniformed team on its way to you now, sir," said the dispatcher in her singsong intonations, interspersed with crackling from a speaker that had not been improved by the grease-laden air of a commercial kitchen. "Full medical will follow as soon as possible. You must understand that there have been many calls this shift, very many."

"All right, I'll stand by," said Yates, as though he were more than an innocent bystander himself. He poked the keypad to close the circuit.

"You're from Security, then," said the woman beside him with a quaver that could have been a result of the corpses. Equally, it might mean that she thought he was the murderer. Guts either way, Yates supposed.

"Why are you here?"

A throaty voice, and that was more than the constriction of fear. "Because I asked my division head where a good restaurant was," Yates said, not snapping, but pumped enough to respond in kind to the accusation in the woman's voice.

At home Security meant jack boots and rubber truncheons to a lot of UN members. Over the years Sam Yates had gotten damn good and tired of the way faces froze and eyes took on a glassy patina when he mentioned his job. This woman sounded like an American, but she obviously thought he had something to do with what had happened here.

Whatever the hell that was.

"You know me, now," said the big man. "Who the hell are you?"

He let his eyes travel past her and out into the dining area beyond. Two of the Indians were there, looking very staunch and afraid. Everybody else had run, and none of the people pressing against the glass from the corridor showed any interest in coming in.

The waiter still lay across the overturned table, his face covered with blood and amazement.

"I'm Dr. Elinor Bradley of NYU," the woman replied in a voice too bold to be fearless. "But I'm fully accredited to the General Secretariat, and my studies have the backing of important people in both the Secretariat and the government of my own nation."

You can't push me *around, you dumb cop*, Yates translated mentally. True enough, probably, and because he didn't even want to—this wasn't *his* job, for Chrissake—the security man found her attitude amusing rather than a challenge.

The crowd outside the door rippled away like chilled molasses when an open car holding four uniformed patrolmen pulled up in the corridor. Yates realized belatedly that the clear panel was still locked. Swallowing the question he was about to ask Bradley, he moved toward the door in a forgetfully-mighty stride. His foot lifted another of the tables against the wall and back again with a violent crash.

The two Indians, both males, skittered to the opposite side of the room, reasonably concerned about where the Downsider's clumsiness was going to take him next.

The uniformed lieutenant let herself and her patrol in with

a pass key, a computer identification card no thicker than Yates' own.

The lieutenant braced him—caught him, really. It wasn't Yates' day.

Though his day was going a lot better than that of the four Arabs sprawled in the restaurant.

"I was just eating here," said Yates, letting his card ID him for the uniforms. The lieutenant's name tag read Yesilkov, and the short hair beneath her cap was pale blond. "The guy coughed blood, then hemorrhaged like he'd been opened up with a machete. Didn't hear the shot, and there's three more the same way in the kitchen, with a live one in shock."

"Todd, Shedron," the lieutenant ordered, gesturing a pair of her men toward the kitchen with two fingers. She looked chunky and competent. Yates might be two pay grades higher than a uniformed lieutenant in bookkeeping's scheme of things, but he was just another witness for the moment.

The third patrolman was already bending over the waiter's corpse, setting up a field diagnostic trellis from the satchel he carried.

"Four deaths-by-violence," Lieutenant Yesilkov grumbled as she eyed the room: Yates; the Indians, stiff enough to be expecting a firing squad; Elinor Bradley, moving toward Yates with tiny steps too precise to be described as "drifting closer." "And they tell me it'll be an hour before they can get us a full medical." She swore in Russian.,

"Ah," said Yates. "That one—her name's Bradley, she was at another table. She's a doctor."

"Officer, I'm an anthropologist," said Bradley in haste, with an angry glance at Yates, as if she thought the security man had scored off her deliberately. "I can't help with the, ah, with these, but perhaps I could talk to the woman who's in shock?"

Yesilkov might have given the anthropologist more than an amused grimace if the black-haired woman had bothered to get the rank right. As it was, the lieutenant said, "Thanks, madam, but no problem." She toed the satchel beside the waiter's body. "Todd'll bring her out of it. Better living through chemistry, you know.''

The third patrolman had deployed his diagnostic trellis over the corpse and was keying preset questions into the control box which also acted as the base to which the sensors were attached. A tracery of probes, elbowed and crossed for stiffness, covered the body like a silver cobweb. The tip of each wire touched the waiter's skin, generally after having penetrated his garments.

"Dead seven minutes thirty, Sonya," said the patrolman. "Unless he was running a fever?" The man looked up, at Yates rather than at his superior.

Yates shrugged, spreading his hands palms up to explain that he hadn't the faintest idea of the waiter's state of health. He'd forgotten about the blood until he saw Bradley and the two uniforms start as their eyes followed the gesture.

"I was, you know, holding him when he died," the big security man said, feeling more than a little awkward. Things had cooled off enough that his mind was becoming that of a social animal and no longer that of a hunted one surrounded by death.

"Right," said the lieutenant, perhaps to ease the embarrassment, and she motioned her subordinate back to his usual work with a curve of her left index finger. Yates noted that she always used her left hand for conversational gestures, though her right could not be said exactly to hover over the needle stunner in its cut-away holster. "There were more people here when it happened?"

"Yes," said the anthropologist, interjecting herself into the conversation from which the others' eyes had excluded her. "All the seats were occupied."

"They were part of a party of six," Yates added mildly, motioning toward the Indians. It was no skin off his ass if the woman wanted a piece of this. "The rest'll be pretty easy to find from fingerprints, I'd guess. Most people just, you know, bolted because they didn't know what was going on."

It would be nice if the guy from Sky Devon stayed gone, at least until he forgot about Yates throwing him around . . . but what the hell, that'd better go in the formal report. Blame it on nerves.

There was reason enough to be a little nervy, after all.

"No sign of puncture, Sonya," said the patrolman, frowning at the blue-green tungsten-sulfide readout of the trellis control. "I ran it three times, but no skin breaks—just conductivity changes where he puked blood on himself."

"Look, Xao, just gimme hard copy, okay?" said the lieutenant in irritation. With less overt emotion, she continued to Yates, "All right, sir, can you—"

"Sonya, the tape spool on this unit's deadlined," said the patrolman, looking up at his superior. "I can't get hard copy till we're back at the station."

Yesilkov swore again. Yates understood only the tone, but from the analytical look on Bradley's face, he assumed that she had enough Russian to translate. A really scatological language, he'd heard. Maybe he ought to learn it. It'd be useful to describe the way things were going lately.

One of the two patrolmen stepped through the swinging door of the kitchen, supporting the surviving woman. His right arm was around her waist and her left hand in his, as if they were lovers. Her broad, swarthy face was blank, her blue eyes were almost beatifically empty.

The patrolman looked as if he were about to add to the present mess by vomiting. Well, Yates had tossed his cookies the first time he walked into a similar situation, back when he was about the patrolman's age.

"Lieutenant," the patrolman said, "nobody came in and did it, it just happened, she says."

He took off his cap and wiped his forehead with it, then placed his hand back on the survivor's waist—the human support was not all one-sided. She was murmuring words, but they were not in a language Yates understood.

The patrolman added apologetically, "I got the dose too high, Lieutenant. She speaks English okay, but she's down in this now—dunno what it is, but Todd don't think it's Arabic."

Bradley looked at the patrol lieutenant but managed to avoid even the hint of a knowing smile. Yates doubted that he could have managed equal restraint.

"Yeah, well," said Yesilkov, her face set in planes as harsh as those of a drop forge as she stared at her subordinate—and avoided the anthropologist's cool gaze. "Got what we needed for now, I guess. Maybe poison, you know . . ."

She looked at Yates because he was big and maybe support; because she'd fucked up, should've let the anthropologist take a shot at the survivor. Looked that way after the fact, anyhow. "Maybe suicide?"

Sam Yates nodded, sympathetic and more than a little grateful that somebody *else* had put a foot in it tonight.

Before he could say something as well, Xao at the diagnostic trellis looked up and said, "Not poison, Sonya. Virus."

"Huh?"

"Virus," the patrolman repeated, as stolidly as if the information had no personal implications for the speaker. "Cell walls of his lung tissue's been eaten away. It's like soup in there. How quick didja say it happened?"

Xao was looking at Yates. They were *all* looking at Yates, at his hands still black with residues of the waiter's dying spasm.

Everyone was backing away. Xao scrambled to his feet, then bent to snatch the face mask with an osmotic filter from the open satchel. Yates stared into the prismatic eyes of Elinor Bradley, but he could not ignore his own hands. His skin prickled everywhere as the blood withdrew from it . . . but not from its outer surface, from the hands that might have rubbed his eyes, brushed his mouth in some gesture forgotten when other things seemed more important.

Lieutenant Yesilkov took the ground-conduction communicator from her belt sheath and stepped to the wall that was carved from bedrock. "I don't care *what* else they've got on," she said carefully as she planted the antenna against the polished stone. "We need full medical, and we need it *now*."

Chapter 2

HOBSON'S CHOICE

Rodney Beaton was paid as well as an engineer Downside, but his rank at Sky Devon was Technician Class Four—in effect, gofer. His status in the conspiracy was similar, which was why he was at UN Headquarters.

Though the potential payoff here was infinitely greater than anything he could expect from his regular duties, the risk was also enormous.

He was terrified. He was so much afraid that he would curl up in a fetal ball if he even hesitated in carrying out his tasks.

Beaton ran along the first two sections of slideway after he left Le Moulin Rouge. His gait was clumsy and loping. The technician was used to Sky Devon's fifty percent pseudogravity, so he was overmuscled for the Moon. He knew that he should let the rollers carry him at their own speed, along with most of the other people using the system, but he could not bring his body to act on his knowledge until he had burned off some of the hormones that surged through his system.

Until what had happened in the restaurant, Beaton's only emotional involvement with the project had been for the wealth and power it would bring him. He knew what the risks were, of course: he had helped to calculate them. But they were only data, like the growth rates of corn under varying angstrom balances—until the waiter had hemorrhaged over the table, the utensils, and the air in front of Rodney Beaton.

There was a tie-up of some sort in the corridor ahead. The rotating blue lights of emergency vehicles at the scene turned bright-work into cascades of shimmering jewels and stained the stucco of the corridor's roof a sinister color in combination with its normal beige. Private vehicles were being halted, so that liveried chauffeurs and their haughty employers argued loudly with police while pedestrians climbed over the cars like so many hurdles.

The sudden crowding relaxed Beaton, because it made him certain that others were interested in something besides him. He could almost believe that there *was* something important besides Rodney Beaton and the risk he was running.

He could *almost* believe that.

Beaton stepped off the slideway so that he was not rolled against the back of the sturdy-looking black in a djellaba ahead of him. He jostled a trio chattering in an oriental language as they all tried to squeeze past a six-place car whose driver's uniform was much more splendid than that of the female security patrolman with whom he was arguing.

The patrolman looked frail enough, even for a woman, but a determined exercise program could make a major difference in the strength of humans living under conditions of reduced gravity. She seized a double handful of the chauffeur's iridescent bodysuit, holding the front where his lapels would have been if he wore them. Twisting, she dragged the driver half out of his seat and bent him toward the scene behind.

"Look at it, fuckhead!" the patrolman screamed. "And then back the fuck *outa* here or I'll mop it up with yer nose!"

The car's sole passenger was a heavy black woman who wore jewelry of cast gold, including a bracelet whose charms were assayers' weights from ancient Benin. They clinked warmly as she rose from her seat. Beaton, stepping into the vehicle as an obstacle to be crossed, was drawn also to look at what had caused the trouble.

There were perhaps a dozen uniformed patrolmen. Most of them were trying to reroute traffic while white-coated medical personnel knelt and muttered and jumped up to get additional equipment from the pair of ambulances parked on the island between lengths of slideway.

There were three bodies. They must have been riding the slideway when they collapsed, because they were sprawled at the edge of the island while the rolling surface continued to jiggle them into a semblance of life. The turban of one of them had begun to unroll beyond him.

There was enough blood on the clothes and startled faces of the victims to have begun painting the corridor. Beaton, struck by dreadful surmise, looked back at the slideway on which he as well as the corpses had been riding. The streaks on the moving surface, unnoticed even by travelers less distracted than the technician had been, was blood smeared along the continuous belt by the rollers inside.

Blood that contained the same virus had been rubbed into Beaton's clothing by the man at Le Moulin Rouge.

The only thing that saved the British technician from immediate screaming panic was the camera woven into his lapel and the reflex that made him shift for a better angle and begin to subvocalize, "One male adult, one female adult, one pubescent female"—the child's veil of tiny beads had been pulled away between the slideway and the lip of the island—"at corridor reference . . ."

Beaton glanced behind him, found the tile glowing on the wall. "Reference D-D two-ought-one," he continued. No need to give the time—the recorder's microprocessor did that automatically—but . . .

The technician turned and bent forward a little so that the lens array could pan the slideway beneath the feet of further travelers. "Residues on the moving belt indicate the event took place some minutes before."

The chauffeur settled back into his seat. Unexpectedly, his passenger vomited over the gorgeous print patterns of her dress.

They hadn't expected so much *blood*. Beaton hadn't, at any rate. He trembled as he scurried past the island, almost colliding with the sweaty man in Bureau of Utilities orange who had been summoned to shut down the affected section of slideway.

Dead, of course. But they should have died quietly, hunching over like the white rats and snuffling the floor until they were racked by an uncontrollable tremor and all movement ceased. Instead of this—gore. Beaton had seen nothing comparable except for the time he had opened the chest cavity of a living pigeon. Blood everywhere, bright and crawling with the virus.

Blood on Rodney Beaton, on his clothing and perhaps his skin.

Perhaps in his lungs.

The technician was running again, but his conduct was less likely to attract attention now. A car that had been turned at the police cordon sped down the sidewalk, its occupants white-faced and frozen. Other pedestrians—some of them sparked by Beaton, perhaps—began to shuffle faster, looking back over their shoulders at the carnage they had passed.

"D-D two-ought-three," Beaton muttered to himself; and at the next island where a corridor crossed, "D-L niner-one-niner."

An ambulance sped down the central aisle of the cross corridor, its flashers and two-tone hooter blaring warnings. The technician stepped in front of the vehicle. It missed him only by the amount its driver swerved up on a moving slideway. Beaton loped onward, oblivious to his near escape and to the curses the two ambulance attendants rained back over him.

The bloody-jowled Arab on the back of the ambulance was too obviously a corpse to have required that amount of haste.

Beaton had assumed that the other fatalities came from air being recirculated through the restaurant by the colony's atmosphere plant. That might cover the family at DD201—they might have passed Le Moulin Rouge on their route to hemorrhage and death—but it did not explain this latest body on the ambulance.

The aerosol phial the technician now carried empty in his pocket had been brought to the restaurant sealed under negative pressure. There should not have been any chance of release before the planned moment, and the exterior of the phial had been sterilized with ultraviolet radiation as soon as it was filled.

Something had escaped early or had been spread by unexpected vectors. If they—he and his superiors—had underestimated one aspect of what they were doing, then they could have made another mistake as well.

"L-L fiver-three-one," mumbled Beaton pointlessly, fearfully.

Suit rooms with airlocks to the lunar surface were scattered throughout the colony, but the British technician needed a specific location.

The colony's waste disposal was handled by surface lines fed by pumps instead of gravity-powered collectors buried under the streets, as was usual in those nations Downside that had heard of sewer systems. The energy to run the pumps was cheap, and collectors laid on the open surface could receive taps or be doubled in capacity without adding to the colony's horrendous traffic problems.

Although they were heated, the sewer lines—like the water and air supply lines which paralleled them—sometimes froze. They could be blocked by caking sediment and could fracture out of sheer cussedness, dumping recyclable nutrients in splendid plumes which sublimed into vacuum at lunar dawn.

The crews of the Bureau of Utilities had to have frequent access to the surface—though human nature being what it was, all options of dealing with a problem from inside were going to be exhausted before anybody went out into the void. The air locks placed for Utility use served the purpose of Beaton and his superiors as well.

Beaton's mind was back in its mechanical mode again. If he permitted himself to drift into emotional data, the technician would break, would fling everything aside until he had cleansed his body and destroyed all the clothing he had worn in Le Moulin Rouge.

But the bodies on the slideway and in the ambulance showed how vain such attempts would be. If he abandoned his task in panic, he would lose the chance of wealth and power for which he had risked his life.

Was still risking his life.

"L-L fiver-three-niner," the technician's tongue mumbled, but he had already stepped onto the next section of slideway before his brain processed the information. This island was his destination.

Beaton turned and jumped back the way he had come, colliding with a pair of men in medal-fronted Argentinian military uniforms. Other travelers had been only a gray blur to the technician since he passed the ambulance at DL919, like the corridor walls and every part of his surroundings save the location tiles at intersections.

The two Latin Americans threw everything back in focus. Not only did they fling the technician aside with a vigor that proved they were recent arrivals from Downside, but one of them reached under the breast of his jacket to touch a bulge which might not have been a needle stunner.

Beaton sprawled on the central aisle while the moving belt carried the Argentinians away. They snarled invective in Spanish over their shoulders for the initial thirty meters while other travelers looked around in detached curiosity.

The man from Sky Devon got to his feet slowly and walked the few steps back to the island and the access door in one wall of it. He hoped the men had Arab blood in them, lots of Arab blood. They were swarthy and greasy-looking enough, Jesus knew. They shouldn't have limited the test to Arabs anyway. They should have gone for all wogs, all the scum that had spread over Britain and had driven a true Englishman to risk his life by working on an orbital habitat.

And to risk his life much more greatly than that.

Beaton walked to the access door, using exaggerated care to keep from bumping any of those crossing from one section of slidewalk to the next. The edge of physical violence the Argentinians offered when they thought their manhood was challenged, had appalled him. They had been willing to hurt him—to *kill* him, perhaps—because of a trivial accident. As if there weren't dangers enough, without imbeciles exploding like emotional gelignite. . . .

The access door was a sandwich of thin metal stiffened with glass sponge. It might as well have covered a broom closet.

The exterior of the panel was marked with the numerals 137 and a slashed circle to forbid entry. An English legend, Authorized Personnel Only, would have been understood by at least ninety percent of the adults in Headquarters Colony; but the political problems of using a single language here were as awesome as the practical problems of adding the hundred-odd other national languages and major dialects.

The door was locked, but an Afrikaner had given Beaton the simple magnetic key when he arrived. The key card had been supplied originally by the same Bureau of Utilities superintendant who had promised to keep this suit room out of normal service for a week, in return for more money than he would ordinarily earn in a month.

There was no certainty the superintendant could keep his crews out of lock 137, since it was in the nature of the job that emergencies would occur—but that was not really crucial. Any crewmen who saw Beaton when they were heading topside or returning after rodding a line, would think the same thing their superintendant did: that there was a smuggling operation going on, and that it wasn't up to them to do Security's job.

In a way, they were correct; but what the Sky Devon technician was smuggling was information.

He swung open the flimsy door, stepped inside, and latched it behind him. The glowstrip that was supposed to light the base of the ladder was faulty, barely able to illuminate its own leprous surface. The strip at the top landing beside the air-lock door was sufficient, especially since Beaton had already entered the suit room once.

The only way of sending a message off-Moon from within Headquarters Colony was to use the regular communications net. The three meters of rock covering the colony were as impervious to radio signals as they were to the cosmic rays against which they armored the residents.

The data that Rodney Beaton had collected could not wait for his personal return to Sky Devon, a laborious process because there was no direct shuttle from the Moon to that habitat. Neither were his superiors willing to entrust to regular channels a block of data with the implications that this had.

The choice was for Beaton to transmit his data directly from the lunar surface.

The technician punched the big latch plate of the air lock at the top of the ladder. The mechanism hesitated briefly while it determined that the door at the other end of the suit room was sealed. Then the pressure door sighed outward, forcing Beaton to move to the edge of the landing so that he wouldn't be brushed aside. The access shaft was close quarters, even now that he wasn't burdened by the laser communications gear he had stored in the suit room upon arrival.

The shaft smelled musty. The suit room wore a muted reek composed of excretions from utility crewmen who had worked in the stored space suits over the years, then compounded by minute arcs in the suit mechanisms and charging equipment. Though the atmosphere was voided every time the outer lock opened, residues from the suits of returning crewmen were always sufficient to color the volume of the small room again.

Beaton touched the inner latch plate of the shaft door. The lock pistoned shut obediently. The brief compression wave in the suit room raised a sympathetic shudder from the technician's body.

Four suits stood ready in the charging rack. They were sized from small through large, though in theory all were universals, usable by anyone who fit within their hinged halves.

Beaton ignored them for the moment. The communications gear was in what looked like an ordinary sewer-crew tool chest, shelved with two others across from the suit rack. The .1 cubic-meter chest Beaton had brought from Sky Devon was locked, and he had fused its casing to the titanium shelf by setting off a high-voltage welding strip between the metal surfaces.

The case would remain after Beaton's mission was completed, but it would suggest no more than horseplay among the Utility personnel.

The British technician unlocked the tool chest with a key card externally identical to the one that had opened the access door below. His tracking-and-sending unit was inside, its spidery legs and antenna quills collapsed for storage. Until the solidity of the unit's handle reassured him, Beaton did not realize how much he had feared that this crucial device would have disappeared, would somehow dissolve in smoke even as the cover lifted to display it.

He set the communicator down beside the chest in which it had been concealed and reached for the flat videochip recorder hooked to his waistband. In sudden revulsion, the British technician stripped off his tweed jacket and flung it with its blood smears into a corner. The thin leads from the lens array to the control box broke, dangling like wisps of cobwebs as his trembling fingers opened the recorder and removed its data chip.

First he would cleanse himself of the information he had acquired. Then he would bathe in antiseptic-charged water for as long as it took to wash away memory of the security man grabbing him with red, virulent hands.

Beaton carefully plugged the data chip from the recorder into the transmit socket of the laser communicator. He was very close to success—to completion, to *escape*—and he could not let his shuddering body betray him now.

The chip locked home.

Beaton stood up, angry at his momentary dizziness and the clamminess of his palms. He had not eaten for too long. He would do that very soon.

He stepped to the charging rack and wrestled the end suit, the smallest one, from the bayonet connectors that kept its air and power topped off while the garment was out of service. The suit was an awkward burden, even under gravity much lower than the technician was used to. At least it did not flop around. Micromagnets kept the suit's skin rigid until someone wearing it moved so that the servoreceptors in the lining had a command to transmit.

The suit's white outer surface was dulled by dust and scratches, and the reflective face shield was scarred badly enough that it would probably be dazzling if Beaton faced in the direction of the sun. The sloppiness offended him—the lab he maintained at Sky Devon was always spotless—but it wouldn't prevent him from accomplishing his final task.

Beaton was perspiring, in part from the effort. He knew that experienced crewmen opened the suits while they were still racked in, then closed the unit around them and stepped away, letting the garment's power assist do the work. The technician was afraid that he would break off the air nozzle if he tried that, jamming the filler valve open into a void that would kill him as soon as he opened the pressure door.

He set the suit down with the right glove poised just over the communicator's handle. One arm was attached to the suit back, the other to the front. The remainder of the unit, including the legs and helmet, clamshelled open and closed in a tongue-and-groove seam. The junction was sealed by the same micromagnets that flexed the suit under the control of the wearer's muscles.

Beaton pressed the release button under the left armpit to open the suit. He had worn hard suits before on occasion, and he dreaded the feel of the inner lining expanding to grip his whole body beneath the neck. He had taken off his jacket, but the rest of his clothing and his skin were surely contaminated. Invisible flecks of blood and sputum holding a virus that might not be dead, might not be—

An Arab in orange coveralls fell out of the opening suit, into Beaton's instinctive grasp. The inside of the face plate was covered with the blood the man had coughed out in his last instants of life.

Beaton screamed and hurtled sprawling as he leaped away and tripped over the laser communicator. He crashed into the three suits still on the rack and howled again, as if they, too, were corpses. Perhaps they *did* contain more Arabs who had suited up and died of their infection before they could move again.

He had forgotten his task, forgotten his dreams, forgotten everything but anguished faces gouting blood toward him. It should not have been so *messy*.

The technician slapped the latch plate. He had no idea of what he would do after he escaped this charnel house. His wild appearance would attract attention in the corridors below, and the jacket he was leaving behind might lead to his identification. Beaton could no more have picked up the bloody tweed again than he could have enclosed himself in the space suit from which the utility crewman had slumped.

The silence when the flaps closed over the air vents would have warned him if he hadn't been so distraught. As it was, Beaton didn't realize that he had opened the wrong pressure door until the suit room voided its atmosphere across the Moon's surface in a fan of crystallizing water vapor.

By then it was too late even to scream.

Chapter 3

TAKING CARE OF
BUSINESS

When the blood-spewing Arab waiter crashed backward over his table, Piet van Zell realized that they had won. He would be going home—not today, but someday soon—to the farm outside Pietermaritzburg where he was born, or to anywhere else in sub-Saharan Africa that he and his fellows chose. They would be the only ones who were prepared.

It was just a matter of arriving at a price. That negotiation was in the hands of other men, but van Zell could not imagine that the sum could not be found for a prize so great.

The tall Afrikaner stood up, brushing his beard free of jewels of water flung there when his goblet was shattered by the Arab's body. The woman across from him wore a look of horrified surmise, her arm raised to ward off an imagined attack by the bloody-handed customer who had been holding the waiter during his final hemorrhage.

Van Zell glanced down at the Arab again. Dead beyond question. He had spewed up at least a quart of bright blood from his lungs. There was no mistaking the color if you had ever seen the face plate of a pressure suit whose wearer had begun to scream when a joint ruptured his atmosphere into the vacuum.

And since van Zell had been one of the Afrikaners who emigrated to space when the Republic of South Africa shattered into a dozen black states, he had seen that sort of death many times.

Theirs was a race with skills and courage, but by the time they were displaced from their homes with nothing but their lives saved, they were loathed as generally by developed states as they were in the third world. Their Dutch ancestors

29

had begun to colonize the southern tip of Africa at the beginning of the sixteenth century, the same time the Bantu-speaking immigrants began to trickle south into what would become the Transvaal.

Between them, the Dutch and the Bantus—Kaffirs—had virtually exterminated the indigenous peoples, the race that became the Bushmen when their few survivors were driven into the Bush. The victors had fought bloodily over the spoils, as was the way of history; and white had defeated and subjugated black, as was the will of God.

The forces of Satan had reversed that process, turning the whole world against South Africa and putting automatic rifles in the hands of folk raised only a half step above the apes and other beasts. And now it was clear that God, after a time of testing his people, was ready to reassert his will anew.

Beaton, the technician from Sky Devon, shuddered back into glassy-eyed function and bent over the waiter's body, oblivious of van Zell. The Englishman had a videochip recorder woven into his right lapel. The unit's thirty subminiature recording lenses used adaptive optics and a microprocessor to create an image almost as sharp as that of an ordinary lens, even if the fabric of which they were a part flexed during recording.

The technician would make a scientific report on the test, van Zell presumed, but that was no concern of the Afrikaner nor of those who had sent him to observe at this time and place. The tool worked, and van Zell would report that. How it worked was immaterial. His ancestors had not pored over the ballistics and metallurgy of their long muskets before they crushed the Kaffirs at Blood River.

The big, blond-haired customer bolted for the kitchen with Beaton trailing stiffly in his wake like a mechanical remora. Van Zell turned to the corridor exit. Men at another table had rushed out as soon as the waiter collapsed, without waiting to learn what had happened or why.

An indeterminate number of strangers stared through the clean panel, freezing the Afrikaner as the preceding events had not.

Van Zell had been so frightened that the test would fail—

so *certain* that it would fail—that the fears which would usually have gripped him had been subsumed in the greater concern. He could have eaten the meal he'd ordered from the Arab waiter, treating his food and the expensive ambiance to as little notice as he gave the protein rations in plastic tubes, which he was used to. But with the stunning success that weltered in its blood on the floor, everything changed back to normal—or worse.

Afrikaners like van Zell crewed most orbital construction sites and many of the survey craft that prospected in the asteroid belt—on behalf of other nations and conglomerates in which no Afrikaner had a share. Space had welcomed them when Earth turned her back. Their virtues—courage, self-reliance, and a faith in God to sustain them when the material universe went awry—admirably suited them for their new duties.

Being stiff-necked and aloof meant that Afrikaners could maintain mental distance in living conditions more crowded than those of third world prisons—while they constructed great volumes and vistas for permanent colonists to inhabit. They were hugely wasteful of any resources that were not in short supply—God had created the universe for them, after all—but equally, they were capable of undergoing the most extreme hardship and privation when need arose.

And finally their rigidity—the fierce determination to bull ahead despite any counsel or change in circumstances—was about as likely to carry them through a crisis as it was to get them killed. If they were killed, then whoever had employed the victims hired more of their ilk to complete the job.

But while van Zell was used to crowding, he was *not* used to strangers. The mass of unfamiliar faces goggling at him through the door was a scene from Hell. He started, momentarily as horrified as any of those who stared past him at the waiter's bloody corpse, but the motion the tall Afrikaner had begun toward the door set the other diners in motion like billiards cannoning from the cue ball.

The party of Indian diplomats broke apart. Two of the men stayed behind, while the other three streamed after the woman in the sari who strode for the door with a determination that added bulk to her birdlike figure.

She slapped the emergency exit plate. When the spectators outside kept the door from opening more than a hand's breadth, she hectored them shrilly in a voice whose language was indeterminate but whose scorpion-raining fury drove them back.

The door sprang wide, and Piet van Zell plunged through it in the wake of the quartet of diplomats.

Slideways ran in both directions down the main corridors throughout the UN colony. They moved people at the rate of seven kilometers per hour, a rate that could be doubled easily by those who wished to stride along the moving surface.

The slideways weren't particularly energy efficient, but power was cheap here. A mirror in lunar orbit directed sunlight onto banks of solar cells on the colony's surface, providing a constant and easily-expandable power source no matter where the cells were in relation to true daylight. Once the initial installation had been completed, the only significant cost was that of fuel to maintain the mirror's orbit and attitude against the effects of Earth's gravity.

Room to store and operate individual vehicles was at a premium where energy was not. In theory, a pair of slideways flanked and separated by narrow stationary sidewalks provided for all the direct needs of the colony residents. Emergency vehicles would operate on the sidewalks in the rare instances that became necessary.

The only problem with the theory came when it was applied to the ambassadors and chiefs of mission who controlled the colony's funding—and thus the funding of the Directorate of Security which would enforce the ban on private vehicles.

The result was a compromise that worked as badly as such things usually did. Each mission was informally rationed to a pair of vehicles—but there were over a hundred sixty states accredited to the UN. The situation would have been a disaster, even if the rationing had been generally observed and if high officials of the Secretariat refrained from flaunting their status with vehicles of their own.

There were three open-topped, six-place cars parked outside Le Moulin Rouge; a fourth pulled away as hastily as

its batteries could accelerate the direct-current motors in its
wheel hubs. The chauffeurs of two of the remaining cars
had stowed their wiping rags when the pair of European
diners bolted from the restaurant and into their vehicle.

Van Zell shook himself clear of the spectators as if their
touch were foul-smelling rain on his body. His height and
grim expression made his path easy, even though the Afrikaner's musculature was by now better suited to
weightlessness than it was to even the low gravity of the
Moon.

He had a natural sense of direction, sharpened by a decade
of work under conditions where the ability to locate objects
in the surrounding sphere might be the margin for survival.
Though he had traveled the route only once before—and
that in the opposite direction—van Zell strode without hesitation to the southbound lane of the slideway fronting the
restaurant. His mind was already reviewing the junctions
where the paired monomer belts ended at square islands and
he would choose which of three corridors to follow next.

Now that van Zell was back in the midst of his task, the
feeling of panic disappeared. He could look around him
with the detached loathing he would expend on an unpleasant
image in a holovision tank.

The slideways were crowded, and many of the people
van Zell stood near were women—polyglot and dressed in
various fashions. He had been married once, but that had
ended twenty years before, in an ambush of the convoy
carrying dependents to Durban and hope of safety. Over
three thousand of them, mostly women and children, with
a scattering of overage males for defense.

The women had fought, too, and the older children, just
as in the days of the Great Trek . . . but when the guerrillas
were done, the lucky whites were those who had died before
their bodies were flung back onto the burning trucks.

Van Zell had been with his unit on the Angolan border
when the massacre occurred . . . and when they were with-
drawn for counterinsurgency operations, to cover their own
dead with mounds of Kaffir flesh, armies crashed southward
from Angola, Zimbabwe, and Mozambique in Russian
tanks. Guerrillas cannot win a war alone, but in South Af-

rica—as in South Vietnam and Occupied France during earlier generations—irregulars could divert attention from the hostile armies which alone smash other armies.

Piet van Zell had survived, but the sight of women in large numbers made him uneasy for reasons he was too unimaginative to discover.

In the central portion of the UN colony, most of the corridor walls were dikes of living rock, hollowed out behind for living areas and cut through for doors. The low intensity of lunar seismic activity made it safe to have foundation, support walls, and overburden all part of the same mass of rock, and the construction equipment available early on in the colony's existence made it the most practical method as well.

The Transient Barracks were new construction. They had already been moved twice during the colony's short lifespan, each time to the new rim of the expanding colony. Space near the hub was at a premium, particularly because of the difficulty of traveling long distances through the corridors.

As the slideways rolled van Zell outward in two-hundred-meter segments, his surroundings changed. At first the corridors themselves became wider to make utility service easier and to permit the slideway capacity to be doubled when the load came to require it.

The support walls were assemblages of titanium girders, processed from lunar ilmenite in huge solar furnaces. Panels of foamed silica, generally beige but sometimes suffused with some other pastel dye, covered them. The construction was superficially identical to that of an orbital habitat, but here the girders were braced to withstand the actual weight of rock rather than the centrifugal stresses that provided pseudogravity for habitats.

The outermost belt of construction had been developed by the techniques currently in use. Instead of tunneling, the surface was gouged away by a combination of cratering charges and mirror-focused sunlight that exceeded the melting point of the refractory rock. The molten glass was sucked out through heated lines and dumped on a suitable disposal area—often a portion of the site where construction had proceeded further.

The building went on under vacuum conditions in the open pit, girders and prefabricated panels being muscled into place by men in hard suits. Van Zell had been employed on a section a few years before. It was more difficult work than orbital construction, because the solid base for support machinery did not wholly erase the problems caused by real gravity.

The sections were spanned by titanium roof trussses, customized during extrusion to match the expected load. Overengineering was extreme by Downside standards: a collapsing beam, too weak for the stress laid on it, could void the air from additional hectares of the colony as well.

When the box sections were completed, sealed, and tested, crews backfilled them with rubble from later construction or spoil pits, providing the several meters of lunar rubble that would block cosmic rays as effectively as Earth's kilometers of atmosphere. Even before the internal finish work was done, people would be moving into the new section—desperate to claim the space allotted to them or jumping another's allotment in confidence that it would be years before they could be evicted through the colony's ponderous, multilayered legal system.

Piet van Zell looked around as the slideways rolled him toward his destination. Panels of raw, press-formed slag. Fabric hangings; generally industrial-grade fiberglass, because not even the paneling had arrived. Occasionally a shopfront that could have been transferred whole from Fifth Avenue or the Champs Elysées, a facade of crystal or polished metal—and in front of one such, a worried-looking woman arguing with a trio of men in the orange coveralls of the Bureau of Utilities.

Why would anyone struggle for a portion of *this*? Here they were at the sufferance of the air plant, at the sufferance of the bureaucracy—there were no freeholds in the colony; at the sufferance of the heads of state who moved UN Headquarters to the Moon and who could as easily move it back, now that it was clear that anyone with real power, both among the Secretariat staff and the accredited missions, managed to stay on Earth anyway.

And why would a man balk at any act, any tool, that

would regain him the land and open sky God meant him to occupy on Earth?

The Transient Barracks were at the end of the line—almost beyond it, because though the last segment of slideway was in working condition, the outward-bound two hundred meters immediately previous was static. A team of men in coveralls waited, some of them playing cards, while a party of engineers, architects, and administrative staff wearing the suits and formal scarves of current Downside fashion argued over the problem and the responsibility for it.

The men and the handful of women trudging past the dead section of slideway glowered at both groups indiscriminately.

Standing while the track rolled beneath him had been a conscious burden on van Zell. Walking the two hundred meters required real effort—he had spent the previous nine months beyond Mars, assaying planetoids for Mitsubishi. Every time the tall Afrikaner reexperienced gravity, a part of his mind questioned his plan—their Plan—to return to Earth.

But the body's questions could not compete with the soul's dream, when only that dream made life endurable.

There was no problem with squatters attempting to fence off portions of the Transient Barracks for their own permanent use. A few of the persons allotted bunk and locker space in the barracks were business visitors, troubleshooters sent to deal with refractory equipment—problems that simply could not be solved by anyone on Earth at the end of a microwave link.

These white-collar transients themselves gazed with nervous apprehension at the construction workers who filled the majority of the barracks space. Almost all the latter were men who had too little to lose on Earth to keep them there—used to brutal conditions, heavy labor, and sudden death. A squatter who tried to appropriate the bunk area assigned to these men would be removed. His condition when they flung him onto an inbound slideway would be determined not by the force necessary to the purpose but rather by the force it amused the construction workers to use.

The corridor that dead-ended now between the Transient

Barracks had been constructed with an eye toward its use in a decade or two, so there was plenty of room in the passageway for squatters of a type.

The type that follows men when their families can't.

The whores and drug dealers, dram shops and card rooms, were an unusual problem here because of the peculiar—and some might have said peculiarly bad—structure of the UN. The attitude taken at most off-Earth construction sites was the same as that of the authorities near a Downside military base: it's going to be there anyway, so keep it under reasonable control—and don't turn down a buck if some entrepreneur offers it to you under the table.

Most UN member countries would have been perfectly willing to have the fringes of Headquarters Colony policed the same way. Most of the UN budget, however, came from democracies, where there was always someone out of office and ready to make political hay if his opponents winked at open UN corruption.

Nobody who had anything to do with getting things done—as opposed to politics—thought that men became saints when they were removed to a construction site in the heavens. On the other hand, nobody volunteered to sign off on an order formally authorizing activities at Headquarters Colony which were illegal, at least on paper, in virtually every UN member country.

The solution turned out to be ceding UN ownership of the corridor fronting the paired Transient Barracks. It was designated a construction site, under control of the developers until it received final acceptance by the Secretariat's Bureau of Construction.

Final acceptance came when the barracks were moved outward again—to a *new* "construction site." Until then, anyone with a problem about what went on in the corridor could take it up with the developers—who, multinational corporations and private citizens under U.S. (for example), law, could tell the nosy bastard where to stuff his or her problem.

Van Zell rode the slideway to its terminus, past most of the recreational activity going on between the in- and outbound ways. A pair of men were crying and shouting bitterly at one another in Russian. Each held one hand of a doe-eyed, olive-skinned boy whose expression could be ethereal or ennuied, depending on the angle from which van Zell glimpsed him.

That was nothing to the Afrikaner, and of no especial interest even to the pair of company police moving toward the altercation: turbaned Sikhs wearing needle stunners and the shoulder patch of their employer, Pacific Architects and Engineers.

It was not to anyone's advantage that the Strip be run wide open. The Site Monitors—company police—kept a lid on the violence that was endemic at any location where the pleasures of a thousand men were distilled.

Beyond that obvious need were the inspectors and administrative staff. They checked the women and boys for disease, seeing to the cure of those with simple problems and the deportation of others. Drugs were tested—not for purity, which was the purchasers' problem, but rather for the presence of dangerous additives like the strychnine and powdered rock that raised the dealer's profit margin at the cost of damage to laborers whom the company had brought expensively to the Moon. Liquor was examined to make sure that it was ethanol rather than one of the even more poisonous industrial alcohols, and that it contained only the usual complement of aromatic esters which collapsed human circulatory systems in the name of flavor.

The developers kept the games honest also. Nothing led to uncontrollable violence faster than a fleeced worker returning to the card room with the remainder of his crew and the tools they had brought for the purpose from the construction site. Quite apart from work time lost to death and wounds, that sort of incident was certain to get media exposure Downside and might well lead to an end of the arrangement that kept the recreational services operating.

Even under normal circumstances van Zell rarely used the Strip outside a construction site. Occasionally a woman; always a black. More often, enough gin to hammer the memories out of his mind for a time . . . but never a long time, and the veins that throbbed when he returned to consciousness mimicked the rage he felt when he first saw camera footage of the massacre in which his family died. Now—he had his duty. He had a call to make.

At each of the twenty off-Moon phones was a line as long as the queues for the most popular prostitutes between the slideways. Van Zell got into the line that looked shortest—it wouldn't be, it never was, but that did not concern him.

The Afrikaner had learned above all during his exile how to wait. Not only for big things, for the mystical Plan that was as far beyond his comprehension as the Virgin Birth and as much an article of his faith. He had waited for others to move beams so that he could weld them; waited to enter and exit air locks that were a tight fit for a single man; waited to be picked up by spidery "taxis" at the end of shifts, with nothing but the stars and his thoughts for company.

He always counted the posts of the barbed-wire fence he could see from his stoop, letting his mind play over the gray, weathered surface of the wood against the sere grass and the pale, friendless sky. He was counting them yet again when the Ghanaian before him in line finished his call and left the open-fronted phone booth.

A Turk from the next line over tried to push in front of van Zell. The Afrikaner braced his arm on the edge of the booth and used his bony elbow to block the interloper. The exchange was without rancor, almost instinctive from the long experience of both men in similar circumstances. They did not speak to one another, but as the Afrikaner slid his ID card into the phone, the Turk was noisily attempting to reclaim his place in the line from which he had jumped.

Van Zell's card was the standard type which provided data on construction workers all over the solar system. It was attached to his left wrist by a coil of beryllium monomer which would stretch as much as a half meter. The monomer could be broken, but it would be easier to sever the wearer's wrist—and either event would put a warning tick in data retrieved through the card thereafter.

The card simply accessed the wearer's file. Any medical, economic, employment, or other data loaded into the records system could be brought up as required. Normally a con-

struction company took a full dump from Central Records
in Geneva on every worker it employed and then purged its
own files when employment terminated, but it was possible
for someone to have separate files in a number of computer
banks.

The financial data in van Zell's file at Headquarters Colony showed a credit balance greater than his earnings during
a decade of well-paid work in vacuum. It would cover un-
limited off-Moon phoning and virtually anything that could
be bought here, including the chief of a fair-sized diplomatic
mission.

The Afrikaner began entering the laboriously memorized
twenty-one-digit code while the card flexed to him was still
being digested with clicks and whirrs within the guts of the
phone. He hit the keys solidly with his right index finger,
punching each number as if he were trying to drive it out
of the pad. Ambient noise, voices of men at the other phones
and the cries of those involved in the pursuits of the Strip,
thinned and faded as he concentrated on his task.

The phone clucked happily, and the speaker plate began
to echo a pulsating whine which the caller assumed was a
ringing signal.

Off-Moon calls could be placed or received on any phone
in Headquarters Colony, but it was general practice to use
a dedicated instrument which bypassed the degradation of
an internal processing stage. There were banks of public
off-Moon phones scattered throughout the colony, though
only these by the Transient Barracks were in constant use.
Most large offices had a unit on-premises.

The signal went through optical cables to the bank of
microwave antennas on the surface. These beamed the digi-
tally-converted words to one of the trio of communications
satellites held with difficulty in lunar orbit. Further switching
took place in the satellite, before it shot the message on to
a final destination. That could be another Moon colony;
Earth or a habitat in Earth orbit; or a mining party in the
asteroid belt, so long as their location had been filed and
updated with the gigantic data bank at the Shaft in Pittsboro,
North Carolina.

Piet van Zell had no idea of who would be on the other

end of his call, nor of where they were located.

"Yes?" said a voice in heavy English.

"This is Piet," replied van Zell in Afrikaans, realizing as he did so that he might be stepping on the other man's side of the conversation. There would be a transmission lag, of course, but only experience would tell him whether it was a matter of seconds or upwards of fifteen minutes.

"Well, go on, man," said the other impatiently, having switched to Afrikaans as well.

Eight to ten seconds of delay. Earth or Earth orbit, then. Not that it mattered. "Everything here is proper," continued van Zell. "We must direct our partners to go on."

The delay this time stemmed from more than the distance of transmission, and there was a note of caution—even fear—in the other speaker's voice when he said, "What is done, is proper, but what is *not* done—that is proper also, you are telling me?"

No code or system of scrambling was truly unbreakable. Any form of transposition, however frequently changed within the text of the message, could be read in clear if enough computers were arrayed, crunching numbers until garbage solidified into nuggets of meaning.

There were ways of sidestepping the problem. For the Afrikaners using open communications channels, the best choice was to keep the message brief and to provide no key words that could possibly be chosen to pluck their conversation from among the millions of others taking place simultaneously.

"Yes, yes, all is proper," van Zell repeated with a note of irritation. If the tall Afrikaner had been imaginative enough to understand what the other speaker feared, he would not have been willing to observe the test the way he had done. "What am I to do now?"

"Wait," said the other decisively. Any hope van Zell had that the direction would be amplified ended eight seconds later with an electronic pop and the hum of an open line.

The Afrikaner agent retrieved his ID card from the bowels of the phone and stepped aside, jostled by the next man in line but not really aware of the fact.

He was to wait, then. All right. He would eat, first, in

one of the restaurants close to the Transient Barracks. He was hungry now that his mind was no longer so involved with his task that it blocked out all the signals his body was sending.

Sighing to himself—mentally and physically exhausted, but relaxed in a way that he had never achieved through sex—van Zell stepped onto the outward-bound slideway.

There was violent commotion between the moving strips. One of the Russians who had been arguing earlier burst through the fabric wall of a crib. His broad, gleamingly white body was nude, and the nude body of the boy cradled in his arms looked by contrast even darker than the rich olive it really was.

Everyone but the company police scattered, partly because of the nerve-shattering sound the Russian was making—a squeal as loud and piercing as that of a boar being gelded. Sikh policemen converged from several directions, drawing their stunners as they moved in.

The Russian's waist and thighs were covered with blood which had sprayed from the mouth of the boy he carried. The boy's head and limbs dangled like rope ends. The indifference that had been in his doelike Arab eyes before was being covered, like leaves beneath the surface of a freezing pond, by the glaze of death.

As stunners crackled behind him, snapping electrically-charged needles into the body of the Russian whom the police thought was a berserk murderer, Piet van Zell wondered whether he should call his off-Moon contact again. he decided not to. This incident was within what had been described to him as the expected parameters of the test.

And besides, he was very hungry.

Chapter 4

ELLA BRADLEY

Dear God, don't let me get it. . . don't let me get sick ran the litany in Ella Bradley's mind, over and over like a tape loop or a Top-40 song. She couldn't escape the prayerful mantra, like she couldn't escape her memories of what should have been a quiet, mildly celebratory dinner.

Hell of a way to celebrate turning thirty-five. Watching someone cough his lungs out over the people at the next table, and then . . .

She shut her eyes as if she could shut out the vision of the waiter with the napkin to his mouth. Of the big man, Yates, reaching for him while orange-bright blood flew and Yates' chair bounced against the nearby table that a sextet of Indians were already fleeing . . .

Ella Bradley was in the bathroom of her apartment, running a very expensive tub of steaming water while a meter set discreetly beside the shower head clicked off the cost.

She had no illusions that a hot bath with Dead Sea salts was going to protect her from the disease, although all sorts of curative powers were attributed to the salts a friend had sent her. But the bath would insulate her from the aftershocks of recollection. She hoped.

She hadn't taken a full bath since she'd gotten here, just quick, careful showers in "budget bags" which lowered the cost because they trapped every molecule for recycling. Tonight the budget bag hanging from the shower door reminded her too much of a body bag—same zipper that closed over your head. . . . She just couldn't handle it.

She poured a palmful of sea salts into the bath and thrust her hand in, wrist deep, after them. The skin beneath the

43

water reddened immediately, despite the tinted liquid. The water was almost scalding.

She didn't pull her hand out, but pressed her lips together and held it there. She'd adjust to the temperature that made her hand feel like someone was massaging it with a glove made from a thousand needles—adjust before the water cooled. She was paying for it.

She clambered onto the tub's rim and thrust both feet in, calf deep, grimacing. Then, slowly, she began to lower herself into the steaming water. Once it stopped hurting, it was going to feel wonderful.

Still in water so hot that she had to turn slowly, once on her knees, to shut off the tap, she began to shiver. Part reaction, part relaxation: just what she needed, at any price.

Slowly she sank down until she was sitting on her heels. Her skin reacted with a flare of red wherever the water lapped for the first time; beneath the surface, where she'd adjusted to the heat, the salts made her body seem tinged with green.

Olive. Olive like the casts of the dead faces she'd seen in the restaurant. Olive and fish-belly white and speckled with bright, arterial blood . . . Ella Bradley slid back in the tub until only the nipples of her breasts and her shoulders were above the surface, and closed her eyes. There was the waiter again, and the big security officer called Yates.

Sam Yates on his feet surrounded by panicked civilians and pulmonary blood. Sam Yates banging through the kitchen door, from which the smell of burning flesh was wafting . . .

And then, when she'd followed, the blue-eyed Kabyle girl in shock, the three dead bodies in their pools of blood: one still lying across the stove; one covered in salad that was drenched not in wine-vinegar, but more blood; one more, sprawled behind the door. And the little man from Yates' table, who'd gone with him into the kitchen . . .

Or had the little man pushed through the kitchen door first? Or followed? She couldn't remember.

Ella Bradley was an anthropologist, a scientist. As she lowered her erect nipples carefully under the surface of the steaming water, she began considering for the first time that her obsession with the horror in Le Moulin Rouge (the right name, that was for sure) might be more tham simple, retroactive terror.

Her mind was trying to collate what she'd seen. Make sense of it. Deduce something from it. Something besides how big the security man was, or how matter-of-fact he'd seemed on the phone, telling someone from Emergency not to "just leave it for the next patrol, okay?" while the little fellow in the bloodied suit slipped by her as she'd paused in the doorway.

She'd made a fool of herself in that kitchen, asking the big man stupid questions: was he from Security? why was he there? As if she had some right.

But it had thrown her back to field days, seeing all that blood: massacres in the African bush when you were trying to get the tribes to talk and you couldn't be sure that whites hadn't provoked any particular piece of slaughter—especially in southern Africa, where it took so little. . . . So she'd looked at the big white man among all those dead nonwhites she thought of as "indigs," and remembered the Pretorians.

She opened her eyes and came up out of the water like a sounding whale. Everybody who'd died in that restaurant had been nonwhite. Everyone had had a melanin content consistent with that description.

"No, no, easy now," she told herself. She was just trying to promise herself that she wasn't going to contract whatever disease this was. And yet, she kept seeing the shocky, blue eyes of the Kabyle girl. The girl who'd survived.

But survived what? Ella Bradley was remembering the ways she'd brayed at Yates: "fully accredited to the General Secretariat . . . the backing of important people . . ."

What an ass she'd made of herself. The man was a fellow American, part of the security contingent. He was a possible ally. More possible than the Russian woman who'd come in on his heels, Yesilkov.

Back into the water, this time more quickly. "What do you want to ally yourself *against*?" she asked out loud. Her mind wasn't ready to answer. It was chasing itself: Indians in that restaurant; lots of people, dark, light—nobody else had died yet.

Or she didn't know about any more deaths yet. "Face it, Bradley, you don't want it to be something you can catch." She wanted it to be something confined to kitchen help, or something the staff had eaten for breakfast, or even some sort of terrorist attack—lots of these people brought their regional hatreds with them. There was probably some Persian poison at the root of the problem, she postulated hopefully.

But her mind wouldn't buy it. *Officer, I'm an anthropologist. I can't help with the, ah, with those, but perhaps I could talk to the woman who's in shock?* That was what she'd said to the Russian, who'd snubbed her with a dismissive smile.

And then the patrolman who'd been fussing with his diagnostics over one corpse had said something to Yates, and Yates had raised his big hands . . . big, gory, bloodied hands.

If this thing was virulent, the security man was going to catch it. If he didn't get sick . . . Ella Bradley was absently arching and relaxing her back now, ducking her nipples in and out of the cooling water. She was going to go see Yates, see how he was feeling; see if he'd realized that everybody in that kitchen who'd died was of the same racial—and cultural—group.

Everyone. The Kabyle girl they'd oversedated hadn't been affected by the virus. Yet.

Virus. The diagnosing patrolman had been sure of that. Ella Bradley sat straight up in her bath. She could pull enough strings to see the Kabyle girl, if she dared. She could definitely manage it, though she might have to call down to New York for support. She was here to document, assess, and hopefully predict the adaptive changes certain cultural groups with which she was familiar would undergo. Since those groups included North as well as Central and South African nations, she could make a good case for interviewing the Kabyle.

If she dared. She stood up in the tub and reached for a towel. If they were dealing with a virus, she'd already been exposed. If they were dealing with some ancient poison that happened to simulate a virus when viewed under a diagnostic trellis, none of these glorified beat cops were going to even think of checking in that direction.

Wrapping the towel around her, she stepped regretfully from the tub. She'd check her office's data base, see if anyone else had died in similar circumstances. Then she'd set up an interview with Kabyle girl.

Then, and only then, was she going to visit Supervisor Sam Yates, from Security's Entry section—if, of course, one or both of them didn't catch the damn bug and die first.

PART TWO

Chapter 5

DATA SEARCH

Tenting his fingers in a gesture that looked ruminative unless one noticed the tips were white with pressure, Sam Yates stared at the hologram tank in the center of his tiny office. The unit, about the size of a fishbowl mounted waist high on a pedestal of scarred black plastic, fluoresced silently in patterns of changing pastels.

The security man rotated his chair and poked one of the presets on his desk phone.

"Yoshimura," grumbled the speaker plate after a moment.

"Barney, this is Sam," Yates said. The fact his call was answered promptly kept him from trying to slap the holotank against the far wall, but the best he could manage in his voice was control—not friendliness. "Is there some sorta problem with that Watch List from Interpol? I was supposed to have it an hour ago."

"Gee, Sam," said the voice of the man in Communications Section. "I think it's been received. Lemme make sure the feed's been sent out. Might be a problem in your hardware, you know."

"Too fuckin' right, I know," Yates said, glaring at the holotank again as he took his finger off the call button to break the connection.

"Supervisor Yates, you have a visitor at Reception," said the speaker plate, the voice different but momentarily unidentified while Yates sat in a brown study.

"Huh?" said Yates.

"Shall I send her in?" It was the intercom circuit, and of course the voice was that of Echeverria at the front desk.

He was a replacement for the shift's usual receptionist, a very attractive Pakistani girl whom Yates had catalogued for future reference when he was first being shown around the office.

That was last week's plan, and it might not have worked out anyway because she turned out to have a husband, a diplomat here. They were found together in their apartment, covered in blood and scraps of lung tissue, two of more than five hundred virus-related deaths within a few hours.

"Sir?"

"Yeah, right, send her—" Jesus *Christ,* it couldn't be Cecile, could it? "Send her in." When the receptionist activated intercom mode, an orange light glowed above receiver's keypad and the speakers were voice-tripped. It let Yates think about other things for the moment . . . though surely somebody would have said, "Hey Sam, this your wife on the list?" even if he'd missed that file himself.

A slim hand wearing an opal ring parted the strands that curtained the doorway and were supposed—actually, they weren't that bad—to do a better job of deadening sound than a solid panel would. The security man slid his chair back so that he could stand. It banged hard against the hologram viewer. A week hadn't been near long enough to learn control in low gravity.

"Supervisor Yates?" said the woman who stepped into the office with a care that reminded Yates of just how small a cubbyhole it was.

Thank God, it wasn't anybody he'd ever seen before!

"Supervisor Yates, we met a few days ago," the woman went on. She extended her hand to him. She was wearing a dress of shifting pale grays, natural fabrics and probably not cheap even before somebody freighted it from Earth to here. "Ella Bradley? At the restaurant four days—"

"Omigod, sure," said the security man, shaking the offered hand with embarrassment. His hesitation must have been obvious. Hell of a thing. As pretty a girl as this one was, and he hadn't remembered a thing about her except the prismatic contact lenses—which she wasn't wearing today.

Though it was harder to catalogue breasts than eye colors,

and he'd wound up the night with a lot of other things on his mind.

"I'm sure you had a lot of other things on your mind," said Bradley, with that transfiguring smile the security man had noticed before. "I'm glad that it turned out—not badly for you."

"Join the club," said Yates, remembering the way the image of his bloody hands had swelled until they pushed everything else out of his mind. Thick with dead virus, the analytic computers in Central Medical had said; but no sign of live virus, and no sign of damage—even entry—to his system.

"I don't think I've ever been so scared in my life," he added wryly, "at least for longer'n thirty seconds or so. Will you have a chair?"

Yates folded down the pair of seats built into the front of the data bank and hard-copy files across from his desk. He gestured Bradley into the one whose cushion filled with air properly when the unit locked down. He took the other, faulty, one for himself. You didn't need a real cushion in this gravity anyway; and if either he or his visitor sat in the swivel chair at the desk, the holotank would separate them like a table-center bouquet at dinner.

"I wanted to talk to you about that, Supervisor Yates," the woman said, settling herself into the seat. He turned at the waist to face her, but when her legs swung with her torso, their knees bumped. Her expression did not change, but she shifted her legs to miss him.

So . . . Not real skittish, but for sure not coming on. More's the pity. "Are you part of the investigation, then?" the security man asked.

She'd said she wasn't an MD, hadn't she? Or was that somebody else? Anyway, everybody and his brother seemed to have been tapped to help the fact-finding committee one way or another. Besides which, at least a dozen nations were setting up their own panels to parallel the Secretariat's efforts. The influx of people wasn't making Entry Division's job any easier—especially with a shift supervisor too new to have learned all the ins and outs of the system here at Headquarters.

He'd learned that *he* was definitely an out, if Arjanian on second shift had anything to say about it, though.

"No, I'm *not* part of the investigation," Bradley said, "and I realize that I'm intruding on your time . . . but I'd like to talk to someone in Security about what happened at Le Moulin Rouge and . . . everywhere. And I was very impressed by the way you handled matters that night, Supervisor."

"Can't say I impressed myself that much," said Yates, who preferred candor as a response to unearned compliments. He seemed to have gotten through that business with his ass and his job intact, but no thanks to his own behavior, so far as he could tell.

"But"—candid again—"flattery'll get you most places. How can I help you—ah, understanding that I know less about what happened than you do, if you've had time to follow the news?"

"I'm an anthropologist, Supervisor Yates," said the woman. "I'm here to document the way cultures change—or don't—when they're transplanted into this totally artificial environment. For that I have data on origins and ethnicity which probably isn't available—hasn't been culled out— anywhere else." She tapped the data bank behind her, and in so doing brushed Yates' knee again.

"So I just wanted to make sure," she concluded with an inflection that made it a query, "that Security has realized that all of those who died four days ago were Arabs?"

Marvelous, thought Yates, aware that muscles in his cheeks were shifting his face into a set of planes as forbidding as crated ammunition. A nut with a conspiracy theory, and coming to *him* with it. He remembered Ella Bradley now, the bitch who'd stared at him as if he'd just blown the waiter away and was likely to do the same to her.

Damn shame she hadn't held that thought. Then she wouldn't be screwing up his morning besides.

"Mistress Bradley," the security man said, "one thing I *am* sure of is that this wasn't a mass poisoning, it was real disease. I spent a *long* time in Central Medical, and I made sure"—sometimes the fear that Security aroused was a hell of a good way to learn things that weren't properly your business; as a patient, for instance—"that it was a virus and not some other sort of, ah, problem that I'd been exposed to."

"A virus that attacked Arabs," the woman said. She didn't seem to be concerned by the sudden hardening of Yates' face and attitude. In fact, she seemed to have relaxed a little, and she didn't jerk her knee back as abruptly when they bumped a third time. "Only Arabs."

"*Not* only Arabs," the security man said, "and by no means *all* Arabs. The—okay, right there in the restaurant kitchen, the Moulin Rouge—four people, three dead and one no worse off'n I am except for shock."

"Ayesha, yes, the daughter-in-law," replied Bradley as she ripped through the argument with the assurance of a circle saw. "Her bloodline back two generations is pure Kabyle—not an Arab among the eight grandparents. In fact, she's got an uncle who's the Minister of Education under the new regime, but she elected to stay with her husband after the revolution instead of going back to Algeria alone."

"Oh," said Yates, relaxing minusculy. He was impressed, though no more nearly convinced than he had been to start with. Maybe he ought to shunt Bradley to somebody on the investigation staff . . .

His phone pinged on the other side of the office.

He raised a finger, silently asking the woman for a minute, and called, "Yates."

The green light above the keypad went on as the phone's brain compared the word with the voiceprint and instructions in its memory, then opened the circuit. "Sam," said the speaker plate at a volume cracklingly adjusted for the supervisor's location in his office. "This is Barney at Communications. I'm sorry as hell, but there was some slippage and the feed went to your, ah, went to the office in Sector Twelve—"

"Shit," said Yates, too softly to trip the speaker but with a level of emotion that caused the woman's eyes to widen as they had when she stared at him past the waiter's body.

"—instead of here. Ah, do you want the data now?"

"Yeah," said the big man, leaning forward to check that the holotank was still set to receive. "Hey, wait a minute,

Barney. You got your people sorted out?''

''You bet, Sam. It was just an old key list, and I've purged it myself.'' It sounded like he meant it. Yoshimura didn't like screw-ups, least of all in his own shop.

''Then hold for just a bit and send me over the file of virus casualties first,'' the big security man said. ''D'ye have them sorted?''

The speaker plate gave a rattling laugh. ''Sorted? yeah, you could kinda say that. I'm going to punch 'em over to you myself without having to look up the access number. That tell you something?''

''Sorry, Barney.''

''No sweat, Sam. Why should you have the only office in the Secretariat that hasn't had the files downloaded?''

''I—''

''Nothing like a real tragedy to liven up conversation on the party circuit,'' Yoshimura concluded. ''Hold on, now— here it comes.''

The green light on the phone winked out with a faint click from the speaker. The tank began to hum. Yates poked the button marked ECHO on the pedestal's control board.

''The supervisor on second shift,'' Yates said, partly to fill time before the hardware locked in, and somewhat to take his mind off Yoshimura's amusement at his nosy colleagues. ''Has a nephew in this section, which ain't great all by itself, but he moved the kid into this office between when the previous guy left and I arrived.''

He gestured. The look on Bradley's face as she followed the sweep of his hand around the office reminded Yates of what a ridiculous cubbyhole he'd fought for. Seemed to be his morning to make people smile.

Still, the fight hadn't been one over space but rather pecking order. That had been occupying Terran life forms since before they grew backbones.

Yates laughed, breaking Ella Bradley's careful control into a broad grin of her own.

''Anyhow,'' the security man continued, ''Arjanian tried to get me shunted out to the Annex in Sector Twelve, even though my orders gave me a space allotment here at Central. Downside didn't say *where* at Central.''

The holotank chuckled happily, settling its pastel colors into the features of a dark, glowering man who certainly could pass for an Arab. The face dissolved into another and more at the rate of one a second, the rate at which files were being downloaded from the main system to the data banks in Yates' office.

The holograms were from the victims' travel documents, showing them as they had been in life, but Yates and Bradley both tensed as their minds supplied the blood and empty eyes of the similar faces that had stared at them in Le Moulin Rouge.

No question about similar either. Yates tugged his lower lip between his front teeth as they stared at cascading holo-grams that lent nothing but support to Bradley's notion. Facial appearance didn't *prove* anything about race, but the security man figured that the scattering of blue-eyed blondes he expected would send his visitor on her way gently.

Gently enough that he might get to know her a little better off-duty.

Thing was, it still looked like she might be correct.

"Our section head," said Yates, continuing the story but keeping his eyes on the tank. Talking made him feel less like the stage magician whose hat didn't have a bunny in it after all. "He's not real big on tough decisions, you see. Thought it'd be nice if I went out to the Annex 'until he straightened things out' . . . but he couldn't *order* me, you see, without getting Personnel in New York to cut a change."

Christ, there'd been a lot of them. Scattered throughout Headquarters Colony the way they'd been, there hadn't been a single event significantly worse than what had happened in the restaurant. But seeing the faces in order like this, every second ticking off another corpse, was starting to get on Sam Yates' nerves.

"He finally gave you the office, then?" said Ella in a pleasant tone that made up for the lack of eye contact. Like the security man, she was watching the display, and he was quite sure that she would call out as quickly as he if an evident non-Arab cycled by.

Christ, there were a lot.

"I had Communications run me hard copy of everything I might need, you know, for the job," Yates explained. He was little embarrassed now about the childishness of what he'd done; but the hell with that, he'd gotten the office he was supposed to have.

"Anyhow, I stacked it all in the corridor outside the section head's office and hunkered down to read it," he continued. "You could just about get past me if you had to"—he grinned—"but you know, my legs're pretty long, and I—you know, people generally don't like to make an issue of things with me, face to face."

The woman giggled.

"It took about half an hour," Yates said, patting Bradley's knee in a gesture of camaradarie that he hadn't planned, "and I had a crew to help me move the kid's traps out of this office."

They laughed together and met each other's eyes. Then, as they turned back to the holotank with their grins fading, Bradley clutched the security man's arm and pointed with her free hand, calling, "*There*, Superv—"

"Sam'll do just fine," said Yates, who was already bending forward, his grim tone a reflection of what he had seen rather than the words he spoke. This viewer had voice controls, but they worked about half the time—which made them totally useless, so far as Yates was concerned.

His fingers made firm, precise stabs at the control board, blanking the Echo into pastels again, though the data continued to course through the system with tiny clicks and beeps. Yates continued to prod the controls while the woman watched him, kneading together the fingers of her left hand.

A swarthy, smiling face congealed in the tank and was replaced a second later by a child so similar in features that she was probably related. The files loaded before Yates hit the control scrolled backward while the security man poised to lock on the face that had struck both him and his visitor.

"Looks like you were right," Bradley said to the back of the kneeling security man. "Though most—*there!*"

Yates stabbed, then blipped the data forward again to get the correct file. He poked one more button before shifting backward into the seat from which he had jumped to catch the controls.

"Be hard copy in a moment," he said to Bradley as the data bank behind her eeped. "Ella, you go by?"

"Ella," she agreed as she took the sheet of flimsy feeding from the slot beside her head. She handed it to the security man unread. "I must not have had all the names, or else I missed one when I keyed in the search commands. I don't have a staff here, you see, and I didn't want to wait for the department to get around to my request Downside."

"You recognize him, don't you?" Yates said, looking at the woman with a frown and then to the printout. He held the sheet so that he could glance past it at the face in the holo tank.

"Well . . ." Bradley temporized as she frowned at the hologram.

The fellow certainly wasn't memorable. A little moustache, slightly darker than the sandy hair on his scalp. No beard, though one would have been useful to hide the weak chin. Eyes more brown than blue, and skin pale enough for the breasts of a fat woman.

"Well," she repeated, "he certainly isn't an Arab. You're right about that."

"Beaton, Rodney Alan Thomas," Yates read from the flimsy. "He was in the restaurant. Sat down at my table just before—" The security man met Bradley's eyes, then spun his finger in the air as a catchall gesture covering the waiter's death and the minutes following.

"*Oh,*" the woman said, nodding in fierce agreement. "Yes. Yes. He went into the kitchen with you, that's right, when you went to call."

"Something like—" Yates said. His throat constricted before the next word came out. "*That,*" he added as an effort of will.

Sam Yates had killed the little man. He'd squeezed fresh, disease-laden blood onto Beaton, maybe through a break in the skin. All the security man remembered was the unexpected slickness of what he'd thought was tweed—but he didn't remember much connectedly about that night. Maybe he'd touched Beaton's face, maybe slapped the citizen's open mouth.

"Sam?" said Ella Bradley with concern.

"Yeah," said Yates. "Sorry."

Sorry indeed, but he wasn't about to blurt what had happened to this woman—who might have seen the incident but apparently hadn't—or to any of those investigating the disease outbreak. They might wonder why a virus with an obvious penchant for Arabs had struck down a single Northern European as well, but that wasn't reason enough for Yates to immolate himself.

It wasn't the first time he'd killed somebody by accident, though this time he hadn't used an automatic rifle.

The phone pinged.

"Yates," said the big man, pleased at the control in his voice as he listened from a mental distance.

"That's the lot, Sam," rattled Barney Yoshimura from the speaker plate. "What the Watch List now?"

"Barney," said Yates, squinting at the sheet of hard copy, "can you shunt the full file on Beaton, Rodney Alan Thomas, K-R one-five-zero, four-two-zero-two, zero-three-six? And then the Interprol feed, straight through."

"We've got clerks over here, you know, if there's something wrong with the computer link," grumbled the communications supervisor; but it had been a clerk's screw-up that put him on the line to Yates, and he wasn't going to insist on requests through channels—with their attendant delay—just now. "Hang on."

Yoshimura had not asked for a repeat of the victim's entry number. The security man had barely enough time to reset the pedestal controls before Beaton's face formed again in the tank. The printer purred, rolling out the data as quickly as the base unit received it.

"Same hologram?" said Bradley, nodding toward the vacuous face in the tank.

"They didn't run 'after' pictures in the general files they're giving out," Yates explained, calm though just a little emptier inside now that he'd come to his realization about Beaton's death. "Not, I'd guess, that there's not a chief of mission or two with a set for his private viewing.''

Why would anybody want to look at dead bodies? But people did.

"Ah," the security man continued aloud, "you may not have flubbed it when you keyed in the list." He handed Bradley the original sheet of flimsy. "This guy and another were found late, in a utility locker or something."

"What was a tourist from Sky Devon doing in suit room number 137?" asked the woman as she scanned the brief data from the victim list.

Not a bad question, Yates thought as he pulled the new printout from the slot, all the information that his section had on Rodney Beaton. "Not a bad que—" he began aloud. "Son of a *bitch*!"

When Ella Bradley leaned over to read the file data, her breast rubbed the man's right biceps. He was damned well aware of the contact, and he assumed she was also; but even though she shifted slightly, the two of them remained close enough together that warmth kept the memory alive.

It was a great improvement over the recent past, especially when added to the fact that he had one fewer death on his conscience than he'd figured.

"The victim list hadn't been updated either," the security man explained, since he wasn't sure Ella would see at once the crucial bit of information that had unburdened him. "When they did a full medical on Beaton, it turned out he didn't die of a pulmonary virus. He stepped out onto the surface without a suit, and blew his lungs into vacuum."

He let the woman take the file sheet with her as she straightened slowly away. "Ah," said Yates, returning to the initial problem, "that may mean that your, ah"—he caught himself before his tongue said "notion"—"theory is still supportable. I'll set you up with . . ."

Just who *would* be the right person to handle this officially? Somebody in the Bureau of Adminstration might—

"What was he doing with camera equipment woven into his coat?" Bradley asked as she pored over part of the file the security man had skimmed.

"Huh?" said Yates, bending over the woman in turn.

"Say, is there anything here about him having an implanted microphone? The way he was mumbling at the table, that'd explain . . ."

He and his visitor looked at one another. Neither of them spoke for a moment, until Yates said, "You know, I wouldn't mind knowing a little more about Rodney, here." He tapped the sheet which rustled in Bradley's grip.

"The virus . . ." the woman began carefully. "What they've decided happened," she went on, "was that cosmic-ray exposure on a shuttle to here caused a virus to mutate freakishly."

"And now it doesn't look like it was a virus," Yates said, in agreement with what he understood to have been the woman's idea when she first began to explain her theory.

Bradley shook her head sharply. "I don't know that," she emphasized. "I'd think that the med staff could tell beyond question. But the *precision* was too great for the . . . for little *bugs*. Somebody must have directed doses of the virus to every Arab he could find.

"Somebody human."

Not a little paranoid, are we? thought Yates as he met the woman's burning, steady gaze.

On the other hand, she seemed to be right.

"I'll make some inquiries about Beaton," the security man said with a grimace. "Somebody walking into space like that ought to rate a formal investigation, even with all the rest going on right now. But—he raised his hand, palm down but fingers toward Bradley in caution—"you understand, I don't have any authority in . . . in a criminal investigation, if that's what's going on."

"I'll get the background on Beaton myself," said the woman calmly as she stood up.

On Bradley's right hip was a large purse attached to her belt by a coil of memory plastic. She drew the purse away, opened it, and tucked in the folded printout. It was a low-gravity style whose form but not function had been copied Downside. The plastic coil drew the bag slowly but firmly to the woman's side when she released it. Downside, a purse of similar size would have to be empty, a mere fashion accessory, or it would throw its wearer into hip-shot awk-wardness.

"I don't think—" Yates began, the phrase a placeholder until he determined just what he *did* think.

"Supervisor," said Ella. Her face brightened and her whole body shifted, perhaps relaxed just a trifle, into a posture that made her beautiful. "Sam. Look, if I go through official channels with my present data—"

If I *go*, she'd said, noted the security man.

"—I'll be passed off as a crazy. Crazy *bitch*, which won't help. It would have been one thing if I were just pointing out that the virus struck Arab ethnics, but the suggestion that this Beaton"—her hand flicked the surface of the holotank—"was prepared to record the event as it occurred . . ." She laughed.

"Yeah, well," said Yates as he stood also, uncomfortable because of the ease with which he could imagine Ella being treated as a nut.

Years ago a psychiatrist friend had told him, "Just because somebody's paranoid, it doesn't follow that there *aren't* people plotting against him." The height difference when both of them were standing made it harder for him to take the woman seriously, but Yates was familiar enough with that quirk in his personality to know how to compensate for it.

"If there's more involved than one person." Bradley went on, "then an official inquiry's going to warn the others that they're at risk. I'll simply have to request for information on Beaton—as a visitor to Headquarters Colony—sent to Sky Devon through my Downside office at NYU."

"Might be interesting to learn if Beaton was orphaned when a mob in Cairo piled his parents on a bonfire," Yates said in what was as close as he could bring himself to agreement with a plan that still bothered him. Civilians shouldn't get involved in what was *real* police business; and on this one, Sam Yates was as much a civilian as the woman herself.

He couldn't think of a quicker route out of UN Security than an attempt to ram this conspiracy notion up the formal chain of command, though. The choice was to let it go, to trust that somebody else would follow it up—when only he and Bradley knew the technician had been in Le Moulin Rouge before the deaths began . . .

"I don't guess," Yates said aloud, "that I'll ever get so used to murder that I'll look aside t' keep from getting involved."

Bradley's face lost its smile but not its beauty. "Yes," she said, "I agree," though the security man could not be sure that she meant what he meant. "We'll be in touch, then?"

"Do you have plans for dinner?" Yates asked with his voice and eyes both level.

Bradley's relaxed appearance hardened, but not to the bowstring tautness she had exhibited when she first entered the office. "Dinner would be nice," she said after a pause in which her eyes had not left the man's.

"Nineteen hundred, then," said Yates, "And I'll let you suggest the place. So long—" his smile was grim enough to remind his visitor that they had business together, that she needn't freeze up—"as it's not French. I had a bad experience the last time I went out for French food."

"Twenty hours," she replied with a nod and a quirk of her mouth indicating that she accepted the humor for what it was. "I want to have some information, if possible, and New York's five hours behind us here. Pick me up at my apartment. My office is there. I'm sure"—she nodded toward the data bank—"that you can find the address yourself."

Cool, aren't we? Yates thought. "I'll look forward to it," he said aloud. "And maybe I'll have learned something by then also."

Watching the anthropologist's series of maneuvers, real put-offs or else coyness, gave the security man an idea about how he might learn more about Beaton's death.

He was pretty sure he'd better not tell Ella Bradley what he had in mind, though.

Chapter 6

SOMEBODY ELSE'S JOB

The monitor beside the door of Patrol Substation Central Four showed that the reception desk was empty, but Sam Yates' ID card let him into the unit without need to touch the call button. The door was hydraulically actuated, a necessity because it was of thick titanium plate instead of the foam sandwich construction normal in the colony. The partition walls that separated the substation from the corridor had been armored with titanium plate on the inside also.

The hallway within was narrowed by lockers against the outer wall. They faced doorways, most of which were closed. The door nearest to the right of the reception desk was ajar. Yates pushed it fully open to meet the stare of a uniformed patrolman young enough to be irritated at the intrusion but junior enough to remain deferential.

"I'm looking for Lieutenant Yesilkov," the security supervisor said. "Information says she's here."

The patrolman shrugged. "Yeah, she's here—three doors down. But she won't thank you, buddy. We're all fuckin' buried, and she's trying to catch up on paperwork while Todd handles the street."

"Thanks," Yates said neutrally as he closed the door again. That news wasn't great for his purposes, but Yesilkov wouldn't have been around here if she weren't busy; and most people, not just bureaucrats, were willing to grab any excuse that rescued them from necessary drudgery. He knocked on the indicated door.

"What the hell is it?" snarled the voice of the patrol lieutenant throught the flimsy panel. There were three names in tungsten sulfide letters on the plate; none of them were hers.

Yates opened the door instead of speaking to it. Yesilkov was at the desk console of a room smaller than the supervisor's own office. Metal boxes were stacked waist high in the narrow space surrounding the desk, but the sole chair to the left of the door was clear.

"Lieutenant Yesilkov?" the big man said to the lieutenant's professionally-blanked expression. "We met last—."

"*Yeah,*" Yesilkov agreed. She spoke with the same pleasure at recognition that Yates himself had felt when he was able to place Ella Bradley earlier that morning. "Sure, Yates, Samuel—surpervisor from . . . Commo?" She stood and reached over the desktop to shake her visitor's hand.

"Entry Division," Yates said in a tone of agreement. "But yeah, that's me. I'm just in a lot better shape 'n I was when you last saw me." He paused before adding, "Ah, I know you're busy, but can I have a minute?"

"Have what you need," said the lieutenant, waving to the chair by the door and sitting down again herself. Her grip had been firm, dry, and warm to Yates' own palm. "After all, I figure you saved me about an hour by not dyin' and adding another name t' my report backlog."

Yates laughed with both his mouth and his eyes. He could see the left side of Yesilkov's face quirk in a grin of approval: he'd passed a private test of her own, let her know that he wasn't going to turn civilian and report her if she got loose enough to joke with him.

"Look," the security man said more soberly, "this won't make your job easier, but it just *might* lead to a result. All the disease deaths, that's the problem, right?" He gestured at the console.

Yesilkov laced her fingers behind the blond hair fluffing at the nape of her neck, and arched to stretch herself over the seat back. She looked a damn sight less chunky in that posture, uniform or not; and though she was aware of Yates' interest, she clearly didn't disapprove.

"All the ones my team investigated, yeah," she said, "which was fourteen, all told. A great night. Plus all the rest of the crap because of the confusion—looting, accidents, you name it. You know . . ."

She leaned forward, lowering her voice. Her visitor almost certainly didn't know, and it did her soul good to blurt it to an outsider. "You know, the Kenyan ambassador ran his car up on the Mexican ambassador's when traffic, you know, tied up sudden? They started swinging at each other, and one of the chauffeurs was pulling a knife just as we got there."

She grimaced. "Had t' pop him, damn near had t' put down the whole damn *lot* of 'em. You think *that's* a fun report t' write and keep my job?"

"I got my share of the third world," said Yates, taking a risk of his own, "in Nicaragua. And some days I think that job was simpler."

If her visitor had not stuck his own neck out—that statement wouldn't have had to go far up the Secretariat hierarchy to net Yates a fierce reprimand—the patrol lieutenant would have tensed up at what she had said to him. That was the last thing Yates needed; and anyway, he didn't have any apologies for his own words.

Yesilkov grinned and flexed her elbows back again, not really for exercise this time. "Okay, big guy," she said. "Make my life tougher."

"I gave you a description of the other customers while we were waiting for Medical," the Entry supervisor said. "I don't know how lucid I was?"

He cocked an eyebrow at Yesilkov.

She shrugged. "Not bad, considering," she said. "we found the Yugoslavs—second secretaries. They won't admit they were there, but there's fingerprints all *over* the place settings. And . . ."

Yesilkov's grin narrowed into a slightly-forced chuckle. "We found the other four Indians, who were pretty clear that, well, somebody fitting your description had a violent argument with the waiter before cutting him with a knife and running into the kitchen to finish the job.

"The other two," she continued, "the guy you thought might be from a habitat and the guy with the beard—who the woman at the next table confirms, though no details— they must not 'a touched anything at the table, and they haven't come forward t' help.

"Not," she concluded with her full-face frown, "that they were likely to, but it'd let me close things a little neater on that one."

"I found one of them," said Yates, flexing his right leg to rest his foot on the storage boxes beside the desk. He was frowning as he tried to remember the evening, not just the customers as individuals.

He was *sure* that Beaton had picked up his water glass. Maybe the tumbler had been shattered beyond reconstruction for prints in the hasty investigation made necessary by the number of incidents. Maybe Beaton had carried the glass off with him.

And maybe the technician's skin had been coated with an osmotic barrier, a standard laboratory precaution which would keep his fingerprints from showing up at the same time it prevented possible contaminants from reaching his skin.

"Ah," said the big man, aware of the expectant Yesilkov again. "He was dead, stepped out into vacuum, and the preliminary in my files looked . . . funny." He reached over the desk to give the lieutenant a copy of the Entry Division printout.

"Stepped?" said Yesilkov, accepting the hard copy but keeping her eyes on her visitor for the moment.

"Fell, jumped, or was pushed," said Yates, using the Downside phrase for which there was not as yet an equivalent off-Earth shorthand. "I'd be *real* interested to know what the full investigation turned up on that guy. If he had something to do with what happened in the restaurant, then, well . . ."

The security man intended to keep his voice light, but he heard it harden and realized just how emotionally involved he was in this businees, if there *were* a business—"he gave me a real bad night, and he gave a lot of other people a worse one, all over the colony."

"What d'ye suppose he was doing with a camera in his jacket weave?" asked the lieutenant mildly. She frowned at the printout, holding it in her right hand as her left keyed Beaton's ID number into the pad on her console by feel.

Data flashed on the flat screen, visible but not readable from the angle at which Yates sat. Yesilkov stared at it for a moment before continuing in the same quizzical tone, "And why d'ye suppose he'd have a plug filter in his left nostril?"

"If I had to guess," said Yates, playful the way a cat is playful with a wounded bird, "I'd bet he sneezed the other one out when his lungs burst, but nobody noticed it outside the air lock when they hauled him in."

The lieutenant nodded slowly as she continued to read the screen.

"You might check," the security man added, going back to his earlier thought, "whether his hands weren't covered with osmotic gel. A lab barrier, you know—wash it off with alcohol after you're done."

"Hands and face," Yesilkov agreed, still nodding. She touched another key and the printer at the side of her console began to whine.

"You can give a firm ID on this guy being at the scene?" she asked as she turned to Yates and put her hands behind her neck again.

"Yes," Yates said flatly. "I picked his hologram out of the victim list, just by chance."

"Right," said Yesilkov. The printer paused, then resumed its function. She nodded to the sheet of copy feeding from the machine and said, "I'm burnin' you off one, too, but you don't need to tell anybody where it came from. Officially, I'll be in touch with you about the investigation. Probably have you eyeball the body."

She chuckled with the same grim humor she'd displayed earlier. "Have t' bring him in to do that. They got 'em warehoused on the surface. Thank God for vacuum, huh?"

"I—" Yates said, standing and extending his hand to the woman. He'd started to say "I appreciate this," and he did; but it was Yesilkov's job, after all. "I'll be interested to hear what you get on this," he said instead.

The patrol officer rose and gave Yates the printout before she shook hands. "You're new up here, aren't you?" she said, easing back against her chair to look the man over carefully.

"A week," Yates agreed evenly. "My wife broke things off, and I figured taking a slot up here might be a good idea in a lot of ways."

"I see," said the blond woman, nodding as she slowly sat back down. "Well, you're luckier 'n me. My husband wouldn't leave me if I put a gun to his head."

Her eyes met those of her visitor. Neither of them blinked. She was too solid to look small, even seated while the tall man looked down at her. "You know," she continued, "you wouldn't think there was *any*body couldn't hold a job up here, as tight as things are, but he says his painting's the only thing his heart's in."

Yates made a grimace of understanding.

"Yeah," said the lieutenant. "I wouldn't even mind *that* so much if he could bring himself to sell one, now and again. Wouldn't be real art, then, I suppose."

She shrugged. "Neither here nor there, I suppose. I figure"—she paused—"I'll be talking to you again."

"I figure so too," said Yates, smiling much as the woman had when she joked about the stored corpses. "I'll look forward to that."

He thought of something else as he left the office, headed back to his own work, but it would have been the wrong note to interject just now.

The next time he talked to the patrol lieutenant, however, he'd have to mention the bearded man who'd sat at Ella Bradley's table.

Because he'd touched his tableware also, and there should have been fingerprints . . . unless he, too, had been protected by lab gel.

Chapter 7

DOWNSIDE

"I tell you, I'm *expected*," said Karel Pretorius in growing irritation. The best thing he could say about New York City was simply that it was on Earth; and now the sky had begun to drizzle besides.

"That's great," said one of the trio of men in dark suits. "Then I'll let you in. When I'm told to."

"Hold this please, sir," said another of the guards, offering Pretorius a pair of metal tubes T'ed into wire leads. "Yes sir, one in either hand."

It was humiliating, but the Afrikaner representative accepted the handgrips. The leads were connected to the box strapped around the guard's waist, and the display screen was tilted up toward his eyes.

The metal was cold, and its touch permitted Pretorius to imagine that he could feel the electricity being fed into him through the leads. Consciously he knew that was not the case: the current was at ultra-high frequencies and of negligible wattage, just enough to build a charge over the conductive surface of his body.

Anomalies in that charge limned on the guard's display a picture of everything the Afrikaner wore over his body and anything unusually conductive—metallic—beneath the surface of his flesh. He could probably enter the building with an unnoticed charge of explosive carried up his anus— but its lead azide detonator would show up on the screen.

Besides, Pretorius doubted that he would be permitted to go to the bathroom alone after he got inside.

"He's clean," the guard with the search apparatus said regretfully, but he kept his eyes on the display a moment longer, as if in hope that a weapon would spring into sight as soon as it heard the coast was clear.

Pretorius released the grips. They flickered in the streetlights as their leads recoiled against the base unit. The fleshy Afrikaner had learned at his first meeting in this building not to carry anything to which the guards might object. They had removed his card case—the microcircuitry within each card might not be what it appeared; and his dictation wand—the meeting was not to be recorded, at least by him; and the trio of writing styluses which he carried.

The guards were not concerned that the styluses might contain weapons. Rather, they knew that anything with a sharp point *was* a deadly weapon if rammed into an eye or throat. The guards were not paid to take chances; and they were not concerned about an Afrikaner, though he was spokesman for his people to a world that did not choose to listen.

While one guard watched Pretorius and another was poring over the research apparatus, the third kept his eyes on the street. He looked nowhere in particular—or rather, he looked everywhere, scanning the vehicles that passed and the patterns their lights drew in puddles, flicking over building fronts and even toward roof lines hidden by mist and distance. There was surveillance equipment more sophisticated than the human eye; but a trained eye can be very useful, and these eyes were coupled by predatory reflexes to the plasma gun the guard held beneath his coat.

"They say for him to go up," said the guard with the search apparatus to the one who watched the visitor.

"Do they?" the guard replied. After a pause that was as deliberately insulting as the gesture with which he opened the door—pushing it with his foot—he thumbed Pretorius into the building.

The Afrikaner could feel the third guard's eyes brush him as he stepped past. The look made Pretorius' skin shiver as if someone had poured ether down his spine and the evaporating fluid were sucking all the heat out of his body.

The door opened on to an elevator car, not the ground floor proper, and as soon as the door closed again, the car began to rise. Pretorius was sure that there were controls hidden behind the mirror-finished walls, but touching them would have been foolish—suicidal—even if he were sure of their location.

Instead he stared perforce at the images of himself which filled a space that could have held a dozen other men as well. He wished he were younger and that he had real hair instead of a synthetic mat color-keyed to the remaining white fringe at the base of his neck.

And he wished that these men and women, this *Club*, would recognize that they needed him, instead of treating him like muck on which they would not deign to walk.

The car stopped. Pretorius assumed he was on the top floor of the ten-story building, but he could not be sure. Only the direction in which the elevator accelerated convinced him that it rose instead of dropping into some armored subbasement beneath the parking garage and the entrance by which the Club members themselves entered.

Sometimes his imagination confused the sensory loops in his inner ears, so that Pretorius was convinced that he had plunged all the way down to Hell and that he would step out of the elevator into an inferno. That was never literally true.

"You're expected sir," said the attendant—not a guard; the Afrikaner never *saw* a guard here in the circular hall surrounding the meeting room, though he knew he was the object of eyes and weapons as deadly as those of the men at the street entrance.

"Yes, yes," said Pretorius as he left the elevator, careful to keep his voice clear of the irritation he felt at being rebuked by a woman—and a Kaffir besides.

She had spoken in a neutral tone tinged with an American accent as velvety as the texture of the skin visible beyond the scarlet tights she wore. The threat in the bland words was as glaring as her hair, teeth, and irises, all colored to match the fabric of her costume. The members of the Club expected Karel Pretorius, and if he balked them by twenty seconds because he was daydreaming in their elevator—who knew what they would do to him? If it had not been for the Plan . . .

But it *was* for the Plan; and in order to return his people to their home and their destiny, Karel Pretorius would have accepted worse treatment than what the Club meted out to him.

He walked toward the door that split to admit him, the weight of its lead core carried silently on massive trunnions.

There were fifteen people at the semicircular table facing the door and the ovoid chair placed for their visitor. Pretorius sat down without needing to be directed. His age and weight made him cautious, but he had no hesitation in gripping the armrest and leaning back against the cushions which he knew monitored everything from his heart rate to the patterns traced by his brain waves.

He had no need to lie to these people, nothing to conceal from the Club. The position that he espoused openly as spokesman for the Afrikaner nation was the reason that they had come to him.

"We are not wholly satisfied with the results of the test," said the man at one end of the table in what Pretorius suspected, despite the electronic deconstruction and rebuilding of the words, was an Oriental accent.

There were not always the same number of Club members present at these meetings, but the Afrikaner had never seen more than the fifteen who watched him now. They were screened from him—and possibly from one another—by hologram projections, patterns of shifting light and shade, that made them individual lumps behind an insubstantial curtain.

Pretorius could have guessed at who some of the members were, despite their camouflage; but he did not really care about their identity. All that mattered was that no member of the Club was a Kaffir.

And of that there could be no doubt.

"I don't understand your lack of satisfaction," said the Afrikaner honestly. A negative remark by his . . . patrons, should have frightened him, but this was so unexpected that he could not believe it was seriously meant. "Of course, you have sources of information more precise than those open to me . . . but both the public media and my personal informants are in agreement that the test was an unexampled success."

One of the Club members wheezed as he or she breathed, but Pretorius could not identify the person through the barrier of disrupted light and sound. For long moments there was nothing else in the room to hear.

"There was to be a limited number of test units," said the voice of a woman seated near the center of the table. The dim light made her thin, precise voice a communication from beyond the grave. "No less than three, no more than a dozen."

"There were over five *hundred*," said the man beside her, needlessly completing the thought and identifying himself as the member who wheezed.

"The outbreak was nevertheless limited in all *important* ways," Pretorius noted, frowning to himself and delivering the opinion slowly so that his brain could check and recheck it to be sure that he was not overlooking some point of crucial significance. "There was no involvement—so far as I have been able to learn—outside the targeted racial category."

Perhaps they were concerned that the sheer size of the "disaster" focused world attention on it. But what better source of misdirection could there be than an extinct virus that had attacked Arabs—on the Moon?

"Why did so many die?" asked the woman who was the voice of death. She ignored Pretorius' statement as completely as if she had not heard it.

"The test was to be limited mechanically," said the Afrikaner, reaching up to stroke the goatee that he had shaved off years before, when the hair grew coarse and white, "to one or two rooms in a colony that was itself isolated from the general population."

None of them spoke. They were staring at him, he presumed, but even that was uncertain behind their curtains of light.

"But more important," Pretorius continued, "the virus was to be *self*-limiting, to be unable to replicate beyond a fixed number of times no matter how ideal conditions for reproduction may otherwise be. And in this the test was wholly successful. There was an Arab crew member and two Jordanian passengers on the shuttle that docked within ninety minutes of the test release, and none of the three experienced any ill effects.''

That depended on how you looked at the problem, of course. The passengers had driven straight to the Jordanian mission premises; before, as it turned out, any survivor had reported the events there. One of the new arrivals had made a hysterical call to Security, and the other was still hospitalized—crooning to the wife whose head he'd been cradling when a patrol arrived.

''Why wasn't it limited to a single *room*?'' said one of the shadow figures harshly. Hands moved, wringing themselves in rage or grief behind the rippling hologram. ''How did it get *out*?''

The Club had access to all the information gathered by the governments and multinational corporations to which its members belonged. They were not always—not often, Pretorius suspected—the persons in formal control of their organizations. But there is apparent power and real power, and it was the latter that reeked through the layers of armor and obscurity the Club set between itself and its visitor.

But they did not know what Karel Pretorius knew, because any direct attempt they made to gather information would risk the wider discovery of the truth and possibly their own involvement.

They *needed* Pretorius, as a conduit. And they would need his folk in the near future, to step forward while the world reeled in shock—a race loathed equally by all, and therefore equally acceptable to all as the new rulers of Sub-Saharan Africa.

If there were no government in place to sign concessions, there would be chaos and war among the powers . . . and that was undesirable.

''The test revealed two misconceptions about the process,'' said the Afrikaner, slowly this time so that he could be accurate while reporting matters beyond his normal expertise. He had always been a quick study—that was a major reason he held his position as spokesman—but he was concerned not to say anything that the experts who would dissect his words might think had been meant to mislead.

''The outer container in which the sample was transported,'' Pretorius continued, ''had been irradiated and was free of contamination. There was no outbreak of disease on either of the shuttles involved, nor at Transfer Station Two, where the courier passed through.''

Pretorius was sure there was a spike on the instruments monitoring him when he said that. He also had staged through that transfer station on his way from Florida to Sky Devon. It was only later that he understood the risk he had taken.

''The inner container, the phial from which the planned release was made,'' the Afrikaner said, his accent and years of practice concealing from his listeners any of the emotions that their instruments would nevertheless snatch directly from his nerve impulses. ''That appears to have been contaminated. There was an incident in the suit room where the courier is believed to have opened the lead container. The outer container.''

''That was a failure,'' snapped one of the members.

''Yes, madam,'' said Pretorius, ''it was a failure—but not a significant one.''

Had the speaker not been a woman, the Afrikaner might have modified his words. Certainly he would have avoided the patronizing tone which he knew was a mistake even as it sounded in his ears.

It was not the woman but a man near the left end of the table who sprang to his feet and shouted, ''Not significant? Fellows, give me this buffoon for a few hours, so that his successor will know the standard of competence we expect!''

The accent was pure Oxford, but the features that wavered higher and farther back than the focal plane of the hologram curtain were those of a Saudi prince.

The outburst frightened Pretorius, but—unlike most of the others in the room—he had faced guns and the probability of torture in the past. ''Sirs and mesdames,'' he said, calmer in some ways than he had been when he was describing biotechnical events, ''my apologies for misspeaking. But the event was a test, and it was clear to you as well as to the principals involved that not all the results were foreseeable.''

The persons across the curved table were whispering

among themselves. Two had risen to touch and remonstrate with the Saudi. Pretorius deliberately looked away from the trio lest he recognize other members of the Club—and be doomed by those recorded spikes of knowledge if his words had not been enough for the purpose.

"Go on," said the man who had first addressed the visitor. "You said there had been *two* misconceptions."

"Yes, that is correct," said the Afrikaner while his peripheral vision caught the movement at the other end of the table. The Saudi and the pair who had mollified him were seating themselves again. "The other and more important error was the belief that the viral strain would replicate itself even under conditions that were less than genetically ideal for it. That is . . ."

He paused, miming the next phrase with his lips and tongue before he spoke the words aloud. "It was believed that most or all of those who were exposed to the virus would exhibit some symptoms, but that serious effects would be limited to those test units whose DNA contained the specific bundle of genes to which the strain had been tailored."

Pretorius had not said "Arabs," a mistake of phrasing he might have made except for the Saudi's previous outburst. There was no wind but blew some good . . . and there was nothing of real value that came without risk.

God knew that there was risk enough in this business, for Karel Pretorius and his folk—and for these others as well.

"In fact," the Afrikaner continued, "the principals believe that replication—infection—was solely limited to the tissues of the target group. This is an unexpected level of precision, and it had important positive consequences for the . . . planned endeavor."

For the Plan. For his folk's trek back to their home, and to more.

The—possible—Oriental did not speak at once, but the wheezing fat man said, "There would have been fewer deaths then. Instead there were more, many more. Are you"—the head that was a bullet-shaped shadow set necklessly on a haystack-shaped shadow shifted, the eyes

looking toward the Saudi prince—"trying to mislead us . . .
boy?"

"No sir," said Pretorius as calmly as if he did not know
his mind had flashed an impulse to kill across the monitors.
"Because the genetic delay designed into the strain was on
the basis of numbers of replications rather than time—which
I understand would not have been possible—the fact that
the virus spread only when it was certain to kill meant that
it did not use itself up within a few minutes of release, as
had been intended."

There was quiet conversation around the table, scarcely
a buzz to the Afrikaner's ears.

"I should add," Pretorius said, because it was his nature
as well as his duty to be precise, "that the principals themselves are unclear on the matter. Their courier died in an
accident before he could transmit the detailed information
they had expected."

"Committed suicide," snapped a member who was
speaking for the first time. "*He* knew it had been botched.
Botched."

"I bow to your greater knowledge," said the Afrikaner,
more in truth than for effect. All that his own sources could
tell him was that the technician from Sky Devon had walked
out into vacuum without a space suit. His folk had no access
to official reports on the matter, but suicide was a probable
enough explanation.

It wouldn't be the first time a human tool broke in the
course of duties for which it had not been tempered.

"But," Pretorius continued, "despite its undesired side
effects, the test proves that a very great level of specificity
is possible. Not certain: the principals will not promise that
a different virus tailored to radically different genetic bundles
will act with the same . . . razor-edged, one might say, care."

He waved his right hand in the gesture of a man throwing
away a bit of trash. "Even if they promised, it would be
the act of a fool to believe them, and you would not support
me if I were a fool.

"But the precision is now *possible,* sirs and mesdames,"
Pretorius concluded, leaning forward in his chair. "Proba-

ble, even, as it was not before. The test that tells us that cannot be considered wholly an unsuccess.''

"We'll take your opinion under advisement," said the fat Club member, the last syllable as much a wheeze as part of a word. "I think"—the pause was for noisy breathing, not thought or rhetoric—"that you should leave now."

The big head shimmered in slow movement. From the end of the table the Oriental said, "You'll be summoned when we next wish to see you."

Pretorius accepted the brusque dismissal as he always did, neutrally: unpleasant, but a factor that had to be expected—like the flies that had bitten him the times he lay in ambush with heat waves shimmering from the receiver of his machine gun. He got up with the deliberation of age, levering himself out of the deep chair with his hands and the back of his calves instead of trusting solely to the muscles of his thighs and lower back.

"Wait," called a Club member harshly.

"Sir?" Pretorius responded to the shadowy blur that had been a Saudi prince when the member's anger had been a touch fiercer.

"You've seen to it that there won't be any slipups afterward?" the Oxford accent demanded. "When the laboratory will have become a liability."

"The one who has been entrusted with that duty is a long-time associate of mine," said the old Afrikaner. He almost seated himself again within the battery of monitors, but instruments could tell these faceless creatures nothing that was not clear in his quietly assured voice. "He will not fail in this duty."

The dignity of Pretorius' response took the Saudi aback. He grunted to clear his throat, a disconcerting sound when the electronic screen had finished fragmenting and reassembling it.

"You had better be right," said the Club member, choosing to take the last word, though he knew he had already been bested in the exchange. "The test would not have been allowed to proceed had we not been guaranteed it would be limited. A false guarantee."

The Afrikaner bowed without speaking and began to walk

toward the armored doors which would roll when he reached them.

He wondered whether the strain of virus tested on the Moon were really extinct. If a further sample could be procured; if it could be spread on his cuff, perhaps, just before he entered the building for his next interview with the Club . . .

There would be a risk, of course.

But not, he suspected, as much personal risk for Karel Pretorius as there was in letting the Plan come to fruition while the Saudi was still alive.

Chapter 8

THE CLUB

The meeting room dimmed when the doors closed behind Karel Pretorius because the hologram screening shut off also and its diffracted light no longer played over the features of the Club members. Al-Fahd first mumbled in his own language, then began to talk of retribution in English; but there was far more important business at hand.

"Obviously we cannot expect the technicians' assessment of the new strain to be any more accurate than their predictions for the test variety," said Sakai, whose artificial left eye was so nearly perfect that it could be noticed only by the fact its pupil did not expand under the present conditions. "It may have the designed limitations, it may not. The risk is unacceptable."

"We knew there were risks," growled Heidigger, one of the generals in the room. "The Dutchman's right, you know: it didn't do exactly what they said it would, but it did better." He nodded crisply to the Saudi beside him and added, "Sure, I'm sorry about the collateral damage, but the—hell, the couple *thousand* pneumonia cases we expected weren't going to be a picnic either."

"There's a level of truth to that," said Pleyal as she rubbed her nose in obvious distaste at agreeing with any opinion of Heidigger's. "After all, we didn't expect any geographical limitation on the main release."

"Wouldn't want one," said Lee, whose accent was American though his features were not. "There'll be disruption, certainly, but the long-term benefits outweigh them."

A smile quirked his expression into that of a moon-faced pixie. "The short-term benefits as well, for those of us who

82

are prepared to take advantage of them.''

Blake, who had been laboriously sucking in a breath while Lee spoke, now said, "What we expected didn't include a kill ratio of a hundred percent either.''

All eyes in the room turned to the grotesquely fat man in the center of the table. He glared around him like a bear baited by dogs while his lungs struggled to fill themselves for another statement.

"Ah, surely," said Mahavishtu in the oily voice that made even flat truth sound like a lie when it came from his lips, "there was nothing undesirable about a more complete success than we expected?''

"Not if it's limited to coloreds, like we plan," said Blake with a harshness that was as much venom at life as it was a result of the battle that speech always cost him. "Like they promise *this* time.''

In the frozen silence that followed Blake's concluding wheeze, Sakai remarked, "To return to Madame Pleyal's observation"—he nodded toward the angular woman—"I think in fact we *can* count on geographical limitations when we direct the main release.''

Heidigger gave a loud snort that began as an even more disdainful obscenity. "A tiny sample ran through UN Headquarters in a coupla hours. Do you really think that multiple releases in Africa are going to stop at the Mediterranean? Or even the *Atlantic*.''

"I think they'll stop at the atmosphere," responded the Japanese industrialist sharply enough to cut through the sudden babble of voices.

There was silence, then another confusion of words and even languages.

"A moment, please," demanded Mahavishtu with the surprising volume he could summon at need. "What our colleague has suggested is very interesting. But will it not cause comment if we, many of whom have never left Earth, should do so at the same time . . . and at a time which will later be the subject of much scrutiny, scrutiny that even we will not be able to control?''

"Not," said Sakai, "if we are attending the celebrations at United Nations Headquarters. Are there any of us here who would seem out of place at the Twentieth Anniversary Commemoration?''

He looked blandly at his fellows, neither eye blinking. The slight disparity in pupil size give him a subliminal psychic advantage over those who met his gaze but were not consciously aware of its details.

Heidigger guffawed. No one else spoke for a moment.

"You can arrange invitations, Mistress Undersecretary?" Sakai prompted, focusing—and not—on the woman to his immediate left.

"There'll be a delay, of course?" al-Fahd protested, drawn back into the deliberations when they intersected his own preoccupation. "Cancellation, even, because of the . . . disaster?"

"Could they cancel a war?" argued Lee coolly, turning his head in challenge to the Saudi. "Could they cancel a rainstorm?"

"Yes, that is correct," said Perilla, planning while her lips pursed in the direction of her ring, a cameo much older than Portugal—let alone Brazil. "The celebration is to go ahead . . . There will be individuals who choose not to attend at the last minute. That will make changes more easy—"

She looked up, sweeping her fellow Club members with her hazel eyes. "That would not have been difficult in any case. Not too difficult."

"Then," said Pleyal with a crispness hinting that she liked the other female in the Club as little as she did General Heidigger, "we will proceed on that basis with our individual arrangements—and with the timing of the main release."

"It is no more than a slum there, you realize," added Perilla, speaking sadly in the direction of her cameo. "Twenty years ago they broke ground, and by today they have accomplished a slum to which no one is transferred who can avoid it."

She glanced around imperiously, her eyes flashing like the jewel-encrusted combs in her hair, the emeralds and topazes that she could not wear as a public functionary but wore here. "I would never have gone there, you realize.

But now, for a few days, it will be"—she flicked her fingers—"acceptable to me."

"I wonder," said Mahavishtu in a musing tone, "whether we should not see to it that a large Sub-Saharan contingent attends the ceremonies?"

"Why the hell?" demanded Heidigger, while other faces around the table blanked or frowned.

"Why, for breeding stock," the Indian explained. "We can house them, do you not think, next to the okapis and the tigers?"

Someone swore under his breath. There was general motion as Club members slid their chairs back and rose from the table.

Mahavishtu remained seated. "Another species becomes extinct," he said. "So sad."

He was still giggling as he left the room.

Chapter 9

IMPROVISING

The only rich color bathed by the light reflected into the room was the spray of huge roses grown here on Sky Devon. The antiseptic array of blacks and whites that otherwise furnished the office of Director Sutcliffe-Bowles was in contrast to the pungency of pig manure which permeated the atmosphere of the entire orbital habitat. The odor did not seem to bother Sutcliffe-Bowles, but Dr. Kathleen Spenser was willing to kill to avoid it.

She had already murdered 517 people at UN Headquarters in order to free herself from Sky Devon on terms that she found acceptable.

The tall, spare woman cleared her throat as she waited for her superior, tilted back in a chair that looked complex enough to be remotely pilotable, to acknowledge her presence in response to his summons. Sutcliffe-Bowles raised a hand to silence her. Though he did not open his eyes, his pinkish face wrinkled up in displeasure at the hint of interruption.

Spenser held herself almost motionless, smoothing the edge of her white lab smock while her mind drew in considerable detail a picture of the director with his limbs blackening and sloughing off as gangrene attacked his tissues. The trouble was, she and Sutcliffe-Bowles were almost identical in ethnic background.

She had double-checked to be, regretfully, sure.

There was a swelling climax to the music that filled the director's office as thoroughly and offensively as did the reek of hog feces. The director's eyes opened and his chair

86

tilted him upright as if the three events had been programmed together.

"Magnificent," said Sutcliffe-Bowles with proprietary certainty. "The Immolation of the Gods and Valhalla, of course. We live in the best of ages, my dear: we have now achieved technical perfection in the creation and recording of sound—and we have the genius of Wagner from the past. Mere mechanical skill would be of small benefit without the work of genius to infuse it."

"So I understand," said Dr. Spenser, uttering a collection of syllables past experience had taught her to mouth in response to the director's absurdities. It was incredible that anyone could visit Sky Devon, much less run it, and believe that humanity had reached the summit of progress in any technical art.

And as for Wagner, she would prefer pig shit if that were the only choice.

The director opened a flat dispenser of varicolored euphoric tablets, chose one for himself, and offered the remainder to this subordinate. "For you?"

"No thank you, Director," Spenser said distantly. "I'm working. You called me from my laboratory to see you at once."

"Yes, yes, I did," agreed Sutcliffe-Bowles with neither embarrassment nor anger at the implied rebuke. "We had a request, what was it. . . ?"

More sharply and with a frown toward the sheet of uncluttered black boro-cadmium monomer that formed his desktop, the director said, "The note for Kathie."

A sheet of hard copy fed soundlessly from a slot in the desktop which had been invisible until it disgorged its printed burden. "There," said the director, gesturing toward the brief document which Spenser had to lean across the broad desk to reach. "He's from your lab, isn't he?"

The microbiologist felt her knees waver a moment before she lost all sense of the body that nevertheless continued to support her. The sheet she had just skimmed expanded into duplicates of itself, then shrank back down to a single document whose letters burned her mind.

Around Spenser's neck was a silver chain. Her left hand now touched the lump of the pendant hidden beneath her clothing. It was a spherical drop of crystal the size of her thumb at the first joint, wrapped in wire that only a metallurgist might have guessed was tungsten rather than one of the rare metals more common in jewelry.

"Yes, Director," she heard herself say. "Or rather, he used to be. Technician Beaton died a week ago in an accident while he was on vacation."

"Well," said Sutcliffe-Bowles with a flutter of his hands, "that's why they want information, then. Take care of it, will you, like a good girl."

"You may have misinterpreted the request, Director," said Spenser, her eyes on the flimsy and her mind filled with shifting images—some of them news holograms fed from the bloody corridors of Headquarters Colony. "This appears to be part of a university study of off-Earth cultural patterns rather than something connected with the accident. An on-going study."

"Well, take *care* of it, won't you, Kathie?" ordered Sutcliffe-Bowles, frowning and making a little fluttering motion with his hands as his chair rocked him into a semirecline again. "The Prelude to Tannhauser, I think," he called to his desk.

"Always nice to chat with you, m'gel," the director added, opening his eyes when he did not feel the movement of his subordinate leaving the room, "but I've a great deal of planning to do today, what with the shareholders' meeting looming on the horizon."

"I was just wondering, sir," said the microbiologist, "if we'd even gotten a request like this before. I'm sure other members of the staff have visited UN Headquarters."

She had done so herself, as part of the run-up to the test release.

"Well, how would *I* know?" demanded Sutcliffe-Bowles, his face darkening. The music swelling to fill the office had an emotional content as pervasive as the miasma surrounding a bushel of rotting peaches.

You would ask your desk's artificial intelligence, thought Spenser, the *only* intelligence that regularly occupies this office, and it would give us the answer in a matter in seconds.

Aloud she said, "I'm sorry, Director. I'll go take care of this at once."

One way or another she would take care of it.

"Always glad to see my staff," said Sutcliffe-Bowles with his eyes closed and his face to the ceiling. Spenser was not sure that he heard her words, but when the mul-tisheeted door panels closed behind her, their motion threw patterns of light like the wings of morpho butterflies across his face.

She was terrified as she stepped toward the transit station, though she didn't suppose her stiffness would strike as un-usual anyone who knew her. All her life there'd been laugh-ter, jokes. She'd lost track of the times she'd heard around a corner or behind a not-quite-sheltering hand, "Walks like she's got a poker up her arse."

Perhaps no burden came without a corresponding benefit. If her normal demeanor during her post-pubescent years permitted her to conceal her agitation at this time, then the four decades of snickers might have been worthwhile.

Almost worthwhile.

An anticlockwise car glided up to the platform, braking smoothly as the drive magnet reversed polarity over the center rail while the suspension magnets in the outriggers continued to poise the vehicle a millimeter above the friction of any solid surface.

Other passengers entered the car with her, but Spenser ignored them except to wait for a chance to key her stop, seventeen, into the destination pad. The transit vehicles sensed and stopped for people waiting on station platforms, but they could not read minds.

Kathleen Spenser was not herself sure of what was going on in her mind.

She was still clutching the data request she had brought from the director's office. The car was enclosed against the wind of its own velocity, but the crinkling of the document as Spenser sat down recalled it to her attention. She touched the latch of her briefcase, the only way that the case could be opened without force since the combination lock that usually supplemented the thumbprint had been disconnected.

When the flimsy was safely inside, she snapped the lid of leather-covered titanium firmly over it.

If only it were possible to close off the implications of the request as completely.

The car slowed to a stop with perfect smoothness, but Spenser and the other passengers swayed as they transferred their inertia to the vehicle through their seats and the arms that braced them in the direction of motion. Two men got off when the doors opened; a woman got on; and the squeals from the feeding pens only underscored what the methane-pungent atmosphere made obvious.

If the odor of hog excrement penetrated every part of the habitat, here at Section Eighteen it roiled. Farming the animals in Sky Devon had been a mistake obvious from the start, but one of the project's major backers was the largest breeder of Poland Chinas in Europe.

The animals were clean, so long as they did not have to wallow in mud to protect their tender skin from insect pests, but the odor of their feces was inescapable in a closed atmosphere, no matter what stages of filtration took place in the recirculating blowers. That omnipresent discomfort for habitat residents would not have kept hog breeding from economic success here—and anyway, Director Sutcliffe-Bowles' acceptance was more typical of the way arrivals at Sky Devon adapted than was Dr. Spenser's continued revulsion.

The real trouble was that Arabs and Jews were only the largest of the cultural and religious groups that refused to eat pork. Caterers who were responsible for off-Earth colonies had no margin for error; and only a fool would chance aborting a project because a workman went berserk or a score of them rioted at the deadly insult.

By definition, any human being off-Earth was under abnormal pressure.

The luxury trade in pork could have been handled from Downside, but Sky Devon was gearing up for a volume business that would probably never exist because the margins of survival within even a large colony were too narrow. Failure had been dictated by circumstances that should not have intruded on rational planning—but had done so nonetheless.

Much the same was true of the way Kathleen Spenser's life had progressed.

The car whisked through a long section of grainfields, stacked from base level to high above the tracks and lighted by a system of reflectors and diffraction gratings. The direct sun was never visible from within Sky Devon, but the huge mirror that hung in space above the hub was only the first of the prisms and reflectors that redirected light onto the agricultural areas.

The light was too bright, and it did not illuminate the real questions looming before the microbiologist.

With a glance around, a fierce warning to her fellow passengers rather than an inspection of them, Spenser reopened her briefcase. Though she did not intend to use it at the moment, there was a communications handset inside— she had the salary and perks of a divison head, even if Sutcliffe-Bowles chose to summon her in person to deal with a clerical task.

Why had he *done* that? Surely the real request for information must have been very different from what the director had given her to test her reactions. . . .

And yet it was inconceivable that anyone who knew anything about Sutcliffe-Bowles would make him a conspirator in a scheme to entrap her—and even less conceivable that the director would carry out his part in such a scheme. The whole affair was within the director's usual profile, focusing on something trivial because he could not grasp anything more complex.

If Sutcliffe-Bowles were playing her, for the Afrikaners or the man *behind* the Afrikaners—there had to be someone else to have escrowed the amount waiting in Spenser's Swiss account—then the implications were terrifying.

She tapped a paging code into her communications unit without lifting the handset. The car's control system would pass the call on to the next transit stop, from which the habitat's communications system would route it to the unit that had been keyed. There was no message, only the paging note; and that should be sufficient to bring Jan de Kuyper to Spenser's laboratory by the time she reached it herself.

The other passengers ignored the microbiologist with the special form of good breeding that alone makes mass living posssible to sane human beings. Sanity was not necessarily a prerequisite for living in the tightly-controlled community of Sky Devon, but those whose madness caused them to intrude directly on their neighbors were quickly shunted Downside.

When Spenser closed the briefcase again, her fingers continued to squeeze it so hard that the flesh beneath her nails blanched.

She did not feel the lack of friends, because she had never had any, only the parents whom she had cared for personally until their deaths freed her to return to her profession—after an absence that made her almost unemployable. In a way, that was a blessing, because she was free to take charge of a magnificent laboratory at Sky Devon when better-established colleagues refused to accept long exile in space.

An enclosed, recirculating habitat did not dare pump poisons into its system to deal with the insect pests that had inevitably hitchhiked aboard with the breeding stock from Earth. Dr. Kathleen Spenser's section was tasked to develop sharply-specific microorganic controls for insect pests.

Sometimes it amused her to remember that nerve gas had also been developed by insecticide researchers.

The car whirred to a halt with a slight roughness suggesting a problem with the drive rail here. Familiarity with the sensation awoke the microbiologist to her surroundings: a housing estate for laborers and technicians in grades three and below; Transit Stop Seventeen.

She got out of the car with two other passengers and strode to the cubicle beside the transit platform. It held the elevator that led down to her laboratory in the bowels of Sky Devon.

Spenser could not feel her weight increase as she descended, but by the time the car stopped, there was a perceptible sluggishness in the way her body behaved. Because the "lowest" levels of the habitat were actually those closest to the rim, they rotated faster than the portions nearer the hub—and the thrust of centrifugal force that counterfeited gravity was correspondingly greater.

It did not bother Spenser that her laboratory was isolated from other occupied portions of the habitat—most of the lowest level was given over to storage and recycling—nor that in her work area artificial light was not supplemented by the sunbeams which hinted that other work areas looked out over the countryside in springtime.

Sometimes it *did* concern her that the designers were naive enough to believe this location—or even the airlock between the section and the rest of the habitat—would prevent disaster if a microorganism got loose in the lab.

There was an entryway between the base of the elevator and the door of the lab. On it was mounted a call switch rather than a latch plate. Huge, insulated lines, some of them a meter in diameter, ran past her and past the enclosed laboratory, sighing and gurgling to themselves.

The attendant within should have been warned when the elevator started to move, but Spenser touched the call switch anyway; and when the air lock did not begin to open on a count of three, her hand moved as it always did now at the onset of anger or fear: to the crystal locket beneath her lab smock.

The door sucked slowly outward.

There was no interlock on these doors. The receptionist saved his job by opening the inner portal simultaneously with the outer one.

"Good afternoon, Dr. Spenser," said the burly receptionist. The sweat that popped out at his hairline demonstrated that he knew he was in trouble.

"Hoyer," snapped the microbiologist, "where *were* you?"

"Ah," interrupted the receptionist, "there was an irradiator to be moved in—"

"You were flirting with Platt, as usual," Spenser interrupted with a cold distinctness which turned each of her words into a sawtooth ripping through her subordinate's soul.

"On your own time I don't care if you have sexual congress with the petrie dishes," she continued. "But when you're on duty at the front desk, that's where you stay unless *I* tell you otherwise. Is that understood?''

Hoyer nodded, his face frozen.

For a moment the tall woman choked on a fury that was directed not at the event but at the implications of which it reminded her. Hoyer would have been ideal for the task she had foreseen as soon as she read the data request in the director's office. He was strong; certainly corruptible; and reliable within reasonable limits.

Unfortunately his male lover—Technician Three Platt— was only corruptible; and even then he did not have the "honest cop's" virtue of staying bought. He would certainly learn of anything Spenser asked the receptionist to do outside his normal duties . . . and therefore Spenser had to go for muscle to a resource she would rather not have used.

"Has the man from Maintenance arrived?" she asked in a tone so similar to the one she had been using that Hoyer did not realize for a moment that the subject had changed.

When the question penetrated to Hoyer's consciousness, his face smoothed and he said, "Oh! Oh, yes, Doctor, de Kuyper's in your office. Something wrong with your air circulation?"

Spenser strode past the receptionist without the retort she might have made if she were not concentrating on the discussion to come.

Several of the laboratory staff murmured greetings which they knew from her face she would ignore. Platt kept out of sight. Dr. Lawrence, who was part of the conspiracy, watched his division head with frightened eyes. Lawrence knew of de Kuyper's involvement, but he did not know why the Afrikaner maintenance supervisor had arrived this afternoon—and he was too frightened to ask directly.

The smell of de Kuyper's inhaler seeped around the edges of the office door. Tobacco smoking was almost extinct as a habit in civilized regions Downside, and the high percentage of oxygen in Sky Devon to speed growth made open flames suicidally dangerous besides.

Cold inhalers were as common as cigarettes had been fifty years earlier, and de Kuyper was typical of many Afrikaners in favoring the odor of strong tobacco laced with other aromatics. When he exhaled, the reek surrounded him; and he was exhaling now as he waited, dour faced, seated in Spenser's chair with his long legs on the desk whose litter he had shoved aside to make room.

The microbiologist would have slammed the door, but the panel—hollow-core titanium—was not dense enough to bang properly.

"I *told* you," she said in a whisper like a whiplash, "not to use that reeking *thing* in my office. In my *laboratory*."

The Afrikaner took the inhaler, the shape and size of a black writing stylus with a gold band near the center, out of his mouth and looked at it. He did not move his legs. "And I told you, goodlady," he replied, "not to call me. Yes?"

He raised his blue eyes coolly to her . . . but when de Kuyper saw the microbiologist reach toward the pendant on her breast, he scrambled to his feet and slipped the inhaler back into a pocket of his gray coveralls.

"Well," he said gruffly, trying to recover his poise without offending the madwoman further. "You called me, I came. What is it that you want?"

"I think," said Spenser, "that we may have a problem which you're better placed than I am to deal with."

She stepped to the other side of her desk so that she faced the slanted screen, shooing de Kuyper around toward the visitors' chair facing her. The Afrikaner moved, but he did not sit down.

"Give me all data requests from . . ." she said to the dimple on the desktop which covered the microphone. She remembered the project number, but the moment her lips began to form the syllables, caution reasserted itself. She thumbed open the briefcase and checked the hard copy before continuing. "NYU Project number thirty-two slash one-four-nine."

The artificial intelligence waited three seconds. Then the screen beeped and threw up the Beaton request that Spenser already held in her hand.

There was a second beep. END SERIES said the screen.

The microbiologist sighed and sat down at her desk. Her pose so closely counterfeited relaxation that de Kuyper said,

"So it's nothing after all? You brought me here for nothing?"

Spenser looked at him with an expression that could have frozen water. "I brought you here," she said, "because someone in UN Headquarters on the Moon seems to be interested in Rodney Beaton."

De Kuyper blinked in obvious confusion and sat down in the chair to avoid the necessity of making a comment when he did not understand the subject.

"The *courier*, man!" snarled the miocrobiologist when she realized the problem. "My technician! Now do you remember?" And as comprehension dawned on her visitor's face, she added, "And no, it's *not* because of the accident. They've made up some cock and bull story about it being some sort of ongoing university project, but this is the first time there's been any notice of it here. So much for 'on-going'— and I don't buy the coincidence."

"Not coincidence, no," the Afrikaner agreed in the slow intonation that always suggested to Spenser that the mind behind the words was slow also.

De Kuyper fished his inhaler absently from the pocket into which he had stuffed it. The microbiologist ignored the act because it was no longer a challenge, only a nervous tick like the way her own fingers played over the supplementary keypad in the surface of her desk.

The two of them were not friends, or even allies in the true sense; but just at the moment they needed one another.

"I will report . . ." said the Afrikaner, a beginning that stopped because there did not appear to be anything he was willing to add to those words. An invisible sphere of brandied tobacco expanded from him as he puffed furiously on the inhaler.

"Will they cancel the project?" asked Spenser with no emotion in her voice or in her eyes.

De Kuyper took the inhaler from his mouth and studied the gold band with an intensity that called for a jeweler's loupe. When he looked up, it was with a resolute expression that proved he understood perfectly what the woman meant: *his* folk would not be deterred from the plan by risk of exposure, but those shadows who were funding them were another matter.

"What else is it that might be done, goodlady?" he said stolidly, overcoming his distaste at treating a woman as, by implication, his superior.

"The request," she said, rising and leaning over her desk to hand the document as far as she could toward de Kuyper. He jumped from his seat to take it, but the flimsy spun a few centimeters toward the floor before the Afrikaner snatched it from the air.

"It asks for information to be sent not to the usual authorities," Spenser continued as she sat again, "but to a university researcher of some sort. That may be false, there may be no such person—"

"Yes, I understand that," said de Kuyper with deep nods as his eyes continued to scan the document. He was reviewing the lines he had already read so that their possible nuances would be clear in a mind that did not normally organize itself in printed words.

"—but if there *is* an Elinor Bradley, Ph.D.," said Spenser, "and her interest in Beaton is personal, for whatever reason—"

"A doxie, do you think, goodlady?" offered the Afrikaner, raising his head with his lips pursed in consideration.

"That seems unlikely," the woman said . . . but perhaps not so very unlikely after all. Her mind had been predisposed to the thought by considering Hoyer and Platt . . . and no doubt the burly man before her understood those things better than she did.

Most people understood those things better than Kathleen Spenser did.

"In any case," she went on crisply, shutting down an area of regret she was sure was biological, not anything to do with her mind, "we don't have sufficient information."

She paused, meeting de Kuyper's waiting eyes. "If your resources," Spenser said, "can determine whether or not this anthropologist exists; and if she *does* exist, what her interest in Beaton may be . . ."

"And dispose of her, of course," said de Kuyper, finishing the sentence dangled before him in a way somewhat different from what the microbiologist had intended. "Yes, I understand."

He was folding the data request to fit his breast pocket as he stood up.

"Wait a minute," said Spenser, rising also and sharply aware that she was about to lose control of the situation. "She mustn't just be killed. If she exists, she'll have information that we *must* have to be safe."

De Kuyper shrugged, very much the man again—very much the old counterterrorist. "Whatever is possible will be done, goodlady," he said. "Capture and interrogation, that may be possible."

He turned, touching the door latch. Before he opened it, however, the Afrikaner looked back over his shoulder. "What I am sure is possible, goodlady," he said, "is that Elinor Bradley be disposed of.

"As she *will* be."

Spenser's eyes were on the Afrikaner's back as he left, but her mind was trying to visualize the appearance of a woman she had never met.

Chapter 10

HOUSE CALL

Piet van Zell knew Steeks and Trimen. The big Afrikaners were construction hogs like himself, and they'd worked together on half a dozen jobs.

Those were paid jobs, unlike this one.

Jantze and van Rooyan were not familiar to him, since years ago they'd moved from general construction into the Bureau of Utilities here at UN Headquarters. Van Zell knew they, too, were reliable, because otherwise they wouldn't have been brought together with him now.

"When—" began Steeks, jumpy with hormones that waiting gave no outlet but nervousness.

"It's all *right*," Jantze said with more snap than solace. The regular utility crewmen were no less nervous than the construction workers in borrowed orange coveralls, but their fears were colored by the possibility that the operation would cost them their regular jobs. "Another shift has been held over fifteen minutes, no more. We can't have them wonder to see us in their work area, not so?"

The team had been assembled by five different calls, all from out of the colony and each giving only a part of the necessary information. There was a sixth important fact as well: a courier would have been much safer, but the orders had come through ordinary communications channels in order to save time.

Therefore there was very little time.

"All right," said van Rooyan, who was monitoring the ground-conduction unit. All five Afrikaners in the small orange van could hear the chatter, but it was meaningless except to those who knew the jargon and locations being grunted out by various service crews. "They're headed back to the barn. We can—"

Steeks was driving the van. Its wheel-hub motors could not jerk the heavy load into motion as his instinct desired, but he squeezed the throttle to its stop position in the attempt.

"—go now," van Rooyan completed.

This could be very bad. If it were not already very bad, they would not have been assembled for a job like this.

Van Rooyan, in the open front of the vehicle, muttered unnecessary directions to Steeks—and tried to get him to drive more cautiously. The construction worker could handle the vehicle as skillfully as anyone on the Moon, but he was not used to driving among pedestrians. The normal arrogance of a man guiding a machine was increased by Steeks' overriding concern with what he—what they all—had to do in a few minutes.

The three Afrikaners in the back of the car jounced against the flimsy metal sides while they tried to steady with their feet the barricades and toolboxes that crowded them. It gave them something to do and to think about, instead of glancing through the window forward or staring at the set faces of their companions.

"The next one," said van Rooyan sharply. "Here, *here*!"

Steeks chopped the throttle instead of easing it down. Loose metal and men's shoulders rocked against the front panel as the drive motors acted as highly efficient electromagnetic brakes.

"Shit for brains!" snarled Jantze, but the curse was directed at the rear door as he lurched to throw it open.

Jantze jumped down, then tried to take both a barricade and one of the toolboxes simultaneously. Travelers on the slideway glanced at the utility van as they rolled by it, but the vehicle and the men in orange coveralls were merely an incident of passage. The Afrikaners ignored the passing onlookers by rigidly concentrating on their task.

They had turned into a narrow passage with no slideways. It gave pedestrians access to residential apartments to either side. The van's width almost blocked it. Van Rooyan stood on his seat to look back over the vehicle. When his fellow utility employee had set the telescoping barricade against both walls of the passageway, van Rooyan said to the driver, "All right, now—quickly!" as if Steeks needed any encouragement to load the motors.

Jantze stared sternly at passersby over the waist-high barricade, ready to stop anyone who tried to enter the corridor during the next few minutes. The toolbox beside his right foot was closed, but unlatched against need.

Steeks stopped again just beyond the door numbered 15. They could not be sure that Bradley was inside, but the chances seemed good since this was both her home and her business address in bureau records. If necessary van Rooyan would move the vehicle ahead to the thoroughfare while van Zell waited in the apartment with Steeks and Trimen.

For the moment, though, Trimen slid past the van to give another barricade and toolbox to van Rooyan. The utility crewman scurried toward the unblocked end of the passage, ready to halt pedestrians just as Jantze did. Steeks remained behind the controls, but he stood so that he could peer at his companions in the rear.

"All right," said Trimen when he saw both barricades were in position. Van Zell pressed the door bell.

"Yes?" said a woman's voice from the speaker below the lens in the center of the door panel.

It was too much to expect that Bradley would open the door at once, but van Zell had hoped for that anyway. "Bureau of Utilities, goodlady," he lied. "There's been a methane leak from one of our waste recovery lines and we need to check all the suites in this corridor."

"I—" said the speaker. The door did not open. Trimen twitched the device he held ready in his hand, looking at his partner in concern equal to that of the woman inside the apartment. "I'm sure there's no gas leak here."

"Goodlady—"

"I'm sorry, you'll have to go away," said the voice with a rising inflection. "I'm very—"

Van Zell nodded to Trimen, who slapped his flat device against the latch plate.

"—busy."

Trimen threw the switch. The lock crasher, fed by a cable to the van's main power supply, sent a surge of high-frequency current through the door's electronic lock. The circuits fried, and the bolt retracted as its electromagnet ceased to force it against spring tension.

Piet van Zell hit the panel with his shoulder, a pry bar ready in his hands in case Bradley had shot a mechanical bolt as well. The door sprang open, and the woman at the telephone across the room turned and screamed as the pair of Afrikaners burst in.

Van Zell grappled with the woman one-handed, and stabbed the pry bar against the wall phone with the other. The phone's cover cracked slightly, not enough to damage the internal workings—had she completed dialing?—and the woman flung him back with unexpected strength, though she did not break his grip on her wrist.

She was the customer who had been seated across from him in Le Moulin Rouge. The Bureau of Utilities uniform was no disguise if she had glimpsed his face through the door lens.

"Help, you fool!" van Zell snarled in Afrikaans to his partner, who was trying to get the drug injector out of the pocket of his coveralls.

Still screaming, the woman thrashed her arm again, forcing van Zell to drop his pry bar and grab her with both hands. Anger flashed him a momentary impulse to strike her with the ridged titanium bar, but he had a personal interest in learning what she knew about the test here at Headquarters Colony. Anyway, his mass and her own efforts had pulled the woman away from the telephone.

Trimen seized Bradley by the other arm. She kicked him in the crotch with a fashionable shoe. Her high, wedge soles must have been as solid as they looked, because the Afrikaner folded like an accordian with a high-pitched scream of his own.

"Steeks, dammit!" van Zell shouted as he twisted instinctively to avoid being crippled the same way. Bradley struck at his head with the hand Trimen had released, then clawed through his long hair in an attempt to tear his ear.

Van Zell kicked sideways at her ankles, hitting her but unable to make her fall. She was at least as strong as he was, thanks to the time he had spent in zero-G.

"Steeks!"

Bradley broke away, reaching for the phone pad again. Steeks fired his needle gun in a long burst from the doorway, pattering tiny darts across the sofa, the wall, and in three dimples on the back of Bradley's dress.

The woman fell onto her back when her legs splayed and her arms began to thrash uncontrollably. Van Zell grabbed one wrist while his partner flopped across the other, his face contorted with the nausea he was trying to deny.

Trimen had not lost the injector when he was kicked. He lifted it toward Bradley's throat while she called him a bastard, her throat muscles far enough from the needle impacts to remain unparalyzed by the high frequency current that leaked into her nerves.

A stunner could kill if the victim's heart gave out or a needle lodged in a major ganglion. Still, van Zell could not fault his fellow's judgment in shooting instead of jumping into a free-for-all in which the advantage had been entirely to the intended victim.

Bradley went limp as Trimen injected chemical muscle relaxant into her carotid. The other side of the injector would bring her around as quickly in the suit room in which they planned to interrogate her under a battery of additional drugs—before disposing of her as the courier from Sky Devon had managed to eliminate himself.

"All right, all right," said Steeks, who snatched the sofa open into a bed and ripped the spread from it. "Cover her with this."

"Shut up, will you?" van Zell muttered, but he was already straightening the woman's limbs so that he and Steeks could roll her in the bedspread while Trimen managed with difficulty to stand. He was cursing under his breath, but they could not be sure whether it was at his pain or at the woman who had kicked him.

Van Zell lifted their victim's torso and shuffled to the door. Steeks took her cloth-bundled legs while grumbling nervously, "I have to drive! Hurry, get her in!"

They folded the woman into the back of the van as if she were no more than the roll of bedding she now resembled.

"Come on!" van Zell called to Jantze at the barricade

as Trimen and Steeks clambered aboard the vehicle.

There was someone arguing with Jantze. That didn't matter now . . . except that when the utility crewman turned, van Zell and the powerful man beyond the barricade met each other's eyes. The man looked vaguely familiar to the bearded Afrikaner.

"Drive!" shouted van Zell as he reached down to open the toolbox still in the back of the van.

Chapter 11

MODIFIED PROGRAM

Duncan, Duncan, you are under arrest, sang Sam Yates' mind a little more tunefully than his lips whistled as he sauntered down the sidewalk. He generally whistled something when he was walking alone, and "Been on the Job Too Long" was a staple of his good moods.

And Duncan shot a hole in Brady's chest!

He wasn't riding the slideway because he was early, bad form for a first date; and he was doing his *damnedest* not to walk at full stride, bounding like an idiot and working up a sweat in his best suit at the wrong time of the evening.

Brady, Brady don't you know you done wrong?

Damn but it felt good to be happy again.

You bust into my bar when the game—

There was a barricade closing one of the residential passages—MM–NN 12. And it was the passage down which Yates had to go.

"Sorry, sir," said the craggy-featured utility worker behind the barrier. He raised a hand—only a gesture, not a threat to push the equally-large security man. The utility worker's voice was harsh with unexplained worry, and he would not meet Yates' eyes, as if that would prevent him from being seen clearly.

Yates took the ID card from his inside breast pocket. He didn't feel anything he'd have called concern, but he sure as hell didn't want Ella steaming in her apartment while he cooled his heels in the corridor for some dick-head reason.

"What seems to be the problem?" he demanded, a little more forcefully than he had intended. An orange van was parked in the passageway while two more crewmen wrestled a tarp or something into the back, but Yates was sure there was room for him to slip past without smearing his good suit.

"Look buddy, I don't *care* who you are," insisted the man behind the barricade. "There's a gas leak and we gotta keep everybody out for just a few"—he looked over his shoulder at the van and his fellows—"just a few—"

One of the utility crewmen slid toward the front of the vehicle, while the other turned and called, "Come on!" to the man at the barricade.

The man who spoke was the bearded Afrikaner from Le Moulin Rouge. That restaurant hadn't catered to flunkies who wore orange coveralls during work hours.

Yates lunged straight at the telescoping barricade because it appeared flimsy. It wasn't, but the aluminum panels buckled enough under the impact of his hip to spring the ends free.

"Hold it!" Yates bellowed at the van, and "Hold it!" grunted the utility worker whose legs were tangled with Yates and the barricade as they sprawled.

The security man thrashed himself clear, using one-G muscles to shed his limbs of encumbrances like a dog shaking water from its fur. The van was accelerating, but he thought he could catch up in a sprint. The worker who had tried to stop him was no problem unless the guy had a weapon, a needle stunner or a—

The man in orange was dragging a plasma discharger from his toolbox.

Yates hadn't deliberately looked back at the man he'd pushed down, another Afrikaner—and maybe that meant something—but his conscious mind was spinning with more data than he could process while his body was controlled by old instincts.

You think you forget, but you never do. If you're lucky, you stay out of situations that trigger memories of jungles and bamboo thickets and bananas planted in rows that give lines of fire in six directions. . . .

The plasma discharger was the length of a man's forearm, with pistol grips at the front and back of the frame and a stock folded against the right side. The barrel was short and fat, covered with a dull black finish like the rest of the metal surfaces, so that the whole weapon seemed to have been stamped from light alloys.

The barrel weighed almost three kilograms. It was a polished forging of tungsten, the only metal refractory enough to survive the jet of plasma from the miniature fusion blasts that powered the weapon.

Sam Yates' mind wondered what an Afrikaner exile was doing with a special-applications weapon that wasn't in general use in any army he'd heard of. All his body cared was that his hands gripped the frame before the other guy could aim the discharger, and that Yates' adrenaline and muscles—still up to Earth standard—could rip the weapon away.

The two men were sitting with their legs splayed and the metal barricade booming as they struggled on it. When Yates got control of the discharger, his torso flopped back and he sprawled full length in the passage.

The Afrikaner grabbed the toolbox to use it as a sharp-cornered club. Yates aimed the plasma discharger at the center of the orange-clad chest and pulled the trigger.

Nothing happened except that the toolbox swung toward Yates' face.

He'd fired a similar weapon once in training, but that was twenty years ago and an experimental model anyway. Rumor was they blew up as often as they didn't—and there was just enough truth to those rumors that the brass wasn't willing even to *test* plasma dischargers under the dust and moisture of field conditions.

Nothing about that experience helped Yates figure out this particular weapon, even if it were U.S.-manufactured . . . but infantry weapons share some basic characteristics, including simplicity of operation. Yates' instinct thumbed the slide switch above the trigger guard, and the weapon recoiled in his hands.

The Afrikaner blew apart in a sunburst.

There was recoil because the plasma spurting through the tungsten muzzle had mass, and it was moving at just below the velocity of light. The Afrikaner exploded because his chest converted the directed energy into enough heat to boil a swimming pool.

His torso did not boil. It flashed away as a ball of live steam.

Yates twisted to a prone position facing down the passage-way and looking for another target, his eyes dazzled by afterimages of his own shot. The passage reflected a thousand copies of the one light source that would seem bright in his half-blinded condition: another bolt of plasma, fired by one of the remaining "utility crewmen."

Three meters of aluminum paneling burned beside the security man. The core of glass sponge inside the wall shattered like a bomb going off.

Yates fired back, using the violet pulse in his retinas as an aiming point because he couldn't see anything else.

"Cartridges" for the plasma discharger were spherical arrays of microlasers aimed at the equally tiny bead of deuterium at their center. There was only one gap in the sphere of lasers, a hole aligned precisely with the tungsten bore of the weapon.

When the lasers tripped, they turned the bead of deuterium into a fusion bomb — and directed its energy down the barrel as a plasma for the microsecond before they were consumed.

The tungsten glowed and some of its inner surface burned away. Targets downrange, with no barrier of coherent light to protect them from the momentary pulse, exploded and burned.

The fellow who had fired at Yates spun when the security man's bolt hit him. His arm was still held by the friend who had been swinging him aboard the utility vehicle, but the limb was no longer connected to his torso, because his shoulders had been vaporized by the blast.

The van had paused to pick up the worker manning the barricade at the far end of the passage. Now the vehicle accelerated again.

Sam Yates wasn't office staff any more, and he'd never had the street experience that ingrains in a true policeman the need to preserve and protect. Part of him was rightly terrified that somebody was going to step out of an intervening doorway or that a burst of plasma was going to miss its intended target and fry a civilian in the busy corridors to either end of the passageway.

That part of him couldn't override the instincts honed in too many firefights he'd survived because nobody on the other side had.

Yates fired again at the back of the orange van as it turned out of the corridor. A fireball of dissociated sheet metal hung at the end of the passage as the rest of the vehicle whined away under all the torque its motors could supply.

Yates dived low out of the mouth of the passage, hitting the sidewalk awkwardly because his shoe had slipped in residues of the man he'd killed here. The bolt of plasma from the van was high anyway, lighting the corridor like a strobe as ceiling panels vaporized fifty meters away.

There were at least a hundred citizens visible up and down the corridor. Two of them were Latins who'd been bounced from the van's fender, against a jewelry shop's window, and back to the sidewalk in a torrent of screaming abuse. The hiss-*crack* of the plasma discharge overhead flattened both as their terms of reference changed from accident to firefight.

The van was halted only forty meters down the corridor, point-blank to plasma weapons that could rip from the Moon to the Earth's atmosphere if anybody wanted to try. You can miss a target right at the end of your gun barrel if the target's shooting back, though, and neither Yates nor the man crouching beside the vehicle hit what they aimed at as they blasted again simultaneously.

The sidewalk in front of Yates exploded in a blinding gout, crushed and bonded lunar slag converted to molten glass by the jet of plasma. The man in orange coveralls ducked from a discharge close enough to make his hair and beard fray out from the induced electrical potential, but it was a wall far down from the corridor that blew up in a ball of crackling rainbows.

Another bolt silhouetted the van as someone behind it fired into the wall.

Yates' optic nerves were already flooded with dancing afterimages and complementary colors, so for a moment he did not realize that the effect was real and not a retinal mirage. Then the man with whom he was exchanging shots ducked behind the van, where his partner must also be hidden.

Yates aimed, waited an instant, then jumped up and charged the vehicle behind the glowing muzzle of his plasma discharger.

Citizens in either direction were bunching on the slideways. Those who realized what was causing the noise and eye-searing light turned in panic, some of them running against the flow of the pavement and knocking over pedestrians still in stupefied wonder at the unusual commotion. A car on the opposite sidewalk rolled past, bumping along the corridor walls after its driver and passengers had bailed out.

The Bureau of Utilities van was wreathed in a bitter haze, but it was not really afire and there was no fuel supply to explode into a real disaster. Yates' bolt as the vehicle turned had vaporzied a torso-sized oval in the rear side panel, but the instantaneous energy transfer that made the plasma so devastating also prevented a shot from achieving any real penetration. Paint had blistered away from the opposite panel, but the thin aluminum there had not melted.

Yates screamed "*Kill!*" and leaped with all his strength, his instincts telling him that his one-G muscles would permit him to go *over* the van and blast the men behind it from an unexpected direction.

His left thigh, seared by the near miss, cramped again. Yates' chest hit the edge of the vehicle's roof hard enough to knock the gun from his hands and the breath from his lungs.

God, he hurt.

If he'd had the strength, Sam Yates would have clung to the roof that had clotheslined him. Dangling there like Absalom caught in the tree was a marginally worse position than the other options available at the moment: sprawling on the sidewalk; or even half in, half out of the back of the van. He squeezed as hard as he could on the slick metal just to prove that he still could control his body against the forces of gravity and momentum.

He couldn't. Burned, battered, and breathless, Yates fell

backward onto the sidewalk. The pull of lunar gravity was so slight that he wondered if the men in orange suits had already killed him.

What in hell were they fighting about anyway?

God, he hurt.

There had been no sound in Yates' world for several seconds. He didn't notice his loss until the screams and traffic noise—but particularly the screams—flooded his consciousness again and prompted him to roll to all fours.

Yates bounded to his feet and collided with the wall because the muscles in his left thigh cramped and his vision on that side was fuzzy, maybe sweat and maybe something a lot worse.

There still wasn't much pain, just enough to warn him that he was in trouble and that the trouble was going to get a lot worse as soon as he stopped to think about it. That wouldn't be for a while. He lurched forward again, throwing the heavy plasma discharger out in his right hand to balance the fact that the opposite leg couldn't take a full stride. Like an undersized bullet in a musket barrel—and equally intent on slaughter—Yates ricocheted down the passage.

The plasma fired in his direction had missed him, but the square meter of wall paneling that burned and melted a few inches away had transferred some of the energy to his left side.

Yates stumbled along in a reek of scorched hair, his own and the smoldering trousers of what had been a very good wool suit. Metal vaporized by the near miss had recondensed on whatever solid surface it touched first. The security man's left cheek and forehead were black with aluminum which had been deposited there in microscopic granules.

There were red cracks across the black that coated his fast-swelling ear. It felt as if each nerve were being bathed in acid. He was *really* going to hurt in the morning if he survived the night.

It wasn't noise that had deafened him but a blow to the head. He couldn't remember what had hit him—the sidewalk when he fell, or some large chunk blasted from the ceiling by one of the shots . . . ?

He *could* remember the back of the plasma discharger

punching him in the solar plexus when the gun's muzzle slammed into the roof edge. That meant the weapon was probably inside the vehicle—how many shots had he fired? How many shots did it *hold*?—and retrieving it was Yates' first priority.

Then he could wonder why nobody'd finished him off while he lay helpless.

There were emergency hooters both up and down the corridor. They might become a problem in a matter of seconds. With luck—and the reasoning part of Yates' mind knew he'd been *damn* lucky this far—the uniformed patrols might be kept away from the source of the trouble by the widely scattered destruction wrought by the plasma bolts.

Yates was pretty sure he didn't want to explain this one to the proper authorities if he could possibly help it. He was *real* sure he didn't want to be disarmed and talking to *anybody* until he knew what had happened to the two or three surviving men with orange coveralls and plasma dischargers.

Two survivors. As Yates crawled into the van he put his hand on what had been the face of the third gunman. The side panel had stopped enough of the plasma to keep the remainder from dismembering the fellow, but his coveralls from the waist up had not survived the fireball.

Neither had the flesh on the left side of his head. His right hand held a needle stunner while his left gripped a drug injector whose two ends were coded red and green.

The soldier, who at the moment worked in Entry division of UN Headquarters Security, shifted his supporting hand and leaned farther into the back of the vehicle to grab his own weapon. Its barrel glowed like a dull beacon against the front panel.

The smoldering bedspread that had covered the head of the woman Yates sprawled across had become disarrayed.

God in heaven, she was Ella Bradley.

Yates snatched up the plasma discharger one handed and swung himself around the van gun fast with a lethal grace he thought he'd lost when his misjudged leap had crashed him back to reality. Nobody was hiding behind the vehicle, but the door that somebody'd blasted open with a jet of plasma showed where they'd gone. The latch and a soup-plate sized disk of the door panel had vaporized, but the rest had swung closed again.

Yates snatched it open. At the motion, a gunman waiting at the top of the stairs triggered a bolt of eye-searing plasma.

The door led up to a suit room. The bearded Afrikaner and his surviving partner were about to escape across the lunar surface, and there was no way in hell they could be pursued directly.

The inner air lock door could not be opened until the outer one was closed, and that wouldn't happen until somebody went to the Central mechanical control room and shut this one. By that time the pair would have reentered the colony by any damn place they chose—and disappeared.

The security man staggered back, blinking and prickly again from the blast down the stairwell. He didn't return the fire. Neither side could hit the other now without being suicidally exposed first—and Sam Yates, for one, was damn glad of an excuse to disengage.

Yates dropped the plasma weapon on the sidewalk and staggered to the back of the van. His left hand brushed along the side panel for support and guidance, until the tears cleared from his stinging eyes.

God! that last bolt had been close. If he'd been a half-step quicker jumping through the open door . . .

A man running away from the destruction downrange stumbled into Yates and clung to him with both hands. "What's happening?" he babbled in French. "What is all this happening?"

"A terrible accident," the security man gasped in the same language. The stranger's grip loosened as the fellow looked into the van, but Yates held his arm and did not let him shy away.

"Very terrible," the big American continued as his free hand pried the drug injector from the grip of the corpse. The plastic tube was slick and an iridescent blur as Yates' eyes struggled to clear. "Tell me, sir, is the green end of this up or down?"

"My God," gasped the stranger.

"Up or down, fuckhead?" Yates screamed.

"It's down!" the French speaker whined as he tried to

jerk free, then a shove from Yates' opening hand boosted him a dozen meters down the sidewalk and off in a shambling run.

The security man leaned over and tripped the injector with the antidote side cradled in the cup of Bradley's throat.

There were more emergency hooters now. Some of them were too close to ignore, but he had to ignore them anyway. His pain was localizing, which was better than being swaddled in general, incapacitating agony.

Of course, most of the *individual* parts of his body still hurt.

Bradley lunged into a sitting position and clawed for his eyes, a stroke that failed only because Yates hadn't been able to unwrap the bedspread completely while the woman lay as a dead weight. "Watch it!" he cried, backing away more hastily than his bruised ribs willingly allowed.

The slashing attack was a memory of what she had been doing at the last moment of consciousness. Bradley's eyes cleared, swept her surroundings, and froze in a stare out the back of the van in an attempt to not have seen the corpse which sprawled half across her.

"Quick," said Yates, looking back over his shoulder to see if uniformed patrolmen were part of the crowd scurrying in opposing directions. Anyone more than a couple of meters away was a blur through the welling tears, but the flashing blue lights were still at some distance.

Bradley scrambled out of the vehicle with the spread still trailing from one heel. She did not look back, but from the way she held her right hand to the side, fingers splayed, Yates was pretty sure she'd set it down—as he had—on the corpse's not-face.

"Where are we?" she asked in a voice so controlled that the security man could barely hear her over the tumult. "Are . . ." She looked around, and he couldn't be certain from the way her voice trailed off that she'd ever had the rest of the sentence in mind.

"Your apartment, fast," said Yates, starting to take her elbow and then drawing back. He didn't want to push her if he didn't have the strength to pick her up and carry her if she balked. Right at the moment he wasn't sure he could even walk the fifty meters or so around the corner unaided.

His suit was a wreck, but the dress she wore had come through as well as the garb of passersby who'd flopped to cover on the concrete. The garment was fawn colored, covering her from shoulders to ankles, but the skirt bloomed away without resistance from the long strides she took.

They shoved past a trio of women gaping into the corridor from the mouth of the residential passage. God only knew what that group or other spectators thought about the chaos. Yates doubted that anyone but him—and the other two gunmen—had a connected idea of what had happened.

Hell, he wasn't real clear on it himself. It had been more like being rocketed at night than any other experience he could recall.

"Here," said Bradley, tugging him by the elbow toward the unlatched door he was about to stumble past. There was a whiff of perfume in her hair, a clean smell among so many other odors at the moment.

She'd been dressed for dinner, and that reminded him that he was hungry, extremely hungry.

He was also, he realized to his own amazement, as horny as he'd ever been in his life.

Chapter 12

BRADLEY'S APARTMENT

Ella Bradley hurt from the stunner darts, pinprick punctures on her back from which networks of shocked nerves pulsed so that her torso felt like a tooth with an air-sensitive cavity.

And her throat hurt too—down in the hollow where drugs had been injected she could feel a raised soreness. As if that weren't enough, she'd pulled a complement of muscles that now chorused angrily: in her thighs, from kicking at her abductors; in her arms, from struggling; across her stomach from she didn't know what.

She wanted, once the door was closed on the nightmare from which she'd just awakened, to collapse on her couch—safe.

But the couch faced the door, and the door's security circuits were fried so that she couldn't electronically lock out the world. And if she could have, Supervisor Yates was in here with her, leaning against that door, his left side singed, his clothes ruined, looking like some New York bag lady after a sex change. . . .

Yates' left ear was blackened like a Cajun steak. He was keeping the weight off his left leg. Through what was left of the fabric, as she approached him wordlessly, Ella could see the raw, wet burns.

Sam Yates needed a doctor. She ought to call one. She would, as soon as she pulled herself together. Right now there were more pressing matters, like getting Yates away from the door so that she could throw the auxiliary dead bolt.

"Please, Supervisor, sit down," she said, as if this were some damned interview, her voice naturally lowering because it always did when what she had to say was important.

She was acutely aware that she sounded foolishly formal, perhaps even addled.

She might *be* addled, for all she knew. Everything hurt and she'd been drugged. . . .

"Yeah, all right, " said the big security man. "It's your furniture."

What was left of it. She didn't remember the struggle being so protracted as to have trashed her front room this way: everything small or fragile seemed to have been crushed or toppled. The tan couch facing the door, however, was nearly untouched—sprinkled with a bit of debris.

Until Yates limped over and sank into it with a difficulty he couldn't quite hide. Then the charred wool from his suit and the charred flakes of epidermal flesh smeared across the twill.

Ella Bradley closed her eyes, threw the manual dead bolt, and leaned her forehead against the door. "What the hell happened back there, Supervisor? And why? Do you know?" she asked without turning.

"My part, or yours?" The man's voice had a whispery quality—or pain added it. "I was doin' my job—nothin' more than your basic corridor firefight with plasma weapons—and then I looked down and the blanket I was lyin' on had you under it."

He couldn't be serious. She turned with a rebuke on her lips and saw the pale face, the sheen of sweat there. And something else. In the middle of all this pain and confusion, Yates' keen eyes were intrusive, possessive, almost proprietary.

"I guess I ought to thank you," she said and took a step forward.

"Maybe later, when I'm feelin' better," he replied with strained machismo.

She suddenly recalled coming up out of her drugged stupor and launching an attack at him. She said, "They broke in here and wrecked the place, doped me, then—" And stopped, realizing he knew all that. When she'd gone for his throat, he'd still had the antidote injector in his hand.

And then she realized she had no way of knowing that he hadn't been part of the attack on her all along. He'd been coming here to pick her up for their dinner date. Maybe it was all planned. To gain her confidence. To make her . . . what? She crossed her arms, halting in midstride halfway to him, the barred door at her back.

"Yeah," he was saying, "I was there, remember? And I don't know about you, but I don't really want to explain all that—what I know's less than what I don't—to anybody. Mind if we just keep this between us, until we find out what's going on?"

"Keep it between us?" she repeated, now pressing her folded arms against her ribs. "If I'm not mistaken, there are a number of dead men littering that corridor, not to mention a wrecked truck and—" Suddenly, the hand she'd put on the seared-away face of one of the casualties tingled. She pulled it from her side and examined it.

Then she sank down on the carpet, still halfway between the man and the door. He was a stranger. Just because he was Security didn't mean he was on her side. And there was definitely a side that wasn't hers in this. Or else none of that would have happened. "They had Afrikaner accents," she muttered, still looking at her hand.

"I thought so," he said, and shifted position with an audible intake of breath.

She looked up quickly, but he wasn't coming at her, just smearing her couch with black char, gooey serum, and a little pink, sticky blood.

She couldn't imagine someone willfully taking that much punishment. So maybe he wasn't part of the enemy. But what he was asking made no sense: "How do you propose we hide what happened out there?"

He shrugged and a grunt came out of him. Very slowly and carefully he sat up, put his right elbow on his right knee for support, and leaned toward her. Every vein in his neck and on his forehead stook out in bold relief as he replied: "We can't hide what happened, but we can obscure our participation—maybe. Get me? I wasn't there, you weren't there?"

"Someone," she said archly, her fingers digging in the rug's pile, "tried to kidnap me. You're asking me not to report it?"

"You reported it to me, if anyone asks. Otherwise, who you going to go to? Yesilkov?"

That struck home. "I'm a UN Mission functionary. I have recourse—"

"Unless you know who did this, and why, I don't think going to the UN Secretariat with it is any kind of good idea. They'll just come back to us, to the Directorate of Security, in any case. And what I'm saying is, *I* don't want to spend the next couple days, or weeks, explaining how come I was shootin' up that corridor with experimental weapons, and why. Not when I can't *say* why, except that you were in that damned blanket—which I didn't know when all hell broke loose out there—and that one of those guys in the orange suits resembled the fellow who was sharing your dining table at the Moulin Rouge the night we met, the night—"

"I remember. The same man, the one with the beard." Again she hugged herself, barely aware of him now, nearly numb with confusion. What did he want with her, that man with the Afrikaner accent and his friends? She'd never done anything in South Africa to make the counterrevolutionaries aware of her. And why now, when the whole lunar colony was half paralyzed with fear and confusion over the virus? Were the two things related? Did someone think there was a serum against the virus, and that her UN group had access to it? Or think there was some plot of which she was a part? There had to be a reason for the attempted abduction—a reason men would die trying to capture her.

"You got some water or something?" Yates asked.

"Yes, surely. Or tea, coffee—real coffee. Or beer or wine."

"Real coffee? Great." He sat back too fast and winced.

She got to her feet, grateful for something mechanical and domestic, something normal, to do. "Black or white?"

"Black," she heard as she sidled past him, stepping over debris from her overturned table, into the pullman kitchen.

In there, where nothing had been disturbed, she started making coffee. "You know," she called out, "you're going to have to see a doctor. How are you going to explain those burns? That—"

From right behind her he answered, "Line of duty. I'm security, remember."

She started, whirled in place. "Don't sneak up on me. I—"

"Sorry." He backed up. "Mind if I look around, see if I can figure what they were after?"

"They were after me—they made no attempt to search this place," she said matter-of-factly, with a surety she didn't understand. "I don't know why. But check my office—I'll bet it hasn't been touched either." She pointed to her office door, and he limped off that way.

When the coffee was done, he hadn't come out, so she brought the coffee, on a tray, into the office.

He was rooting through her files. Fury flashed through her. It was like being violated all over again.

And that errant thought brought everything she'd been suppressing to the surface, so that she started to tremble and managed to put the two cups on her desk just in time to avoid spilling their contents.

"Your coffee," she said in an icy voice. "If you want something in there, I'll be glad to help you."

"Sorry, just trying to see if they'd rifled anything." Yates came to the desk to take his cup, and she realized again how large he was. Large, rawboned, a little on the past-tense side of muscular; what certain people, if they'd seen him, would have referred to as "Ella's type."

And he might have saved her life. There was an awkward pause in which he took his coffee mug and she took hers. She wished he wouldn't look at her like that, so intrusively.

Holding his cup in his seared left hand, he reached out for her hand with his right. Somehow she didn't pull away in time.

"So," Yates said, "we're going to keep this between us for now, okay?"

She slid her hand out from under his. "That means that we'll be working on this investigation together." It was the only arrangement possible under the circumstances; she hadn't meant it to sound like a proposal.

"A deal," he said with a lopsided smile. "Now, let's figure out how we can work this."

How, indeed? He looked like he'd been run over by a

truck and then torched. She said, trying not to let her embarrassment show, "I've got some clothes that somebody left here , . . they might fit you. Those, plus some judicious clean up, and you could probably make it to Central Medical without arousing too much suspicion."

"Terrific," he said with boyish enthusiasm she hoped was real.

At least he hadn't asked about how the clothes had come to be here. Not that it was any of his business. She raised her coffee mug to her lips and said over it: "All right, then. While we're getting you dressed for polite society, we'll concoct some sort of plan."

And you can convince me that you aren't part of whatever it is that's going on, Sam Yates, that there's some good reason you don't want the UN mission to know that we were involved in what happened out there.

Because she couldn't think of a single reason why he hadn't called his office from here, why her apartment wasn't swarming with his colleagues by now, or why he wasn't more concerned with his wounds than with what she would or wouldn't say to any subsequent investigators.

She was even beginning to wonder whether she'd tell him that she'd sent a data request—NYU Project 32/149—via a UN Lunar Headquarters terminal to Sky Devon, asking for everything Devon had on Rodney Beaton.

"Supervisor Yates, if you'll come this way . . ." It sounded stiff and distancing to her own ears, but she was leading the man into her bedroom, where she was about to give him another man's clothes.

He followed her out of the office, coffee cup in hand, saying, "Look, we were on first-name terms before all this happened, Ella. Remember? I'm still Sam, okay?"

She spoke over her shoulder to the man on her heels. "Fine, Sam. Tell me, have any other Le Moulin Rouge customers from that night been attacked . . . or died in odd circumstances—any circumstances different from those of virus-enhanced respiratory failure? In addition to myself and Rodney Beaton, I mean."

"Not yet," he said as he followed her into her bedroom.

His answer was noncritical. Noncommittal, even. And softly, intimately spoken. He meant to asssure her he didn't think she was paranoid, that he wasn't patronizing her.

She swung around to face the big man, suddenly aware that she could have had him wait in her office, in the living room, anywhere else. He could have changed in the bathroom. She hadn't had to bring him in here. And he knew it.

Flustered, she raked her hand through her hair. "Just a second, and I'll have these things for you." She fled to her closet, sliding back one mirrored door.

The bed was between them and it was, she supposed, natural for him to sit on it, his good leg crooked under him—he was injured, after all. Now she felt herself flush, and that made her feel even more foolish.

She rattled the hangers, looking for the clothes Taylor had left here when he'd been recalled to Earth. Taylor McLeod's office, in the U.S. Mission to the lunar UN, had helped Ella ram her innocent-looking request for background material on Rodney Beaton through the data queue to the head of the line.

Helped without question, without a blinked eye or a ruffled feather. Nice to have friends in high places, even when those friends were absent. Taylor wouldn't mind that she'd used his clout or his staff the way he'd mind that she'd loaned another man his clothes.

But it couldn't be helped. Not now. She'd replace the garments before Taylor returned in two weeks, if she was still alive in two weeks. If anything such as where to get real merino cut on Savile Row to McLeod's measurements mattered in two weeks . . .

"Here we are, Sam. The style's loose, so they should fit well enough." *Turn your blood blue in the process, Mister Security Man*. She held out the pale, fine wool fashioned into an unconstructed sports jacket and pleated pants, neatly hung over a Sea Islands cotton shirt and rep tie.

Sam Yates didn't move from the bed. He looked at the clothing and one eyebrow raised. "I wouldn't be caught dead in that, most times, but these aren't most times." There was a challenge in his voice that at first she didn't understand.

She brought the clothes to the bed and held out the hanger stiffly. "I'll be in the living room." Her own voice sounded like a stranger's. She wasn't going to defend or even discuss the taste of the man whose clothes these were, not with someone of Yates' breeding.

"Your boyfriend's?" Yates asked the obvious question as he held out a hand, not to take the hanger from her, but to feel the material between his thumb and forefinger.

"A friend of mine from the diplomatic corps," she said stiffly. Short of tossing the clothing to the bed and stomping out, there was nothing for it but wait until Yates took the hanger from her.

Instead of doing that, he got up slowly, with obvious effort, and moved close.

He reached for the suit and her at the same time.

She thrust the suit on its hanger against his chest, and there was an awkward moment where his good arm was around her, pulling her toward him, and her own was stiffening against his chest with the suit hanger as a pry bar.

Then she managed, "Please, let's not make this any more awkward than—" but the big man was already bending to kiss her.

She should have turned her head, let his lips brush her cheek, but she didn't. His lips were dry and rough where they'd blistered. He'd saved her life, she told herself. Worth a kiss, she thought as she returned a chaste one, her lips firmly closed.

And a hug, to make it more clear that she wasn't being standoffish. But Yates returned that hug with one much more sensual than decorum required.

"If you're worried about him learning," he murmured, "look—*I'm* not gonna tell him."

His lips traveled down her neck when she turned her face away. She had to do something before he got the wrong idea, if he hadn't already. She was suddenly frightened—he was so big, an unknown quantity. She didn't know him at all. His arms around her were far too strong.

"No, not now. I—" She stepped back, and he didn't force her against him. That was something, anyway. Flustered, she said, "We hardly know each other . . . I've had a rough night. I can't—"

He let go of her with pained reluctance and they stood

at arm's length. She could see his chest rise and fall.

He said at last, "Your call, Ella. But really, it doesn't matter about him—"

"It does to me," she said stiffly, and backed three steps. "Come out when you've changed and we'll see how you look."

She left him alone in her bedroom, closing the door on his half-hopeful, half-annoyed smile.

Of course it mattered—even if Taylor and she hadn't been more than friends, it would have mattered. It mattered that Yates said it didn't matter—that he'd consider it acceptable behavior to fool around with another man's woman so casually. And it mattered that he assumed she was of the same disposition.

In Ella Bradley's world you didn't hop into bed with just anyone, merely because the opportunity presented itself. Especially when that someone presumed he was cuckolding someone else.

She decided that she didn't like Supervisor Samuel Yates very well at all. *Well, what did you expect? He's just a glorified beat cop, an ex-soldier—a Nicaraguan vet with some permutation of delayed stress syndrome*. People in Ella Bradley's circle hadn't gone to Nicaragua—unless they went on diplomatic or intelligence assignments, or right out of West Point as part of the Military Assistance Command structure.

The well bred, the well heeled, and the well educated had stayed out of that war as they'd stayed out of every war since the Korean conflict: there were plenty of expendables like Sam Yates to fill America's ranks.

Not that Ella Bradley's peers didn't fight, or sacrifice, in their way. Some, like Ella, ventured deep into the jungles with the Peace Corps or the UN; some, like her absent friend, Taylor, fought shadow wars in hallowed diplomatic halls and exotic back streets. But all of them knew, without question, their place: they were leaders, they were role models, they were the bearers of the torch of civilization which, for Americans, had become epitomized in a single word— democracy.

Ella's peer group fought to promote that democracy— freedom to learn, to think, to live, and to vote—worldwide.

Some of them had brought that struggle to the Moon, because the UN was the real battleground, not some soggy jungle where primitives lobbed grenades at one another in thoughtlesss fury. Taylor McLeod had told her once that each person chose only his appropriate battlefield—that all human existence was warfare; even the claim of noncombatant status or nonviolent protest was warfare by inaction, as effective a strategy in many cases as warfare by direct action.

Ella's specialty was tribal peoples, every disparate group from Kabyles to Zulus who still professed national identity and thus kept representatives at the UN, and every subgroup threatened with extinction by the homogenizing process of civilization and tribal warfare. There were fifty-two wars in progress, down on the placid-looking blue planet called Earth.

Every nation had a representative here on the Moon. Every power bloc sustained by brute force feared America because it feared democracy, the greatest homogenizing force of all. So there were as many possible culprits in her attempted abduction as there were tribal factions who feared Americanization, Ella told herself dreamily, sitting on the couch while she waited for Sam Yates to emerge from her bedroom.

Americanization meant democracy. Democracy meant equal rights—one person, one vote. Sometimes, like tonight, she understood viscerally why so many people perceived democracy as their enemy. Democracy allowed for excellence but inclined toward mediocrity—the presence of Ella Bradley and Sam Yates in the same apartment was sufficient proof of that.

When Yates came out of her bedroom, hitching up the waistband of pants slightly too loose, Ella broke the silence before he could. There was no use of either of them prolonging what had become an uncomfortable situation.

"Before you go, Supervisor, perhaps I'd better tell you that I put through a request for deep background on Rodney Beaton—to Sky Devon."

"Chrissake," said Yates, halting in midstride. "*Now* you tell me."

Chapter 13

CENTRAL MEDICAL

"Feels like you've got me wearing a lead tube," said Yates, rubbing his left thigh as he stepped out of the treatment room. From the way he burned, deep into the muscles, it felt as if the lead had been poured over him to congeal against his flesh. "It's—is it supposed to be this stiff?"

"It'll loosen up as you move, sir," said the medical technician who had supervised Yates' treatment according to the parameters ordered by a doctor and a bank of diagnostic computers. "By tomorrow you won't notice it, almost."

The technician, whose name tag read da Silva and whose delicate features were Filipino, winced sympathetically as he watched the care with which his patient drew on his trousers. "The pain stops in three, four hours, sir. It's part of the healing, really."

"Could've been worse," said Yates, managing a smile to show that he appreciated the med tech's concern. It embarrassed him that his pain was so obvious . . . but then, da Silva had probably seen enough burn victims to know exactly how the transparent cast over Yates' thigh must feel.

The cast replenished fluids that had been seared out of the shrunken muscles; supplied nutrients and antibiotics at a metered rate; and covered the seriously burned area until the skin grew back. Yates' memory of the plasma bolt that had ripped the wall of the passageway beside him was lost in other events. He kept remembering his own shots and the awesome coruscance of the blast which lit the darkened stairwell before him.

But that first shot had damned near done the job. It parboiled his left thigh, despite the considerable insulation provided by the leg of his trousers.

Maybe he ought to replace the now-carbonized gray wool with a white linen suit that'd reflect more radiant heat the *next* time he was a finger's breadth from a plasma discharge.

"Excuse, sir?" said da Silva, warning the security man that he'd been muttering under his breath.

"I was thinking," Yates explained in modified form as he shrugged into the shirt, "that I wouldn't have been wearing my good suit tonight if I'd known there was going to be an explosion beside me.

"Any idea"—he couldn't help the change in his voice, but he covered it by putting on his new jacket—"what it might've been? I just got the hell outa the way, and it wasn't till I was changing clothes that I saw I'd really been hurt."

That was the official story; and the last part of it was pretty close to the truth.

The med tech grimaced in negation as he readied his treatment cubicle to be used again. He was stripping the cover from the couch on which patients were gripped and ministered to by robot arms. Normally, patients walked here from the diagnostic cubicles at the other end of the facility, where more delicate probes and sensors assayed them under the titular control of an MD.

In fact, the MD was as much a caretaker as the med tech here. At need, a patient could be transported from diagnosis to treatment by a robot gurney while the parameters of his care were blipped from machine to machine on a dedicated data link. Untouched by human hands or will, the patient's chance of recovery would be as good as that of others who had the advantage of human oversight.

Barring electronic or mechanical failure.

Which killed only a fraction of those who had succumbed in past decades to doctors with more interest in real estate than diagnosis, and nurses who misread a decimal point in the medication order.

The clothes Ella'd given him were loose. At the time he'd figured maybe all the clothes on that side of the closet were cut the same way—God knew, the fellow who owned 'em didn't have any more taste in color than a camel. Maybe she hadn't, from their few meetings, noticed Yates' preference for tailoring that showed off the lines of a body he was damned proud to have kept at his age—or perhaps she *did* understand and was making her own cool response to the way he was coming on in her apartment.

It struck him now that the woman had simply realized that loose fabric would be a lot more comfortable than garments that prodded his burns every time he moved. He shouldn't take everything so damned personal.

Knowing that she had a live-in—or at least a steady—whom she hadn't bothered to mention, meant that Yates had misjudged how personal she was being on other stuff. Well, you win some, you lose some—and some get rained out.

"Say," Yates said, converting a thought into a request, "do you have a phone I can use? I need to report this, I guess. And I oughta call my office."

"Yes sir," said da Silva. "It's on the end wall."

He also, Yates realized as he punched in the number of Entry Division's front desk, needed to get up with Ella Bradley and retrieve the ID card he'd left in the other suit when he changed. But he wasn't ready to talk to the lady just yet.

"Entry Division," said the speaker. "Rosario."

There was a flurry of noise behind Yates as da Silva scrambled to help a woman whose right arm was in a bloody bandage. There was a man beside her, both of them screaming in an unfamiliar language. The glance Yates threw at them left him in doubt as to whether the man was supporting the woman or threatening to finish her off.

Raising his voice, and hopeful that he wasn't going to get involved in another brawl in a moment, the security man said, "This is Supervisor Yates. I've been involved in an accident, and I may miss the first couple hours of my shift. Leave a message for Emeraud to take my calls till I come in, okay?"

"Supervisor?" said the phone. The receptionist's raised, quizzical voice made Yates wonder how much was getting through the commotion ungarbled. The victim was entering the treatment cubicle, but she continued to cling to her companion with her uninjured hand.

"Yes," Yates said, "yes—Yates here."

"Supervisor, there's an ASAP message for you to call a Lieutenant Yesilkov," the phone said. "She, ah . . . she told me I'd better not drop the ball on this one, sir."

"You haven't, Rosario," the security man said with a smile that reminded him of the blisters spattered on his face by molten glass. "And it sounds like I'd better not mess up either. She leave a number?"

"Yessir," said Rosario's voice with such evident relief that Yates wondered just what threats the patrol lieutenant had made. "One-five"—the general Directorate of Security exchange—"two-three-six-niner."

"Got it," Yates replied, nodding in part at the fact that the two civilians behind him had been separated on the correct sides of the door to the treatment cubicle. The room was quiet again, except for the hum of machinery and the mumbled prayers of the man kneeling in front of the cubicle. "And leave the message for Emeraud, okay?"

He did not wait for a reply. Instead, he tapped the call closed and immediately punched in the lieutenant's number while his surface memory held it.

"Central Four," snarled the voice of a man who was either trying to juggle three things at once or was madder than hell—or mad because he was juggling three things, of course.

"Supervisor Yates returning Lieutenant Yesilkov's call," said the security man, with enough edge to make sure that he wasn't going to get lost in the shuffle because somebody was having a bad day. Hell, his leg hurt like a bear was chewing on it, and he was dotting the i's and crossing the t's like a good citizen, wasn't he?

Acting like a good citizen helped him forget what he'd been doing just an hour ago. He couldn't *believe* the shards of the firefight which his memory was still trying to fit into a connected whole.

"Hold one," said the phone, no happier than before but doing its job. "I'll buzz 'er."

Yates dabbed at the blisters on his face as he waited, head bent toward the phone. The man outside the cubicle was leaning his forehead against the door, but it was hard to tell whether he was even aware of his posture. The blisters had been shrunken flat and all the associated pain deadened at the same time the cubicle exuded the transparent cast around Yates' thigh, but the injured spots didn't move with the skin around them.

Actually, his leg wasn't burning near as bad as at first. Certainly he could flex the big muscles without the stiffness that had begun to weld the limb rigid even before the shooting had stopped.

"Sir, she says where are you?"' demanded the phone with only token courtesy.

"Central Medical," Yates replied. He'd expected the patrol lieutenant to take the line, but apparently she wasn't in her office.

There was another long pause while the security man bent and straightened the injured leg. Da Silva was talking into the console built into the side of the treatment cubicle, trying to get the patient to remove some article of clothing so that the hardware could get on with its work.

Must be easier when the victims were unconscious—and there was a patrolman or two to control hysterical companions. You didn't need humans to deal with medical problems, maybe, but they sure would help on some of the human side effects.

"All right," said the phone. "She says meet her here in twenty, that's two-zero, minutes. Got that?"

"Yeah, I've got it, but hold on," said Yates with his anger rising—though twenty minutes was a good estimate of the distance by slideway, and the fellow on the other end of the line wasn't where these brusque orders originated. "I've been injured in a . . . in an explosion on M-M Corridor, and I think I'd better report it before—"

"We'll take your statement when you get here," interrupted the voice. "We're covering that too."

"You are?" said the security man, startled out of his irritation. "Is M-M in your patrol area?"

"No sir," snapped the phone, "but they've called in adjacent units because of the work load. Which I'll get back to now, if you'll excuse me."

Yates started to apologize, but the click of a broken connection forestalled him.

Waving to the med tech who was still pleading with his patient, Yates walked out the door of Central Medical. An ambulance had just arrived, bearing someone motionless behind two harassed-looking attendants.

Yates hoped that wasn't another side effect of something *he'd* done.

He figured he had enough on his conscience already.

Chapter 14

TEAMWORK

Yates wasn't whistling as he reached the door of the branch station, and his silence wasn't solely a result of the pocks of deadened skin which made it awkward to purse his lips.

He reached toward the announcement plate—as before, there wasn't anyone visible on the door visor. Before his hand touched the plate, Lieutenant Yesilkov called from behind him, "Hang on, I'll catch it."

The overhead light picked out flecks of gray in the patrol officer's hair as she stepped past Yates with her card out, but those colorless strands only brightened the generally pale blond.

"Nice timing," she remarked while the door jacked itself open. Her eyes met Yates' momentarily before she led the way inside and to the left instead of toward the office where he'd found her the day before. "If it's that good in other ways," Yesilkov called back over her shoulder, "you must be real popular with the ladies."

"Couldn't prove it by the time I've spent on the Moon," the big man grumbled; but though his lips moved, he did not quite voice the words.

"Sonya?" called a man whose head popped out a door they had passed. "Did you see the new *duty* roster?"

Yesilkov put a hand on Yates' shoulder as the Entry Division supervisor flattened himself against the lockers that thinned the passage to less than the width in which two humans could pass comfortably. "Herb," she called past Yates without trying to see her questioner, "you got a problem with the roster, you take it up with Ingraham. I don't even talk to her about my own shift anymore, okay?"

Yesilkov turned, ignoring Herb's bleats. With a finger bent as if it were hooked through Yates' lower jaw instead of hovering a meter in front of him, she led the supervisor through the door at the end of the hall. The room they entered was relatively large, with seats for twenty or so. Several patrolmen were already clustered in the front, talking. They looked up as the lieutenant and her visitor came in.

"Squad Room," Yesilkov explained as she slid chairs out of her way instead of following a straggling aisle. "We've only got one holotank in the station, and it's here. It'll be long enough to shift change that we can use it and get out before Fernandez needs the room."

While the patrol officer loaded the holotank with a data chip, Yates rotated two of the movable chairs. The chairs could have been collapsed into fifty-millimeter disks and stacked, but the clutter didn't seem to bother the patrol personnel who used the room.

And if the Squad Room *were* cleared, somebody would probably move lockers into it before the next shift change.

Yesilkov slapped the machine. The equipment looked as doubtful as the unit in Yates' office. One of the projection circuits was out, and the test pattern of colors waving in the tank had a decidedly greenish cast.

The slap didn't appear to help. The lieutenant swore in Russian, and a moment later the ripples snapped to full chromatic life.

"Play," said Yesilkov in a threatening voice. Colors coalesced into moving images, a corridor scene whose fuzziness was probably due to the recording rather than the playback equipment.

"Got a copy of the pictures your friend Beaton was making," Yesilkov said, settling herself in the chair without really relaxing. There was emotion underlying the huskiness of her voice, but Sam Yates couldn't be sure *what* emotion. "Thought you'd like to see 'em. There's an audio commentary, too, and I've heard it—but Third Platoon couldn't copy it till Maintenance finishes with the duplicator."

Her eyes narrowed as she looked the security man over carefully for the first time since they'd met in front of the substation. "Hey," she said. "You look like you died three days back and they just brought you 'round again.''

''This doesn't hurt,'' said Yates, gesturing at his face.
''My leg, though''—he pointed toward his left thigh, but
he did not touch the trouser leg—''hurts like *hell*, and it
doesn't look much better. There was a bomb or something
on M-M Corridor, and I got caught in it.''

''Yeah,'' said the lieutenant in a neutral voice, ''we'll
get to that in a bit.'' She pointed toward the tank—in which
the glazed front door of Le Moulin Rouge had just appeared.

''He switched it on, the cameras, about three blocks down
the corridor,'' the patrol officer explained. ''Doesn't really
help determine where he was coming from, but it's more
likely the tourist hotel where he was staying than the air
lock where his body was found.''

Two more patrolmen entered the room, one of them loudly
demanding coffee while his companion laughed. They
quieted somewhat as Yesilkov turned and the flag of her
short blond hair caught their attention.

Yates grunted, though he did not know he made a sound.
All he was aware of was that the figure swelling to fill the
holotank was the Arab waiter who had died in front of him.
Yates mind insisted on masking the face with blood and
ruptured lung tissue that was not there.

Yet.

The picture wasn't sharp, but as the door opened inward,
the viewers glimpsed Rodney Beaton's reflection in the clear
panel. The British technician's face was set and white, in
sharp contrast to that of the bored waiter who turned to lead
yet another customer to a table.

''There,'' said the security man. *''There.''* His finger
tapped the surface of the holotank as the image within opened
past the waiter's shoulder. ''That's the . . . that's the guy
at the next table, the one I thought might be an Afrikaner.''

Yates' ribs tickled as he realized the man here glimpsed
in hologram might be as dead as the waiter, one of the
''utility workers'' he'd hit with plasma bolts that afternoon.
Maybe not. Yates was pretty sure the fellow in the restaurant
was the same one he'd traded shots with vainly at the end
of the firefight; but the spikes of plasma had been so bright
that his vision still flashed ghostly afterimages, and the five
men in orange coveralls had been pretty much of a type.

There wasn't enough left of the three dead for anyone to swear to their faces now either.

"Good," said the lieutenant mildly as more patrol personnel entered the Squad Room. "We'll keep that in mind."

The holotank filled with the torso and chin of the waiter during what the security man knew was an argument about seating. Occasionally Beaton would shift enough that the lenses in his lapel swept a broader expanse, but only in brief glimpses.

A proper holovision recorder had its lens heads offset a considerable distance apart so that they caught significantly different aspects of the view between them. Even so, only the most elaborate studio rigs truly encircled a subject. Usually, portions of the hologram were created by the microprocessor in either the recording or the playback equipment.

In the present case the hardware was of low sophistication—but the picture was more than adequate for the purpose of the two security officers.

"Not a bad likeness," said Yesilkov with the lack of emotion that was beginning to concern her visitor. The image of the waiter moved away and the recording lenses shifted across the table to a big blond man whom Yates *didn't* think was a great likeness of himself.

Yates' image looked away from Yates' self, the hologram eyes drifting toward the next table and Ella Bradley.

With a deliberation the security man had not suspected while he sat in the restaurant, Beaton shifted his body so the recorder slowly swept everyone in the room. Ella looked up, not quite at the camera. Her expression was detached. It melted minusculy, just the beginning of the smile Yates had seen transfigure the woman once in a while—and then froze into a mask of distaste which meshed perfectly with the security man's memory of the same incident.

"Must not have liked her soup," said Yesilkov.

Yates was sure the patrol lieutenant was joking, but there was no emotion—no archness of suggested meaning—in her voice. Maybe she was just exhausted, flattened by a series of what were obviously double shifts . . . but that wasn't quite what it seemed.

The recording lenses tracked the Arab waiter rigidly as he returned from the kitchen. Watching the hologram, Yates

was sure he could see signs of discomfort, of devastating
illness, in the victim's features.

There hadn't been anything at the time, though, just
another professionally supercilious waiter going through
familiar motions unexceptionably. Maybe the man had been
as ignorant of what was about to happen as—

The Arab coughed.

Sam Yates stood up, the back of his calves shoving his
chair away. He turned around. "Look," he said in a voice
that was so ragged that it shocked him, "I guess I'm pussy
but, you know, I don't want to see this right now. I'm sorry
as hell—"

He breathed quickly, deeply, and wondered if he were
going to need to stick his head between his knees to keep
from fainting. Or would it be less embarrassing to faint. . . .?

Lieutenant Yesilkov said something. It was an instant
before Yates' mind realized that she had snapped "Exit"
to the voice-controlled holotank.

"Look," the big man said softly. He turned and seated
himself again, but he kept his eyes on his lap and hands,
which suddenly felt clammy. "I'd like to say it was the,
you know, the hospital and all that. . . ."

He gestured toward his left leg, though the injury could
not be seen through his trousers, and anyway, it seemed to
have stopped hurting so bad.

There was some good to incipient fainting, it seemed.

He breathed deeply again, and this time let it out slowly.
"Truth is," he said, meeting the lieutenant's worried eyes,
"I can get this way sometimes, not so much remembering
as being there again. And not being able to stop what's
coming. It used to happen, you know, in dreams once in a
while."

It was going to start happening again, while his mind
came to terms with this afternoon.

At least he'd be sleeping alone this time.

"No sweat," said Yesilkov. Though her voice was still
blank, there was knowledge in her expression. "Wanted
you to see that he was really tracking what went on, Beaton
was. Followed you into the kitchen, close shots of the sub-
jects there. Including the, ah, the witness."

Her voice changed very slightly, and perhaps her mouth quirked toward the start of a grin. "Picture degrades a bit from there on out. The lenses in his lapel got a little smeared 'r something."

Yates grimaced. "Yeah," he said to the random colors of the holotank.

Yesilkov shrugged. "People who ain't been there hisself, sometimes they don't understand somebody havin' a temper. Me, I wouldn't worry about it."

"He knew what was going to happen before it did," said the big man, because he didn't know how to thank the lieutenant except with a shrug of his own. "He was there because of it, set to record the killings like it was somebody's election speech."

"That's right," the patrol officer agreed with a nod. "He made sure he caught a good picture of the others when he came across 'em. Made a beeline for the air lock where they found him, but he was still on the job, I'd say."

"Right," said Yates, drawn enough back into the problem that he absentmindedly crossed his right ankle over his left thigh.

He'd been wrong to think his leg had stopped hurting.

Wincing hard enough to close his eyes momentarily while he set both feet squarely on the floor again, the security man continued, "Thing is, where does that leave us?"

"Just now, let's take care of the other business," said Yesilkov coolly.

The Squad Room had continued to fill, unnoticed in Yates' personal agitation, with uniformed men. Several slid into chairs Yesilkov and her visitor had disarrayed to use the holotank.

The lieutenant ignored them. "Play map section four-four-one," she said to the hologram projector while her fingers extracted the data chip she had loaded into it earlier.

The tank obediently retrieved from the central memory bank a monochrome, two-dimensional plan of corridors and cross passages.

"All right," continued Yesilkov to her visitor. "Please indicate the point at which you think you were when the explosion occurred. Just touch the surface of the tank."

Maybe her voice had become so detached because this was a speech she gave by rote with minor variations several times a day.

Yates leaned closer to the tank so that he could see the identifying letters and numbers in miniature on the street plan. He found MM–NN12, the passage to Ella's apartment. He held his hand rigid so that it would not instinctively follow his thought and betray him to the patrol officer . . . and there was cross-passage 10, whose corner with Corridor MM had gouted molten fury when a stray bolt touched it.

"Here," said Yates, fingering the pebbly, warm surface of the tank. An orange dot glowed in hologram within, at the point he meant to indicate.

The security man leaned into his chair again, combing his fingers through the lock of dark blond hair that had fallen onto his forehead. "I was walking past a jewelry store, I think it was"—he'd checked the site and his story on the way to Central Medical—"walking on the sidewalk because I wasn't in any hurry, and the wall, well, it blew up. Burned. I can't really describe it."

That was true enough. The bolt that almost hit him had left only a hazy recollection of rainbow coruscance and a tearing noise that filled the world.

"Ever used a plasma discharger?" Yesilkov asked.

"Once," Yates replied with equal calm, making sure that he had eye contact with his questioner as he delivered the half truth. "In training, a long time ago."

"You were on the receiving end this time," said the lieutenant. "See anything more?"

"Well, not really . . ." the security man replied, wondering what exactly to claim.

He was willing to admit, if necessary, that he had gone to Ella Bradley's apartment after the firefight and that the woman had provided the clothing he now wore. That wasn't something he wanted to say if he could avoid it—especially to Sonya Yesilkov—but he could scarcely avoid mentioning the shot-up van forty meters from passage MM–NN 12.

"There was a car up the street, burning, too, I think, and people running all over the place," Yates decided aloud. "But frankly, I was too shook myself to pay much attention."

"Right," said the lieutenant distantly. "There was a Bureau of Utilities vehicle here."

She touched the screen with a short, capable index finger. An orange pip glowed at about where Yates would have placed it.

Still leaning forward, Yesilkov turned her head to look at her visitor before she continued, "It'd been shot up, plasma dischargers again. And there was a body in it."

She glanced back at the tank and prodded it. "Another body here."

An orange bead at the junction of the corridor and the residential passage. *Hell,* Yates had forgotten the fellow he blew off the back of the van, the one who'd been manning the other barricade. How was he going to explain forgetting that he'd stepped over a corpse on his way to Ella's apartment?

Well, he'd done just that, too wrought up with other things to notice.

Yates wasn't sure that nearly having his leg burned off would have been enough in itself to disconnect him that far from reality . . . but he figured he could convince Yesilkov that it had been.

"Jesus," he said aloud. "I didn't see him."

"Right," the patrol officer said—*agreed* would give too much weight to the flat voice. "Another body here." She tapped the corner of NN and the cross passage.

And now you're lyin' dead on my barroom floor chorused Yates' mind, concluding the stanza it had been singing before he was interrupted by a man who was now a corpse.

"And there was enough shooting besides," Yesilkov continued, "to burn holes in a lotta walls and roof ducts."

Her finger dabbed quickly, sprinkling half a dozen orange dots across the map. These included the passage outside Ella's door—and a shop on Corridor NN, facing the passage. One of the men in utility coveralls must have fired past Yates during the first instants of the engagement, but the security man couldn't remember that for the world. The bolt had been lost in one of his own or the shot that vaporized the wall beside him.

"Damn," Yates muttered, and only the lift of Yesilkov's eyebrows warned him that he'd spoken aloud.

"Yeah," said the woman as she leaned back in her chair, watching Yates with eyes that gave up nothing. "Hell of a thing to have happen in the middle of the colony, ain't it?"

"Sonya?" called the man who had just mounted the dais in front of the room. Collapsible chairs squawked and clattered as the roomful of patrol personnel turned toward the subject of the question.

"Exit," said Yesilkov to the holotank. Then, rising as quiet ripples flooded the disintegrating map, she nodded, "Sorry, Pedro. We can finish this outside. Anybody in Room Three?"

"Not for a couple hours," said the man on the dais. He shrugged. "You need it longer 'n that, let me know, okay?"

Yesilkov threw a salute, both appreciative and sardonic, to her fellow, and led Yates out of the packed room. Her economy of effort impressed the visitor. Most of the patrolmen who moved out of the way were larger than the lieutenant, but it was as much her personality as her rank that opened the passage.

"Where we were before," Yesilkov said as she strode down the narrow hall. Her words were a drift of sound to which the man behind her fitted meaning a few steps later.

A black patrolman, harassed-looking and late, flattened against her open locker as the lieutenant and security man passed. Beads of sweat glimmered on her fashionably-shaven scalp.

"All right," Yesilkov said as she opened the door of an office—the names on the plate weren't the same, but the clutter within hadn't changed—and waved Yates in ahead of her. "Sit down," she added, not quite as a single word. She gestured her visitor to the chair facing the desk while she closed the ceramic-foam door panel.

Yates wasn't surprised when the patrol officer shot the flat manual bolt to lock the door against anything but considerable violence. But he *didn't* expect her to clear hard copy and office paraphernalia from a corner of the desk itself and perch herself there, looking down at her visitor with blank eyes.

The room was so small that if Yesilkov wished, she could rest a boot on the arms of Yates' chair, between the seated man and the door. For the moment she put her right sole flat against the front of the desk and gripped her bent knee with both hands.

"Supervisor Yates," the woman said formally. "I need to see your ID card."

"All right," said Yates, pleased that his voice was placid, and hopeful that it hadn't jumped an octave above normal the way his frightened ears told him it had. "We'll have to go get it, though. The suit I was wearing burned when—" He motioned idly toward his thigh.

Yates' heart rate had shot up, and that was a bad thing because there was nowhere to run.

"I left the card in the other suit when I changed clothes," he concluded with open-faced calm.

Yesilkov took her hands away from her right knee, letting that leg dangle while the toes of her left boot just brushed the floor. She was really very short. . . .

"No, you didn't," she said as her fingers opened the touch-sensitive closure of a breast pocket—not the one in which she was keeping the chip containing Beaton's data. She took out a plastic card and spun it onto the security man's lap with the slow perfection that proved her adaptation to lunar gravity.

It was his, all right. But where—

"You left it at the junction of corridor N-N," Yesilkov said coolly, "and cross-passage twelve."

"Ah . . ." said Yates as his mind searched for a lie.

"*Under* the body of one Jan-Christian Malan," the woman continued, "a foreman with the Bureau of Utilities."

"Ah."

"Jantze to his friends, one of whom was the Michel van Rooyan who provided the corpse at the other end of the passage," Yesilkov said.

She paused, looking the Entry Division supervisor over as if he, too, were a body hunched in the chair for her inspection. "Think you'd like to tell me what really happened, buddy?" she said.

"I think I'd better," said Sam Yates. He was genuinely calm for the first time since the moment before the shooting started. He was being forced to lay out the situation, so none of the results were his responsibility.

The most likely result was that the Secretariat would,

under the terms of the UN Charter, transfer him to the United States authorities to be tried for murder.

And God knew what other charges.

"I'd arranged a meeting with Ella Bradley," Yates said. He would have gotten up to stretch—the room was too small for pacing—but the lieutenant staring down at him might have misinterpreted his intention. "There was a barricade and a man—that would be Malan, but I'd never seen him before. At Bradley's corridor."

Yesilkov nodded, but she did not speak. Her body shifted so that she could raise her right leg and plant it on the desktop. Her forearm rested on the knee in a pose more relaxed than any she'd displayed to her visitor thus far in the afternoon.

"I took out my card, figured it'd get me through the barricade," the big man continued. "Must be there I lost it."

He grimaced. The woman allowed herself a grin.

"He, the guy, he was giving me some crock," Yates went on. He was suddenly nervous again, because he might have some hope after all. "There was a van up the passageway and some more utility people with it, but I didn't think anything about it until one of 'em looked around and it was the guy from the restaurant. The—"

He gestured toward the desk display, where the holotank might have been if they had not left the Squad Room minutes before. Yates did not realize his mistake, continuing, "The guy we've got in holo now, I figure an Afrikaner."

He cleared his throat and went on, as Yesilkov waited without the tension of moments before. "I pushed through the barricade. The guy there had . . . had a plasma gun. I took it away from him."

Yates didn't want to say what came next, not that the woman'd be in much doubt about it, but he said instead, "It was in a regular toolbox, the gun, that's how they kept it hidden."

His face had turned toward a wall of file drawers of no interest to him and of damned little to the uniformed officers whose records they were. Yates forced his eyes back to the waiting Yesilkov and said, "I shot him. Somebody shot from the van, a couple times, I guess, but I only saw the once. I engaged the vehicle with two rounds as it exited the passage. Then I gave pursuit.''

Sam Yates was twenty years younger as he sat in the chair, and the images he was trying to describe kept getting confused with ghostly foliage and the bamboo shacks of villages whose names he never learned.

''The vehicle halted,'' his voice rasped on, shredded by a past in which everything had happened at the same time— not over the years and decades of objective reality. ''I engaged its personnel without effect, then . . . then I think they ran off and I rushed them.''

He was breathing hard, aware that something was wrong with the air but unable to say that the humidity was too low, that it wasn't dripping with moisture wrung from the surrounding foliage by a tropical sun.

''They'd escaped up an air-lock shaft,'' Yates said. ''There were at least two of them, maybe a third, because I couldn't see the front of the vehicle. I—Jesus! Maybe that was before?''

He couldn't remember the sequence. Veins stood out on his wrists and forehead as he strained—not because only the truth could save him from punishment, but rather because he was adrift in a timelesss Hell and every lost memory was another bulwark that had failed him.

''S'okay, man,'' said Sonya Yesilkov. She was standing beside him, though he hadn't seen her move. The fingers of the woman's left hand were kneading the taut muscles at the back of his neck.

''I *killed* the fuckers,'' Yates whispered. ''Just blew their ass away. If anybody else got in the way, I didn't mean it, but I did . . .''

''Nobody else,'' the woman said. ''Nobody near as bad as you. It's okay.''

''The woman, Ella Bradley, was in the vehicle,'' Yates continued. The quiver in his voice was a sign of returning control, not that he was about to lose it. ''She'd been drugged but the antidote was in the hand of the . . . man in there.''

''He was dead?'' said Yesilkov, interjecting a question for the first time since the security man had begun to blurt the true story.

"Oh, yeah," said Yates. His eyes were forward. The woman's hand had slid from his neck to his shoulder. He raised his own hand to clamp it there. "Not much doubt about that, was there? She was under a blanket, Ella was, so she hadn't been . . ."

His free hand gestured nervously in the air. He had a clear, frozen memory of the van's side panel vaporizing in his gunsight—metal burning and gaseous, a superheated bubble which must have flashed across the vehicle's interior.

"When they're shootin' at you," Yates said softly, "all you can think is *make it stop*." His eyes were open, but he continued to look across the desk as if the lieutenant were seated there instead of standing beside him.

"Some people just flatten 'emselves," he continued to the empty chair. "Pretend they're diggin' a hole with their belly button. And some—if you shoot back, maybe it stops, and anyway, maybe you can forget it . . . till it's over."

Yesilkov chuckled harshly.

Yates turned and lifted his head. "You keep doing this to me, lady," he said past the bright blue uniform shirt. "I'm not like this, most times. Long past it."

"Not what I'd've guessed from your box score t'night," the lieutenant said with an eyebrow lifted sardonically. "You musta been hell on wheels before you got all broke down with age."

"You bet," said the big man as his left hand touched Yesilkov's back and ribs to guide, not draw, her face toward him for a kiss.

She did not resist, but her head turned slightly so that his lips met the corner of her mouth. "Do we think we're playing some cute game?" she murmured. "That's going to get us out of trouble that lying couldn't?" Her enunciation was unusually precise.

Sam Yates' mind flashed between two approaches to the problem. He could express anger, which would sound real because his body was momentarily suffused with rage at the possibility its needs would be ignored again. Alternatively, he could be calm and let the woman's body do the convincing.

The uniform cloth had a slick feel that fitted its bright

color, but whatever the lieutenant used to restrain the breast
to which Yates' hand slid must have been of gossamer
insubstantiality.

"If you want," he said aloud, "you can book me for a
triple homicide right now. Just so long as we get five minutes
in here before they lock me up."

God the breast was soft.

"And explain t' my captain why I palmed your ID card
at the scene and didn't list it in the evidence file?" said the
blond woman as she straightened.

Yates thought she might be pulling away. His face
frowned in concern, but his hands did not attempt to restrain
her.

Instead, Yesilkov ran her index finger down the center
of her shirt. The seam, sensitized to the touch that had last
closed it, gaped open. She tugged the shirttail from her
waistband and finished the task while Yates cupped her
breasts.

Not chunky at all. Very white, and the nipples were of
such a pale pink that it was hard to be sure where the areolae
merged with the outer skin. It was not until he tongued one
that Yates realized there was another garment after all, a
bandeau so soft and clear that his eyes and fingers had not
noticed it.

"It rolls up," said Sonya Yesilkov. Her hands led him,
lifted him, out of the chair. "Here," she added. "I'll help
you."

Problem Number One was well on the way to being
solved. That still left the reason for the kidnapping and
firefight, and the virus whose release was planned and observed while it slashed like a scalpel through UN Headquarters.

But those problems could wait.

PART THREE

Chapter 15

THREE ON A MATCH

Yates' office hadn't shrunk, but with both Sonya Yesilkov and Ella Bradley sitting on the fold-down chairs opposite his desk, the hard-won space seemed unbearably confining.

Yates ran his fingers absently through the strands of noise curtain in the doorway as he told the hologram tank, "Play." It didn't.

"Voice commands only work 'bout half the time," he said apologetically into the sub-zero silence as he retreated to his desktop, where he could key into the unit commands it couldn't ignore.

"My equipment is ever so much better . . ." Ella Bradley's statement was as much a critique as an offer to adjourn to her apartment's office.

Yesilkov, beside her, shifted long enough to give her a scathing glance which made Bradley blush.

"I'll take your word for it, thanks, sister. Especially since, t' hear Sam tell it, the last time y' used it t' *research* Beaton, Sam here got parboiled, you got snatched, and the mess left in corridor M-M was *ever* so difficult to explain, don't you know?" The exaggerated send-up of Bradley's diction as Yesilkov tailed off wasn't lost on the slimmer, black-haired woman.

If Bradley hadn't had on her prismatic contacts today, the look she stabbed Yates with might have drawn blood. Still facing Yates, she said, "Patrolman Yesilkov—"

"That's Lieutenant to you," said Yesilkov with a long-suffering sigh.

"Lieutenant," Bradley repeated with barbed pauses between the syllables. "I sent that data request via a UN

149

office, not straight out of my apartment.''

Yates, taking a seat at his desk, wondered what the likelihood was of witnessing a cat fight. He couldn't figure Bradley—Yesikov's combination of possessiveness and combativeness he could understand. Bradley had this way of treating Yesilkov like part of the furniture. Yesilkov had busted her ass making her rank; she wasn't going to take easily to being snubbed by someone who'd have thought she was a menial laborer even if she were three grades higher and the ranking security officer on the Moon.

Maybe Bradley had scoped that there was something going on between Yates and Yesilkov, but Bradley'd had her chance. Yates didn't understand why it would bother her if somebody else was—

"You what?" Yesilkov twisted in her seat, her knees bumping Bradley's as she confronted the darker woman.

"I had a friend of mine in the U.S. Mission bump the priority on my data request," Bradley said.

"Don't do it again," Yesilkov ordered, and turned away from Bradley, shaking her head in Yates' direction. "Not unless you want to say who, and give us some warning—now we've got something else to check on." She crossed her arms over breasts whose softness Yates could almost feel.

"All right, team," said Yates, stabbing with unnecessary concentration at his keypad, trying to set a good example. "Let's start—"

But Bradley was unwilling to let Yesilkov's implication go unanswered: "Lieutenant, are you inferring that someone—anyone—in the U.S. Mission had a hand in my attempted abduction?" Now there was an edge to Bradley's tone that brought Yates' head up from his keypad. Next she was going to threaten to put Yesilkov on report for behavior unbecoming a security officer . . . the emphasis on U.S. had already implied that Yesilkov's Russian nationality might become part of the discussion.

"I ain't 'inferring' nothin'," said Yesilkov in Yates' direction, her back straight, her eyes sparkling. "Am I, Sam?"

Yates treated them both to a pained expression and said, "Let's get this show on the road, ladies, you read me? Ella, if you don't want to tell us what U.S. Mission office you went through, that's fine for now. But if there's anything else as pertinent as your background check on Beaton, y' better level with us. It's your butt they came after, not either of ours."

Bradley digested that with a noncommittal look, and Yesilkov unbent some, satisfied for the moment. When Bradley shook her black-haired head indicating that she had nothing more to say, Yates looked down at his keypad and realized that all his data requests were spooled and ready to run.

He hit the button and got up, because the holotank was going to play its data's front view to the women in the chairs facing it.

The first file that came up was that of Jan-Christian Malan, one of the corpses from the firefight at MM. Bradley drew in a quick breath, and her hand covered her mouth.

Yesilkov shot a look at her and then at Yates, coming around the holotank to lean against one of his file cabinets, and said, "That's a positive ID, I guess." She flicked a thumb at Bradley, still staring wide-eyed over her hand at Malan's file photo.

He tried the voice commands again, and the data from Malan's file scrolled: nickname, Jantze; birthplace, Capetown. "One of your Afrikaners, all right, Ella," Yates said as gently as he could.

"And a Bureau of Utilities employee, to boot—the orange suits weren't missed because, like the truck and the equipment, the guy had a right to be using them." Yesilkov was leaning forward slightly, all business now. "Next file, okay?"

"Right." Yates called it up, still watching Bradley intermittently for signs that seeing these men again was going to be too much for her.

Yates wasn't normally so solicitous about a respondent, not when he was pursuing an investigation. Protecting Bradley from guys with plasma rifles and dope was one thing; protecting her from holographic images was something else again. He'd just begun to worry that maybe he wasn't as impartial about this case as he ought to be, when Yesilkov swore blisteringly in Russian. He glanced at the tank.

Yesilkov was already remarking, "Well, there goes the easy answer—this guy isn't Afrikaner. He's Uruguayan, this Trimen. So much for any simple racial motivation . . . not that that's what I was hopin' for, of course." Again the uneasy glance at Bradley.

Ella Bradley was staring with wide, unreadable eyes at the holotank. *Damn those foolish contact lenses.* Yates said, "He's—he *was* a construction worker, though—same general kind of job. And all sorts of types come out of Uruguay . . . Let's not jump yet, Sonya."

"Who's jumpin'?" Again Yesilkov folded her arms over her breasts, changed her mind, and laced her hands behind her head. "Next," she demanded imperiously.

Yesilkov could see easy as he could that this was tough on Bradley. But then, so had the kidnapping been. He shrugged minutely and called up the next file.

This one was another orange-suited Bureau of Utilities worker named Michel van Rooyan. And he was Afrikaner as well. "Now what's your take, Sonya?" Yates asked quietly, seeing Bradley suddenly bring her knee up, hook her boot on the fold-down chair, and encircle that knee with her arms.

Yesilkov screwed up her wide, Slavic face and fluffed her blond hair with an impatient hand. "Take? From this? We've got three dead guys, two of 'em Afrikaners, one not. Bradley says there were five in all, so two of 'em 're still out there, ain't that likely? Somewhere? Waitin' to try again, maybe?" She grinned wickedly.

Ella Bradley straightened up and folded her hands demurely in her lap, staring at the screen. "Sam," she said in a tiny voice, "none of these are the man with the beard . . . the man from my table at Le Moulin Rouge."

"I know, Ella, I know," he said, and the gentleness there made Yesilkov curl her lip. "I've got a still from the Beaton tape of the Moulin Rouge dinner—didn't think there was any need t' make you watch the whole thing—"

"Let's finish with these guys, okay, Supervisor?" said Yesilkov impatiently.

"Yeah, right away," Yates said, and headed back to his

desk, where he could control the holotank without talking to it.

From there he brought up the employment records of the three men on a split screen.

Yesilkov whistled. "No shit, Sherlock . . . how 'bout that? This Trimen wasn't even here when he died. Cute trick, if you can manage it."

Yesilkov was right: Trimen, the Uruguayan, had a full employment record up until two weeks before the kidnapping, but had logged out for Downside leave. There was, no matter how Yates tried entering his data—under name, job, visual or retinal or handprint ID—no record of his return through customs.

Which made him scour the records of the other two, the Afrikaners.

When they were done going over the data, Yesilkov reprised it: "Okay, let me see if I've got it straight: the two Afrikaners were off-duty, that's nothin' special. The Uruguayan wasn't here a'tall. That's pretty special, but we don't know how these guys could *get* that special—takes some clout to show up on the Moon without never deplaning from nothin'." She cocked her head at Bradley, who'd been ominously silent for far too long. "These guys has got the same kinda connections as our friend Ella, here."

"It's a theory," Yates conceded. It would take better connections than construction workers usually had, to smuggle someone into the colony. But you never could tell—if a construction worker was drinking with a dock loader regular enough, and that guy had a friend in customs, and there was enough money in it, then somebody would know a flight attendant or a baggage handler . . . the possibilities were endless.

"What are you suggesting?" Ella Bradley asked Yesilkov woodenly.

Yates made a mental note never to have these two women in the same place for longer than was absolutely necessary, then said quickly, "Lieutenant Yesilkov's suggesting nothin' about your friends, Ella, except you won't tell us who they are—that doesn't help our confidence. We're try-

ing to keep you out of another one of those trucks, Ella.''
Yates heard the plea in his voice and he didn't like it one
bit. He'd been wearing some other guy's clothes, for Chrissake, some guy who had his own damned tailor. He could
probably have chased the name down just from that—chased
it easier than he could the missing man with the beard who'd
been at Ella's table at Le Moulin Rouge, because the man
with the beard was in this up to his ears and ready for all
comers.

Of which, if Yates understood what was happening here,
Superviser Samuel Yates was going to be one. So he said
to the doctor from NYU, ''Ella, let's all put our cards on
the table. I don't need your friend's name, but it would help
clear away suspicion where there doesn't need to be any if
we knew how you routed that call.''

For Yesilkov's peace of mind, for God's sake.

''Fine.'' Bradley's voice was clipped. ''I made an unoffi-
cial request to the USIA deputy's liasion office at the U.S.
Mission. The deputy—Taylor McLeod—was Downside, but
his assistant, a friend of mine, cut some red tape for me—just
cut through enough red tape that my data request got to the
head of the queue at Sky Devon earlier than it otherwise
might—''

''The goddamn United States Information Agency,''
Yesilkov said with unhidden distaste. ''We're not goin' to
get no help from that buncha spooks.''

''Listen here, Yesilkova, we can do without your provoca-
tive, politicized, and I must say, predictable, comments,''
said Ella Bradley.

Bradley had teeth, that was good to know. And if Yates
wasn't mistaken, he'd been prancing around in Taylor
McLeod's clothes. He ought to see about getting them
cleaned and pressed, in case he had to replace them. Probably
cost a week's salary, maybe more. Wrong woman to hit
on, if those were McLeod's clothes. Wrong, if you cared
how heavy the hitter was when it was your turn on the
pitcher's mound.

Yates wasn't sure that he did care. ''You say McLeod
was Downside? That it was just his assistant who you're
friendly with?'' Assistants didn't have the kind of salary

that allowed for the duds Bradley had handed him.

"I didn't *say* anything that would support the determination you're trying to make, Supervisor Yates." Bradley's dander was up now. Her face was pinched, and he fancied he could see her fury even behind the mirrored contacts. "I have more than one friend in that office." But she wasn't going to tell him which friend's clothes he'd been wearing. "Deputy McLeod's Downside for another ten days or so. It's not unusual, the way things work between his office and mine, for my friends there to do me favors when they can."

"So McLeod probably doesn't know about this?" he prodded, because it was his job now, and he wanted her to tell him that USIA didn't have any stake in whatever was going on.

"Which 'this,' Supervisor? They know about the virus, I'm certain. They don't know about the kidnapping, not from me."

Yesilkov let out a deep sigh, whether of relief or disgust, Yates wasn't certain, because her next words were: "Bullshit, they don't know. With luck, unless the lady goes to them, they'll stay out of it. And I wish she would, else me and my kind *gets* out of it. Before we're 'asked.' "

"Again," Bradley said glacially, "I resent the inference. I didn't want to discuss this with you two at all. I certainly haven't discussed it with the office in question. Nor will I, unless I'm convinced that you, the proper authorities, aren't getting results."

Teeth and claws. Oh well, Yates, teach you to reach above your station. But she wasn't kidding: she hadn't brought USIA into it. Yates had been with Bradley when all her defenses had been down; you learn a lot about a person, fast, during something like the rescue and its aftermath.

"We don't want them in it, neither do you. Let's just make sure it *don't* happen," said Yates, throwing the colloquialism Yesilkov's way companionably.

Damn poor tactics, putting these two bitches together. Especially since the Soviet/American angle had come up, somehow. Shouldn't, not normally. And USIA—he wasn't prepared for that. Somebody like Yates didn't even want that bunch to know he was alive.

But you worked with what you had on hand. Right now that was Bradley and Yesilkov. And lots of unanswered questions that he didn't want ending up on the no doubt immaculate desk of somebody with no Christian name like Taylor McLeod.

"Can we look at this data one more time, and wrap this up? I pulled strings of my own"—Yates let a plaintive tone come and go—"to get priority on Arjanian's shift. This kind of commo use doesn't come cheap, not in Entry section. But now we've got an illict—unauthorized, anyway—entry involved, I can justify it. So we've got somethin' to thank Trimen for. Let's see what we get if we cross-reference to Records . . ."

"Don't bother," said Yesilkov, rising with a hand to the small of her back. "Can't check those Afrikaners, not the way we could have checked Trimen if he wasn't here under some kind of cover. *You* should know, Supervisor." Yesilkov's eyes narrowed suspiciously.

"Yeah, I know—Afrikaners up here get their green cards—resident alien cards and work cards—granted by Latin American countries. Usually because some multinational or other wants it done—special skills, cheap. But I'm going to run an auto check anyhow." He punched it in to punctuate his words.

"Let's see the Moulin Rouge still," Yesilkov prompted, on her feet. She would have paced back and forth if there'd been room in Yates' office.

"Comin' up," he promised, and when the likeness emerged in the holotank, a little squeak of distress came out of Ella Bradley's pale mouth.

Damn, he'd been worried that the sight of the bearded man would give her a double whammy: memories of the dinner that turned into a disaster, and of the kidnapping attempt.

He was moving toward her, just in case she fainted or something, when Yesilkov grabbed his elbow. "If she wants water, she'll ask for it."

Standard interrogation technique. Yesilkov was right—

you used this kind of advantage. Never could tell what you might get out of a flustered, distressed respondent. But Yates just wasn't thinking about Bradley that way.

Yesilkov said, "That the man, honey?"

And Bradley was so upset she just muttered, "Yes, yes that's him."

"Well, here's the bad news," said Yates, between the two women, waiting for Yesilkov to take her hand off his elbow, which she did then. "You see that blinking cursor under the likeness? Means that we can't ID this sucker. He's not data-matched anywhere in our banks."

"How can that be?" Bradley said in a voice like a frightened child's.

"What about credit card receipts?" Yesilkov demanded.

Yates shrugged and said, "Worth a try. We'll see if he paid his restaurant bill. If he did, maybe we've got him. We'll check entry records against restaurant records. . . . Goin' to take a while, Sonya. You want to stay here while I escort Ella home?"

"I'll get her some bodyguards," Yesilkov said, approaching Yates' desk like she owned it, "long as you don't mind me usin' your phone. I need you here, Yates."

"I don't want anybody—" Bradley began.

"Yeah, Sonya, that's fine," he said. And to Bradley: "You take what help you can get, and be thankful we're tryin' to keep you alive."

Chapter 16

ENTRY'S PROBLEM

Yates was still in his office—alone, mercifully—when Arjanian came storming in, looking like hell on wheels.

Arjanian, Entry Division's second shift supervisor, had a bullet-shaped head, a bulldog's nose, and lips Yates couldn't help thinking about as "slobbery." He was overweight for this duty and even in Moon gravity, he was so mad he was puffing as he put pudgy hands on his spare tire and glared. "What d'you think you're doing, Yates? Tying up the whole of commo division with your cockamamie restaurant-receipt checks? And on my goddamn shift. What gives you the right to pull priority access because you didn't like your lunch yesterday, fuckhead?"

"Hiya, Arjanian," Yates said laconically, leaning back in his swivel chair. Very slowly Yates put one foot up on his desk, locked his knee, and crossed his other leg over it. "Somethin' I can do for you?"

Yates didn't like Arjanian any better now than ever. If he'd tied up Entry's computer capacity while sifting restaurant records for the bearded guy's name, then well and good.

"Yessss," said Arjanian with an exaggerated sibilance that sprayed from those wet lips of his. "Give me a straight answer."

"What was the question again?"

"Yates, you better straighten up." Arjanian took his fists off his hips and made one threatening step forward before Yates' legs came down and his own hand went to his belt line. Arjanian had no way of knowing whether a cross-draw holster might be there, under Yates' jacket.

The fat guy checked himself in midstride and said, "I

158

want to know why you're tying up the commo computers on *my* shift. Without so much as a by-your-leave."

"Right," said Yates equably. "I'm lookin' for an ID on a guy who ate at Le Moulin Rouge the night I did . . . the night people started droppin' like flies in there. I got a picture of the guy; he had to pay his bill. I'm also"—he held up his hand to forestall Arjanian's next explosion— "lookin' for every other meal this guy ate, and where, and with who."

"Whom."

"What?"

"I said, 'with whom.' Shit, never mind, you ignorant bastard. Just tell me what you're doing on this investigation in the first place—it's not Entry's business to—"

"It's Entry's business, all right—one of the guys, name of Trimen, who got dead in M-M had no Entry records. Get me? Shouldn't have *been* here; wasn't here, according to all I can find. But he's dead as dead can be, so here I am, in this up to my singed ears."

"I still don't see how it's Entry's problem, Yates. And I'm going to make it my business to—"

"Butt out, is what. It's Entry's problem because the division head says so, and it's *my* problem because of this." Yates pointed to his injured left leg as he propped it again on his desk's edge. "Don't get in the way of this investigation, Arjanian." The warning in his tone wasn't one Arjanian could mistake. Yates hadn't meant it to be so clear, or so promissory.

Arjanian actually retreated a step. "You're way too jacked up over this investigation, buddy," said the fat man, who had beads of sweat on his upper lip now.

"Don't tell me what I am and what I'm not—or what I'm doing or should be doing about this investigation. The guys with the plasma guns aren't the only ones who're real serious about it."

"Yates," said Arjanian with a long slow shake of his head, "I'm going to—"

Yates' phone beeped. "You're going to go on your way, mind your own business, and stay out of my data probes." He grabbed the phone's headset and barked, "What is it?"

It was Yoshimura, who had a third file ready for him. "Send it through," Yates told the man on the other end of the phone. "Supervisor Arjanian is just leaving."

Arjanian didn't move, and Yates half rose from his chair. Arjanian moved, muttering curses as he pushed through the sound curtain.

In the holotank a face was starting to form. Behind Yates' back hard copy was beginning to feed from his printer.

Yates ignored the printout. In the holotank was the face of the bearded man from Le Moulin Rouge. Then he reached behind him, and without looking, grabbed the first sheet of flimsy.

It identified the face as belonging to one Piet van Zell, who, like the dead Uruguayan Trimen and somebody else named Steeks, had been buying his food in the Strip outside the Transient Barracks.

Steeks had come up earlier in the evening, in the first round of computer hunt-and-peck that Yesilkov and he had done together. She already had the company police alerted, ready, and waiting to track this guy named Steeks if he used his card again anywhere on the Strip.

Yates figured it was time to call Yesilkov—congratulate themselves about Steeks anyway. And tell her to add this van Zell guy to the Watch List. He was just reaching for the phone when it rang.

"Yates?" said the voice on the other end of the line. "Yesilkov. We've spotted Steeks. He got take-out food for a coupla guys and he's carried it to a suit room down that way—number 312. But 312's marked Out of Order and locked up tight."

"Don't assume nothin'," Yates said, his slow voice belying his movements as he got a gun and ammo out of his center drawer. "Find out about using the Mechanical control room to override the locks and air system. I'm on my way."

Chapter 17

GONE TO GROUND

"*Look,*" protested Piet van Zell as his hands accepted his platter of chicken-rice casserole, only vaguely warm. "He *has* to tell us more than 'Stay where you are, the Plan needs you.' And then not talk to us at all today."

"I know that," said Steeks, looking at his partner, then down at the meal he had purchased for them on the Strip below, and finally around the fittings of suit room 312. There was no comfort in any of the things the Afrikaner saw.

And there had been none offered by a voice on the other end of the off-Moon line when Steeks called today. The phone had rung unanswered.

"If they will not withdraw us from here," said van Zell, "we must withdraw ourselves. Here we are useless, so we must go someplace we can be of service. To the Plan. To something."

He scowled at his partner. Van Zell was afraid, but even more than that he was angry because the situation had become unimaginably complex. If someone were telling him what to do, things would be simple. If not—Piet van Zell would simplify them himself.

One way or another.

"I don't see . . ." said Steeks, pausing because there were too many ways to complete the sentence, too many things that he neither saw nor understood.

In the silence between words and thought, the air-vent shutters slapped closed like multiple gunshots.

That was the sort of disaster to which the Afrikaners' background fitted them to react.

They moved in opposite directions. Steeks half climbed,

half vaulted, into one of the pressure suits open on the rack, while van Zell jumped toward the inner, colony-side, air lock door.

When the speaker plate of the emergency phone on the wall crackled into life, van Zell twisted in mid motion and snatched up his plasma discharger before his left hand hit the latch.

"Both doors of this air lock are being controlled by the emergency overrides in Central Mechanical," rasped the speaker, harsh with adrenalin and distorted reproduction but still female in its underlying timbre. "I am Lieutenant Yesilkov of Security. You must prepare youself to surrender according to my directions."

The latch should have resisted van Zell's hand, given sluggishly under his pressure. Instead it clacked instantly against its stops, jarring the Afrikaner's arm to the shoulder. Somebody had, just as the crackly voice was saying, disconnected the door from its normal controls within the suit room.

"In a moment," the speaker was saying, "I will open the inner door wide enough for you to drop your weapons through it. If—"

Van Zell screamed a curse and spat at the phone. Then he spun and kicked at the latch plate. The shock threw him back across the cluttered room. The door remained as solid as the rock floor of the suit room.

Steeks had closed his suit. He was reaching for the latch of the outer door lock.

"A squad of armed patrolmen are waiting to take you into custody," lied Sonya Yesilkov through the speaker of the emergency phone. "If you attempt to—"

"*Wait!*" van Zell screamed to his partner. He hadn't—consciously—meant to point his plasma discharger at Steeks, but a use for the weapon might have occurred to him in the next instant if the man in the hard suit had not grabbed for the motion and torn the gun away.

The muscles of both Afrikaners were atrophied to great weakness by Earth standards, but the suit Steeks had donned more than made up for his own lack of strength. His gloved left hand rose with the weapon.

But his right, continuing the motion that had panicked his partner, bounced off the latch to the outer air lock as vainly as Piet van Zell had done from the inner door.

"Your only choice," crackled the speaker, "is whether you come now, uninjured, or you come after we've fired a couple of plasma bolts into the room. Even with suits on—"

Van Zell clung to his erstwhile partner's arm with both hands and all his strength. It was not enough to prevent Steeks from inexorably aiming the plasma discharger at the outer air lock.

"It won't work!" screamed the suitless Afrikaner. "You can't open it by—"

But when he saw the armored finger start to squeeze the trigger, van Zell ducked out of the way. Steeks didn't know if he could burn his way out of the air lock either, but he wouldn't be kept from the attempt by the fact success would leave his partner trying to breathe vacuum.

Van Zell's world exploded.

The jet of plasma blew a cavity from the door the way a meteor dimples the surface of a planet, converting solid matter into a ball of vapor and molten droplets. The first bolt did not punch a hole all the way through to vacuum.

The shock of the confined plasma discharge was a thunderclap that thrust Steeks back a step and deafened him. The front of his suit was a dazzling mirror where the titanium burned from the door had recondensed. The thin but perfectly opaque layer of metal deposited over his face shield would have blinded him, except that the muzzle of the weapon itself had blocked a portion of the expanding cloud. A clear swatch like a petrified shadow fanned across Steeks' helmet, leaving a triangle of face shield still transparent.

The Afrikaner aimed, covered his eyes with his free hand to keep from blinding himself completely, and fired again.

The gun blew up, vaporizing itself and most of the pressure-suited man who held it.

Steeks' first point-blank shot had laid a mirroring coat of titanium over the nose of the next round loaded into his weapon's chamber. When the second, precisely-balanced nuclear explosion took place, the layer of redeposited titanium reflected it for the microsecond that was enough to turn the gun into a fusion bomb in the hands of the man who pulled its trigger.

Piet van Zell had been partly shielded by Steeks' armored body. The heat within the suit room was so intense that when Yesilkov opened the inner door from the Mechanical section's control room, air blasted out at several times normal atmospheric pressure. The tall Afrikaner was alive, but he could not see Yates and Ella Bradley as they dived through the door.

"I said stay *back*!" Yates shouted to the woman who had heard and ignored his orders. The air in suit room 312 was furnace hot, with a greasy, metallic aftertaste.

But there was no other danger within, no need for the needle stunner in Yates' hand. The surviving Afrikaner moaned as he writhed on the floor.

And both of his eyeballs had been melted from their sockets.

Chapter 18

INTERROGATION

Ella Bradley watched with growing horror as Sonya Yesilkov interrogated the blinded, burned Afrikaner still writhing weakly on the floor of the suit room nearly fifteen minutes after Yates and she had burst in here.

"Yates," Ella whispered urgently, hugging herself. "I must insist that you call a doctor for this man." For what was left of him. Ella Bradley kept seeing torched slums north of Capetown and blackened swathes in the Congo where all that remained were awful, akimbo limbs like uprooted trees. The wages of prejudice, the aftermath of societal collisions . . .

Maybe Yates was thinking something similar — or remembering something he'd seen in Nicaragua. His face was sheened with sweat and his eyes kept roaming everywhere but to the tableau of the Russian woman kneeling beside the stricken man, holding a hand-recorder close to his blistered lips.

Yates said, "Yeah, we'll call somebody, soon as we can." But he didn't move toward the phone in the suit room, a phone that probably still worked, shielded from the blast in its nook the way it was.

The man whose beard was singed away was sobbing for a doctor and Yesilkov kept promising him one "as soon as you tell me what I got to know."

Ella wanted to bolt for the phone herself, but she had a feeling that Yates would physically intervene. This man was dying, didn't either of them realize that?

And then she understood why Yates hadn't moved toward that phone, why Yesilkov was methodically and ever so slowly questioning the dying man from Le Moulin Rouge,

and even why no other security personnel were here with
them: Yates and Yesilkov wanted this horrid, blinded thing
that had been a man to die before anyone else could talk to
him.

It was murder. Her blood seemed to congeal in her veins.
On numb, still legs she walked over to the man on the floor,
who twitched and rasped occasional answers to Yesilkov's
questions—walked as if she were a robot, devoid of volition.
And knelt down there, beside the man whose skin now bore
the pattern of the clothing he'd been wearing, as if the
explosion had stamped the weave into his flesh.

Yesilkov and Yates didn't want a living witness to what
had happened on corridor MM. They didn't want anyone
but themselves questioning this man about plasma rifles and
casualties—or about Ella Bradley's abduction. They'd never
reported it; they'd eyed each other in distress when Ella had
mentioned McLeod's office.

They would let this man die rather than admit they'd
withheld what they knew about the slaughter in the corridor—about what Yates had done. So where did that leave
her? Ella Bradley was a principal in the MM kidnapping.
Was she going to end up like this poor fool gasping for
breath on the floor, while Yates watched everying else but
her dying breath, and Yesilkov interrogated her about who
she'd told?

She hadn't told anybody, she wanted to scream. She
hadn't done anything, she wanted to shout. She'd just leave
now, she wanted to whisper. And get out of here before
these two security people secured their own careers by making sure that Ella Bradley couldn't threaten that security.

Just as she was beginning to shiver, to double up, her
arms against her belly in prelude to vomiting, Yates' hand
came down on her shoulder. "Come on, you don't need to
get so close to this."

She shrugged off his hand and said, "Don't I? I'm lucky
that's not me there. I—"

"Shut up, both of you, damn it," Yesilkov whispered
fiercely, her palm shielding the tape recorder's integral microphone from their chatter.

And then Ella listened, for the first time, to what the man
was telling Yesilkov:

"The Plan," he was saying raggedly, coughing little suppressed coughs as he tried to breathe. The effort of concentrating on those words made Bradley's eyes fasten on the Afrikaner's blistered lips and the pink foam at their corners.

"Yeah, y' told me 'bout the Plan, van Zell. Y' told me all about the Plan to wipe out every black on Earth. Now what about the perps? The perpetrators? Who, where, and how, van Zell? C'mon, man. Don't die with this on your conscience. Who is it you report to? Who do you call?"

"Call . . ." Piet van Zell tried to close his lids, what was left of them, over his ravaged eye sockets.

Ella Bradley's hand pressed against her mouth as if she must physically contain her stomach's contents by that means. Yates, now, knelt down beside her on the blackened stone of the suit room floor. He took her other hand, cold and clammy, in his hard, warm, dry one. She hadn't the strength to pull it away.

Piet van Zell was murmuring numbers, and when he'd finished a twenty-one digit string of them, he gasped. "Tha's the code; that's the call. From an off-Moon booth. Call." He coughed. "Test's successful. Arabs, but what the hell? Works, works good."

"Where's the call to, van Zell? Who's doing the testing? Where's the stuff made?"

"Beaton," said van Zell. And laughed. "Ask Beaton, or the Sky Devon . . . lab." And laughed again, a horrible wracking laugh Ella Bradley would never forget, because in the midst of it van Zell fell silent.

"Aw, c'mon, you racist bastard, don't die on me," Yesilkov said softly. She shook the man, then slapped him, then pounded his chest in some flurry of activity.

A flurry that Yates joined.

Bradley realized they were trying to restart van Zell's heart, the way they were pounding his chest. Yates straddled the corpse for a better angle, and Yesilkov pinched his nose, opened the blistered mouth with two fingers, and pressed her own lips to the dead man's.

Ella Bradley turned her head away and gave up the contents of her stomach. When she was done retching, she stumbled to her feet, wiping the back of her mouth with her hand.

Funny, the smell of roast flesh and feces were so strong in the close air of the suit room, she couldn't smell her own vomit—not even taste it.

She leaned against the wall and shook, waiting until the two security people gave up on van Zell.

Yesilkov prodded the body one final time with her booted toe, and the two approached Ella, leaning again the wall by the phone.

Yates was saying, ". . . got to go to Sky Devon, five will get you ten."

Yesilkov responded, "Not till I check this phone number," she shouldered past Bradley to pick up the suit room phone.

"Works," Yesilkov said with a triumphant grin.

"Who's she calling?" Ella asked Yates, trying to see in his narrow eyes whether her own death was next on his agenda.

"Her office: call in the phone number, get a check on where it rings. Won't take long. Then I'll take you home."

"What about. . . ?" she gestured weakly in the direction of the horridly burned corpse. They could have saved this man, with immediate medical attention, she knew. She also knew that they knew it, and that they knew she knew they did.

She wanted to go home, all right. Home to Earth. Failing that, she wanted to go to her apartment, alone, and call Taylor McLeod's office. She needed to tell somebody what was going on up here, somebody who'd follow up if anything terminal happened to her. "Fine, you can take me home, but all I want then is a good night's sleep. Alone." *Clear enough, Yates? I don't trust you worth a damn. Worse, you and your ghoulish lady friend make me sick. There's a puddle on the floor here to prove it.*

Yates had paused, his eyes drawn in the direction Ella had pointed—drawn to the corpse. "What about him, you mean?" he answered her unfinished question. "We're keeping this pretty tight, just between the three of us for now. Yesilkov'll have somebody she can trust pick up the body; we'll log it as a casualty in the pursuit of presumed felons armed with plasma weapons. This guy and his very dead buddy over in the corner there are responsible for the firefight on M-M, sure enough. Got the exploded plasma rifle to prove that. It'll close the case, unless you say something you shouldn't.''

''I won't, really; I won't.'' It came out of her too quickly.

His eyes measured her with all the cold of interstellar space behind them. ''You bet you won't—it was you, maybe still is you, they were after. We don't know who we can trust, so we don't trust anybody. Clear? Not your friend with the fancy clothes, not anybody. You don't say squat about this until Yesilkov and I give you the word. Un—''

''Until we get back from Sky Devon,'' said Yesilkov, palming the phone as she hung it up. ''That's where this phone number rings, Sam—it's the paging system designator assigned through the Sky Devon Division of Pest Control Research. Head there's named Dr. Kathleen Spenser, the next person we've got to see. And see fast.''

''Is that what they're calling 'em now—'pests,' I wonder?'' said Yates in a voice that told Ella he wasn't wondering at all.

Yesilkov grimaced. ''I dunno how much you heard—van Zell was talking about the Plan . . . some bug that'll wipe out any genetic strain selectively. And guess who these Afrikaner buggers are selecting? Ain't white folks, you can bet.'' Yesilkov, for the first time in Ella's memory, seemed actually upset.

''But you can't go to Sky—''

''Whadya mean, Dr. Bradley?'' Yesilkov snapped at her fiercely. ''Why 'can't'? You got somethin' in mind to stop us—like talkin' to your fancy friends? Well, don't—''

''She didn't mean that, Sonya,'' Yates interrupted.

''God,'' Ella Bradley said, scrubbing her eyes with her hands. ''Can't we get out of here? I'm going to—''

''Faint? Puke again? What?'' Yesilkov bore down on her inexorably. ''Look, Ms. Sensibility: your life's in the hands of whoever I assign to protect you while we're gone, 'cause you sure can't protect yourself. Not from this shit—'' She waved behind her, where van Zell's corpse was. Over in the corner were other remains, hardly recognizable as having once been part of another man. ''Y' understand me?''

''I understand,'' quavered Ella, who needed to hold onto something for a moment. The only thing near was Yates' arm, so she grabbed his elbow with both hands.

The big man put an arm around her protectively and said, "Shelve that, we don't need to make this any harder on her, Sonya. I'll take her home and we'll meet"—He consulted his watch—"at your office in, say, three hours. You check the transit schedule to Devon and get us seats."

"Yeah, and I'll find some guy to put on Bradley for security who'll stick, this time."

"Great, I'll stay with her until that somebody shows up," said Yates.

Ella Bradley didn't like the way the two of them talked about her as if she weren't present; she didn't like it at all. But if Sam Yates was taking her home—and if he didn't kill her to keep her quiet—then maybe she could make the big man realize that she wasn't part of the enemy. Not like the corpse on the floor, who stared sightlessly through empty sockets at eternity.

"So, Supervisor Yates, am I under house arrest?" said Ella as Yates, with a flicked salute to the stolid patrolman who waited unspeaking by her apartment's door, took her key card from unresisting fingers and inserted it in the lock.

Yates didn't answer until they were both inside, the door between them and the patrolman in the corridor firmly closed.

Then he said, "I wish you'd stop thinking of me as the enemy. My name's Sam, and all I want is to keep you from ending up wherever van Zell and his playmates were trying to take you."

"I wish I could believe that," she said uncertainly. She'd thought almost the same thing about him, and Yesilkov, that *she* wasn't the enemy. "But you're making it difficult, Sup—"

"Sam."

"Sam."

"Good," he smiled. "That's a start. Now, how am I making it difficult? I don't want to . . ." He was moving by her, and she found herself scurrying from his path as if this were his apartment, not hers.

She thought he was going to sit on the couch, but he didn't. He paused between her and it and finished his sentence, ". . . especially not after what you've been through. The patrolman out there is here for your protection—you don't want him, he's a memory. Just tell me flat out."

He was close enough that she could see the amusement lingering at the corners of his mouth as she shook her head; close enough that, if she fainted, he'd probably be able to catch her before she fell.

She'd never fainted in her life, but she wasn't sure this wouldn't be the first time. Suddenly, in the aftermath of the horror in the suit room, she was debilitated, enervated, devastated, and lost. She wanted to bury her head against the big man's chest and hold on tight; she wanted him to be what he said—her friend, her protector—not what she feared. . . .

She said, "For all I know, you and your girlfriend Yesilkov will kill me like you killed that poor man in the suit room—so nobody will find out about . . . about . . . M-M and the shooting and—"

"Whoa, whoa," he said, and she didn't understand how he'd closed the distance between them so quickly without her seeing him, except that she'd begun to cry.

Then she was leaning against his chest and he was telling her, "Ssh, don't be afraid. You've been doin' fine so far. We all have. We'll beat this thing, I promise."

But she was more conscious of his hands on her back and his lips in her hair. And of her own urge to melt against him, to make sure he *was* on her side, to make it worth it to him to be.

Otherwise she was lost. She had no illusions that Taylor McLeod's office could protect her from some horrendous plot called the Plan and the maniacs who were carrying it out. People willing to slaughter wholesale, to eradicate entire bloodlines, to loose bioengineered viruses upon an unsuspecting world, weren't going to show mercy to an NYU anthropolgist named Bradley because she was nice, or well bred, or promised she wouldn't say a word about what she knew.

Such people would kill her out of hand without even a pause for reflection. In Yates' arms, weeping softly while her body trembled uncontrollably and his palms ran up and down her spine, she reasoned that if Yates and Yesilkov were going to kill her, they'd have done it in the suit room. Because, if she didn't believe that, she couldn't justify the way she was feeling.

She raised her head to Yates and said through her tears, "What about Yesilkov?"

"Ssh," he replied. "Don't worry, I told you. Just let me handle this—it's what I know how to do."

His hands were on her shoulders now. One slid up her neck to cup the back of her head and guide her lips to his. The other slid down to her breast. When it made contact, all the tension she'd been feeling—the doubts, fears, uncertainty, and even the clear knowledge that Yates and Yesilkov were an item—transmuted into something else.

That something was as alien to Ella Bradley as the firefight on MM corridor or the interrogation she'd witnessed in the suit room. It was passion, and she'd never succumbed to it before.

The world went fuzzy around the edges, and its center was a diamond-sharp core: her body, its lips, its breasts, its crotch; and his, every rough-hewn inch of him.

All the differences between them—of class, of education, of avocation, vocation, style, and content, didn't add up to one single cogent objection strong enough to dam the feelings she felt.

Not only did she meet the thrust of his hips with her own, but she fumbled with his clothing as desperately and boldly as he did hers.

By the time he pulled her by the buttocks up and onto him, still standing in a pile of their discarded clothes, she wasn't thinking about any of the myriad reasons that she shouldn't let Sam Yates make love to her.

Even if she had been, it wouldn't have mattered. Ella Bradley had just ventured into uncharted territory and it was too late to turn back.

Chapter 19

TURN-AROUND

Jan de Kuyper, the tall, thin right-hand man of Karel Pretorius—and right now the most important single cog in the Club's wheel—stepped off the inbound shuttle from Sky Devon and immediately inhaled brandied tobacco through his cigar-shaped dispenser.

Around him was the automated docking area that served as both embarkation and debarkation lounge for lunar flights to Devon, at which de Kuyper was Air System Maintenance supervisor. And so much, so very much more.

He'd hated to leave Spenser, who was getting skittish. But de Kuyper had his official responsibilities to tend to, still. His "routine" meeting here at the lunar colony with Lunar Air Systems officials was something that would only become a problem if he broke that routine and thus drew attention to himself.

For the Plan to work, everything must be normal. It was normal for the lunar brass to want de Kuyper's expertise on call regularly; more than ever now, when they worried that some of the evanescent virus might be breeding in the lunar colony's ventilation system—a supercharged Legionaires' Disease with an eye for color.

So he was here on schedule, and damn the Club if it took offense: some Club members, he'd heard from Pretorius (or at least gathered from a drunken innuendo Pretorius had made one night, a single slip), might not be as white as the driven snow themselves. Another reason to balance off against any later criticism that he should have stayed by Spenser, now when they were so close and Spenser was becoming so predictably difficult.

The thing was, de Kuyper knew, to make Spenser dispensible. He grinned around his inhaler, pleased at his play on words, and followed the straggling line toward the baggage wheel where he'd pick up his luggage.

And stopped in his tracks. There, before his eyes, was Ella Bradley. Ella Bradley, whose fate should have been sealed. Steeks, Trimen, and some few others, under the leadership of Piet van Zell, had been ordered to deal with this woman: to take her into custody, to question her, then to dispatch her.

When de Kuyper had given that order, he'd assumed it would be carried out. It was not so difficult for so many men to deal with a single woman. He'd not heard from van Zell before he'd had to leave Sky Devon, but that meant nothing. . . .

Nothing, until now. His brain nearly frozen with panic, de Kuyper watched the woman closely, only cognizant enough not to stare, paused in his tracks like videotape on freeze-frame.

This was the same woman whose hologram he'd gotten through back channels . . . through Arjanian. The likeness Arjanian had provided—for a fee; Arjanian was no part of the Plan—must be put in the hands of someone capable of doing what must be done, and done quickly, if her presence here meant that van Zell's boys had failed.

For de Kuyper's money failure was what the sight of this woman, now embracing a large man in Security garb, must mean.

On the excuse of looking for something he might have dropped on the floor, de Kuyper meandered closer to the NYU anthropologist and the big man. Now he noticed another female, a blond woman, also in Security uniform.

From this distance he could make out that the man was from Entry Division, but not the blond's provenance—she was turned away. And the black-haired woman, Bradley, was again embracing the big man.

There was nervousness about this embrace, as if its propriety were in question. And Bradley said, if de Kuyper's ears did not deceive him, "Oh, Sam, it's so risky. . . . What if you don't make it back?"

The man murmured something in a deep, low voice, and Bradley wiped her hands across her eyes and stepped back with a plucky grin. Then she offered her hand to the blond woman, who shook it, and said, "Good luck, Lieutenant Yesilkov. And a safe return."

The blond addressed as Yesilkov retorted, "Maybe what I was cut out for all along was farming. Maybe I'll just stay there."

All three laughed the nervous, self-conscious laughs of people taking their leave of one another under stress. Then the big man and the blond woman headed into the boarding tube.

Bradley stood watching, her hand raised.

De Kuyper had only a moment to make his decision: he could walk up to Ella Bradley, force her to go with him, and begin improvising a job that van Zell should have done by now. Or he could follow the two security types who were on their way to Sky Devon.

Even if it hadn't been a nonstop flight at the other end of the Devon boarding tube into which the security people had disappeared, de Kuyper would have known where they were bound from what the female lieutenant, Yesilkov, had said about farming.

Farming meant Sky Devon, all right.

Jan de Kuyper reached into his vest pocket, got out his return ticket, and strode to the automated teller, where he fed it into a slot. While the machine whirred and clicked, he prayed to some unnamed, silicon god that the flight wouldn't be full—his was an open return, and if luck was against him, he'd be shunted to the next shuttle.

But luck was with Jan de Kuyper, as it had been all his life. The machine assigned him a seat in coach and as he hurried toward the boarding tube, hearing the loudspeaker call the flight number, he saw Ella Bradley drifting away, a sad and worried look on her face.

And he saw a black security officer step out of the men's room alcove and fall in beside her.

Chapter 20

STRINGS

When she got back to her apartment, Ella offered the security patrolman some coffee. She wanted company. She didn't want to be alone, to face the confusion left in Sam Yates' wake. And she wanted to be close to him. Somehow, the patrolman represented that—being close to Sam.

But the patrolman couldn't have coffee, he explained—unless Ella wanted to bring it to him at his post outside her door.

So she made the coffee, taking the time to steam the milk (steamed, it didn't taste dehydrated), and brought it to the man, who told her, with a bright smile on his pitch-black face, to "Go back inside, ma'am—you're safer in there."

The patrolman wasn't anything like Sam, and he was probably right. Inside, there was just herself to talk to, and that awkward interval in the transit lounge to remember. Damn Yesilkov—Ella was trying to be nice about everything.

But it was as easy for Yesilkov to see that Sam had been with Ella as it had been for Ella to intuit what had been going on between Yesilkov and Sam. It always showed; another woman could always see that sort of thing, unless she didn't want to see it.

And Ella didn't want to see it between Sam and Yesilkov, especially not now. But she wasn't easy with what she'd done either—not with the part of herself she'd discovered, or with the man who'd helped her discover it.

What would Taylor think, if ever he took her in his arms and she started ripping at his buttons and fumbling with his belt? What had come over her? She still wasn't sure. It was probably a result of all the death around her lately, and little if anything to do with Sam Yates, who certainly wasn't the sort of man she could introduce to her friends.

Especially not to Taylor. Taylor McLeod was never going to understand, should he find out what had happened, what Ella Bradley saw in Sam Yates. Worse, he'd probably be offended. It was somehow degrading, in retrospect; Taylor would certainly think so. "Couldn't you do better than that?" he'd ask with his eyes, but never, oh never, with his mouth.

A woman who traveled in Ella's circles could never have an open affair with a man like Yates. Couldn't bring him to a party or introduce him to the right people—he had no business knowing the right people; he'd have no idea what to say or what to do. He'd be bored and they'd be scandalized and it was just no good, no good at all.

But she kept thinking of what it would be like to bring Sam to a University cocktail party or a USIA mixer . . .

It would be hell, that's what it would be.

Everyone would be polite, because she'd brought him and she had the right, of course, to bring whomever she chose to any "plus one" event. But the *embarrassment* of it all. Could Yates even handle a knife and fork when there were a number of both beside his plate? Did he know enough to turn his knife blade in on the right side of his plate when he wasn't using it, or place his fork below, parallel? Did he even know enough to start with the outermost utensils and work in?

More important, would he care to learn?

It was, she told herself as she flopped on the couch, ridiculous to be thinking this way. Taylor McLeod would feel exactly as she herself had when she'd realized that Yates was involved with Yesilkov—people of low degree and questionable repute tainted the party with whom they kept company. And as far as other lovers were concerned, the least one could expect from a lover was other lovers of similar quality . . . so one wasn't embarrassed.

Face it, Bradley, you were slumming. One night, to find out what a man of that sort is like. Now you've found out. You don't have to pretend it was—or could be—more than that. It wasn't. It can't. Even you, my dear, are allowed a one-night stand. As long as no one finds out, of course.

One night stand. It was so . . . cheap. Surely there must be more to what had happened between her and Yates than that. Or must there? She should count herself lucky, and get on with the business of surviving.

It was clear to both of them now that she didn't need Supervisor Samuel Yates, in the flesh, to do that. He'd left her in competent hands; the same hands he'd have left her in, no doubt, if she hadn't fallen into his arms. And he *would* have left her.

That he did leave, while she was so vulnerable, was an act she couldn't fathom. It was, in her terms, an act of betrayal, or at least a devaluation of what they'd shared. In the sorts of novels she read, and the sorts of affairs she'd had, men didn't desert their women in dangerous situations. It wasn't chivalrous.

Sam Yates probably couldn't even spell chivalrous.

"So, you've been had. 'Laid,' I believe, is the term your ignoble savage might use. Leave it at that."

Talking to oneself wasn't the best of signs. She ought to talk to somebody, though. She sat, chin on fist, legs crossed at the ankles, on her couch and stared at her front door while her living room, so full of Sam Yates, whispered to her of memories that really should have been someone else's. *Don't you dare fall in love with that . . . that. . . cop.*

The warning echoed in her inner ear until, to silence it, she reached for her phone. Damn the expense, she was going to call Taylor in Washington. Wake him up, no doubt. But Taylor wouldn't mind.

He'd listen while she talked around the subject, because she'd promised Yates not to divulge specifics, and she never broke her word. He'd understand that something was wrong, and they'd discuss what they could discuss—the virus, perhaps; their friends, for certain.

And she'd ask if he could do something about the report she'd requested on Rodney Beaton—the report that NYU should have had in hand by now . . . NYU in the person of herself.

That was what she'd do. Galvanized because she'd found

an excuse to make the call, she began punching phone codes. She'd be careful not to impugn the effectiveness of McLeod's staff, or to seem too urgent. After all, she'd originally asked only that his office boot her request to the head of the data queue. The slug on the request—NYU PRIORITY—ought to have done the rest.

But it hadn't, and Ella Bradley, as she gave her credit number and waited for Taylor McLeod, in his bed at this hour, Washington time, to pick up, was glad of that.

"Hello, Taylor? Ella, yes. Yes, yes, I'm still on the Moon. . . ."

Chapter 21

A VIEW OF SKY DEVON

The two Security personnel from UN Headquarters were already drifting in the zero gravity of Sky Devon's docking hub when de Kuyper disembarked from his berth, farther to the rear of the shuttle. The Afrikaner ignored his targets with a studiousness that might itself have been suspicious — if suspicion had already been aroused.

De Kuyper'd been careful to keep that from happening.

The docking hub was busy, as usual. Sky Devon was at least ten years short of being self-supporting, and it would be twice as long before the habitat began to turn a profit on the enormous capital investment it represented. Nonetheless, the volume of cargo routed through Sky Devon's docks was equal to that of any port off-Earth — with the possible exception of UN Headquarters.

The influx needed to feed and clothe UN personnel and their hangers-on probably made up for the fact that the colony produced nothing tangible — and virtually nothing of intangible value either.

At the moment a huge cargo flat was being loaded with one-meter cubes of frozen meat. Its spidery girderwork was visible through the transparent dome covering the docking hub which, unlike the remainder of Sky Devon, did not rotate. Eyes as trained as those of Jan de Kuyper could resolve a sparkle of light among the stars beyond into another cargo flat, hanging in space until its turn to be loaded.

Two men in tailored clothing wrangled loudly beside the window and access door to the bucket loader which lifted cargo to a vehicle ready to carry it millions of miles to a destination. A third man in coveralls waited impassively by the controls of the bucket loader. The endless belt was motionless within its enclosing tube, sealed off from the hub proper because its further end projected into vacuum. The supervisors were blaming each other for the fact that part of the cargo in the tube was intended for the flat that still waited to dock.

De Kuyper smiled as he passed the men in an expertly controlled drift. It was sometimes good to be reminded that things went badly wrong for other people also.

And to remind himself that there was nothing that could not be fixed.

The Afrikaner had gone to great lengths in order to prevent his eyes from resting on his targets, the man and woman from UN Headquarters, during the two legs of the shuttle flight and the brief stopover at a trans-shipment satellite between. He did not need to watch them to know where they were going or when they would arrive, and he knew from experience that staring at your quarry was almost certain to alert it—to the attention, if not to you personally.

De Kuyper knew there was a slight chance that he might have overheard the couple discussing something important if he had made an effort to get a berth near them instead of as far away as the shuttle's strait accommodations permitted. Again, the risk outweighed the possible benefits.

The leisurely interrogation that the Afrikaner planned would elicit all the information the couple had to give.

The boarding notice at the transfer station gave de Kuyper the names of his quarry, Yates and Yesilkov—their real names, unless they had gone to the length of booking their transport with false ID cards. He would send the names to Arjanian to learn what the data banks in UN Headquarters said about the couple. The bribe was a trivial cost against the chance it would turn up some information affecting the Plan.

But that could wait.

For the moment Yates and Yesilkov themselves were more important than what they might represent.

The Oversight Room was located in the hub of Sky Devon rather than the wheel because it had been among the first portions of the habitat constructed. It was inconvenient for the oversight crews to have to work in weightless conditions; but there were only six men and women on each shift, and they were among the lowest ranking of Sky Devon's personnel. It would have been far more inconvenient—as well as expensive—to reroute the lines carrying environmental data from every part of the habitat into the Oversight Room.

The oversight crew—four men and a woman under a male foreman—twisted or turned when de Kuyper entered, more interested in their visitor than they were in the screens and data arrays which constituted their work. The grin with which the Afrikaner responded briefly to them was part wolfish, part bemused. He did not close the door. Instead he held it half ajar so that he could watch his quarry at the information pylon in the center of the docking area's floor.

"Sir?" offered one of the oversight crew, perhaps the foreman, but de Kuyper had too little interest to look around and see for sure.

"Go on about your business," he growled. Yates, the man, said something to the woman. They began to move toward the rotating walkway which surrounded the stationary loading bay. Both of the visitors were hopelessly awkward in zero gravity.

Sky Devon was a three-spoked wheel, and the only access between the hub and the rim, which rotated to maintain a semblance of gravity for the habitat's living and production areas, was by means of the paired elevators in the spokes. Once a visitor had reached the rim, the magnetic tramway would carry him to any other point on the circumference— but choosing the spoke closest to his destination would save considerable travel time later.

As de Kuyper watched, Yates and Yesilkov struggled, only half under control, to the head of elevator B. Only then did the Afrikaner close the door and give his attention to the interior of the Oversight Room.

All six of the personnel were still staring at him.

"Go *on*," de Kuyper repeated, his snarl only a flash submerged in his disinterest for these people and what they thought. His left hand fished out his ID card and waved it, too briefly for anyone to have read the data printed on its surface.

They didn't need to read it. De Kuyper's nonchalance proved his authority; the card's blue border indicated he was involved with Air System Maintenance; and the colored square filling the upper left corner marked him as a supervisor, at least.

Nobody in an orbital habitat wanted problems with the men who kept them breathing.

The oversight crew shifted their attention, not so much back to their work as away from the intruder. One of the men turned his head and sniffed the air secretively, as if he could tell anything useful about the composition of the atmosphere that way.

"*No* problem," said the Afrikaner as he tucked his card away again. He was pleased in the same fractional way that he had been irritated before. He was focused on his task, and his immediate surroundings impinged only very slightly on the problems that mattered to him.

There were twenty-four meter-square viewing screens arranged adjacent to one another around the walls of the Oversight Room. The screens were flat, not tanks for holograms, because the greater resolution of a laser-swept flat surface was more important to their use than three-dimensionality would have been.

The only break in the array was for the door by which de Kuyper had entered, and it was to the pair of screens directly across the room that he now drifted. The slight tackiness of his boot soles gave the Afrikaner control without hampering him unduly in zero-gravity conditions.

The shift foreman, who was probably younger than his baldness made him look, approached the interloper again. "Is there something the matter with the air, sir?" he asked obsequiously.

"Not if you keep your mouth shut," de Kuyper said as his hands worked the controls of both screens simultaneously. "This doesn't *have* to be any problem of yours at all."

As the foreman backed away, de Kuyper took an inhaler from his breast pocket. The room began to fill with the odor of brandy-soaked tobacco.

Each of the large screens in the Oversight Room swept slowly across the view of one of the twenty-four sections into which the wheel of Sky Devon was divided. Beneath each vision screen were fifty flat gauges which reported air, soil, and water temperatures at selected locations within the section; atmosphere mix; and the flow of waste and nutrients through the section.

No individual could keep track of everything that went on in acres of grain and vegetables, livestock ranging from cattle to rabbits, and fishponds—layered one atop the other and all mirror-illuminated from the direction of the hub, "up," against the thrust of pseudogravity. In addition everyone on an oversight crew had nominal charge of four adjacent sections, a volume of space and information staggeringly beyond the collection and processing capacity of two eyes and a human brain.

But the Oversight Room was not intended to deal with sudden emergencies: there were automatic alarms and shutdown procedures for that. What trained personnel with this battery of views and sensors *could* do was note a problem before it became an emergency.

Did the slow buildup of methane in a carp tank indicate that an effluent filter was clogged? Did a differential of a few millibars pressure from a section's upper levels to its base mean there was an air leak? Were both the cattle and the sheep in stacked pens avoiding the same corner, suggesting that a distorted mirror was causing a hot spot?

No one Jan de Kuyper knew on an oversight crew was enthusiastic about the job—but their cameras were ideal for the Afrikaner's present needs, about which he was as serious as death.

Elevator B reached "ground level" of the rim, where two sections met. The cross wall, which could be sealed if necessary to contain a disaster in one of the adjacent sections, served here as a structural brace. The three spokes of the habitat's wheel had to balance the asymmetries of mass and rotational velocity throughout the rim. It was critical that those stresses—tiny but additive—be distributed through cross walls instead of merely the skin of the structure.

The Afrikaner's normal duties required him to know the physical layout of Sky Devon as well as anyone in the habitat could. He didn't need the help of the oversight personnel to step directly to the proper screens and begin swinging the camera controls to display people leaving elevator B in either direction.

Each picture was controlled by a handle like that of a joystick, mounted beneath the screen. The control levers did not move under the operator's pressure, but they transmitted the level and direction of force as commands to the battery of cameras feeding the screen.

The two pictures in front of Jan de Kuyper sped toward one another. Smooth motion was punctuated by abrupt changes of perspective as a camera reached the limit of its field of view and the microprocessor switched to the next unit in the correct direction of travel.

"There . . ." de Kuyper muttered under his breath in Afrikaans as the picture in the right-hand screen began to sever itself with the expanding mass of the barrier wall. At its base was the wide plaza onto which the doors of the passenger elevators opened—cargo was loaded and emptied at a still lower level. The doors swelled on the screen as the Afrikaner pushed the control in, increasing the focal length of the mirror-optic lens that the distant camera mounted.

The other side of the cross wall rushed to fill the left-hand screen. De Kuyper grinned around the tube of his inhaler. Only a practiced torturer could have recognized the expression as one of humor.

He didn't need the left picture after all. His targets stepped into sight on the right-hand screen, moving with assurance in the half-G pseudogravity—and staggering slightly because the acceleration of centrifugal force has side effects that true gravity does not. They walked to the transit stop near the elevator head, pausing to check their directions while more familiar travelers pressed past them.

The Afrikaner locked his camera down on the faces, the man and then the shorter, pale-haired woman. He held that close-up so long as the couple stood still. De Kuyper did not learn anything from the pictures, though it occurred to him (as it occasionally had before) that lip-reading would be a useful talent.

In any case, the close-up was a useful preview of how the faces would look over a gun sight.

The woman's head bobbed off the screen. De Kuyper's hand tugged up and pushed sideways on the control, expanding his picture and shifting it to follow the couple striding, as he more or less expected, toward the clockwise transit stop and the magnetic tram just gliding to a halt there.

Yates and Yesilkov had not paused to recover their luggage—one case apiece, and that loaded well below the weight permitted without additional charge on shuttle flights. Yates' hands were free, but the woman carried with her the satchel that had been near her person from the first time de Kuyper saw her in the passenger bay at Headquarters Colony.

The case bore signs of wear—scuffing at the corners, and a black streak on one side which was probably something rubbed on rather than a tear in the sturdy synthetic. There were no markings on the satchel's exterior, but its color was as close to the blue of Security Patrol uniforms as dyes in different materials could achieve.

Most of the oversight personnel had returned to their duties. One of the men hovered in the background, glancing nervously toward the interloper who had ousted him from his position. De Kuyper looked without expression at the fellow—and felt, but did not show, his pleasure when the crewman blanched and spun away.

The tram holding the Afrikaner's targets was gathering speed, but the picture slid along with it in a comfortable panorama under the guidance of de Kuyper's hand. The next transit stop was in the middle of the section where layers of garden truck surrounded a community reserved for personnel above technician class.

No livestock was raised within this segment of Sky Devon. That should have meant there were relatively few complaints about air quality, since the only agricultural effluvia that assailed the inhabitants were those traces that simply could not be filtered from a recirculating air system.

De Kuyper and his crews spent more time here than in any other segment of the habitat. Problems that don't exist are the most difficult ones to cure.

The tram slid on. De Kuyper focused down on the platform to scan the passengers who had disembarked. The high-angle camera he was using showed the top of people's heads, not their faces, and tugging at the control lever did not slide the picture down.

The oversight system was not intended as a tool for human

surveillance. No batteries of cameras had been installed in the communities themselves. Fortunately, Sky Devon had been planned as a chain of tiny hamlets in the midst of farmland. The overlap of the oversight cameras was sufficient for the Afrikaner's present needs.

Unless Yesilkov, with her bright hair and blue satchel, separated from the man Yates.

Well, de Kuyper couldn't watch two targets at the same time anyway. He'd use what he had, and he'd make field decisions on whatever problems arose.

Just as he always had, whether repairing a duct that didn't follow the planned routing or deciding whether to shoot a lone Kaffir or let him walk on without warning the column of guerrillas that perhaps slouched along behind him.

The tram slowed for another stop while de Kuyper stepped to his right with a leisurely motion and took the control for the next screen. Both were the responsibility of the same member of the oversight crew. The woman watching the adjacent screens moved down to the last of her line of four, talking with false animation to the foreman.

Yates and Yesilkov did not leave the tram before it accelerated into the next section of the wheel. Focusing carefully through the windows of the car, the Afrikaner was sure that he could see the splotch of blue that was the satchel. Reflection from the glass—processed out of lunar silicates instead of thermoplasticss which would have had to be lifted expensively from Earth's gravity well—made the windows montages of too many distorted images for de Kuyper to be sure of more than that.

There was a phone beneath every fourth screen so that the oversight personnel could report apparent problems to the workers on the ground. De Kuyper took out his card again while his eyes and right hand tracked the train speeding past tiered livestock byres. He fed the card into the phone slot so that its microcircuitry enabled the Sky Devon paging system.

Pressing zero now would turn the phonepad into a series of presets, each of which dialed a complete number that had been loaded into de Kuyper's card. Presets one through nine had been assigned by the Maintenance Department and were loaded with the extensions the Afrikaner had to call most frequently in the course of his regular duties.

Preset zero rang the phone in Dr. Kathleen Spenser's attaché case.

The tram slowed, halted in a community stacked like the livestock pens to either side of it—housing for Tech Threes and Fours like the oversight crew watching him furtively. The men and women who left and boarded the train here wore coveralls.

Except for a couple who got off. The man's hair was light enough to be called blond in any company save the present, but the locks of the woman behind him were as straight and pale as teased flax.

De Kuyper put the reeking inhaler in his breast pocket; keyed zero to enable the preset; and only then lifted the handset of the phone to cradle it between his shoulder and left ear. He did not look away from the screen.

The couple waited, turning uncertainly while more familiar passengers strode from the transit platform on the way to their farther destinations. The blond woman touched her companion with her left hand and gestured with the satchel in her right toward what the vertical camera angle showed as a small square adjoining the platform: the elevator to the Pest Control Research lab.

The couple were foreshortened to heads on shoulders on the screen. They stepped together in front of the elevator— more than a handshake but not, perhaps, quite an embrace. Then the woman broke away and disappeared within the elevator. Yates turned, laced his fingers together, and bent the joints fiercely backward.

De Kuyper released the camera control and touched zero on the phonepad a second time. Yates' figure was moving in short arcs around the elevator head, as if he were tethered to it.

"Yes?" said Kathleen Spenser's voice in the Afrikaner's ear—as chill and pure as a sword in a bed of ice.

"There is a woman with a blue briefcase coming to you in a few moments only," said de Kuyper, knowing that his accent was all the identification necessary on the microbiologist's private line. "You must not let her leave your laboratory until I get there."

The oversight crew was edging away from the sound of

the intruder's soft, deadly voice. They formed two distinct clots in the corners of the room farthest from him, so that they could not even seem to be listening to the whispered conversation.

"What do you mean?" Spenser demanded, her voice an octave higher than it had been before de Kuyper spoke.

"Any means you please," said the Afrikaner. He stroked the picture control, broadening the field of view until the man Yates was a mote wobbling near the minute square of the elevator. No other person was visible on the screen. "Seal the air lock, if you must. I will arrive soon, but she has a companion who must be gotten out of the way before."

"*I* can't—"

"Mistress Spenser," Jan de Kuyper said. "You must. Do you understand? You *must*."

Spenser's initial shock and uncertainty were gone. "Hurry, then," said the microbiologist.

The line clicked open.

De Kuyper cradled the handset and gave the picture control a quick spin across his palm and fingers to make its previous alignment a matter of doubtful conjecture—if anyone even tried. He thrust himself toward the door of the Oversight Room, letting weightlessness benefit him. He gave the trio of crewmen which included the female a nod of his head as he left them, courteous or grimly threatening as their minds chose to accept it.

The luggage de Kuyper had abandoned when he boarded the outbound shuttle at UN Headquarters contained the plasma discharger he had thought he might need on the Moon. No matter. There were others here.

As he worked his way through the bustle of the docking area, the Afrikaner was inserting his nose filters. They and the gas grenades which they accompanied had made the entire journey from and to Sky Devon in one bellows pocket of his trousers.

Chapter 22

DOWN ON THE FARM

Kathleen Spenser was sure that de Kuyper's odd behavior, his chilling orders, and his urgency which left no time for the occasional "goodmistress" or even a "please," must have something to do with the woman of whom he'd spoken. A woman with a blue briefcase and companion.

Seal the air lock if you must . . . she has a companion who must be gotten out of the way first. . . . You must. Do you understand? You must. Too many musts. Something must, then, be terribly wrong. She'd half expected to hear from de Kuyper—hear about the Bradley woman whom de Kuyper was supposed to be bringing in for interrogation.

The Afrikaner's behavior might not have been so frightening but for the conspicuous lack of success in the case of Ella Bradley. Not even a mention of her, or how it had gone, or when she'd be available for further questioning, or, if not, then why and what that could mean.

Spenser ruminatively stroked the crystal phial hanging from her neck chain. *I will arrive soon,* de Kuyper had said, and she'd told him to hurry.

Hurry before she lost her nerve, before supposition drove her mad, before . . . what? Before the woman with the blue briefcase arrived, if possible. Spenser didn't want to be involved with—

The gentle tone of her desk paging system interrupted her thoughts. "Dr. Spenser?" came the receptionist's voice from the desk's speaker. "There's a Lieutenant Yesilkov here from UN Security who needs to see you on a priority basis? Immediately?" The voice piped from the entryway reception station made everything a question.

Spenser glanced around her littered office once, a quick, furtive check: everything was in its usual disorder, her desk and even the visitor's chair facing it littered with papers. Just as the Pest Control Research head's office should look.

Security. From the UN—probably at the lunar colony, the way their luck had been going lately. Did this visit have something to do with de Kuyper's agitation? But he was on his way. She hesitated transiently. She could tell the security lieutenant she was busy. She would be, momentarily, when the woman with the blue attache case de Kuyper was so concerned about showed up.

But for now she wasn't busy. No need to take chances that the security lieutenant would know that. She touched a colored square on the intercom: "Send the lieutenant in, but I've got another visitor coming. Buzz me when that one arrives."

Good, she thought, a built-in reason to get rid of this snoop. She wished de Kuyper had been more communicative. The last she'd heard, he'd been on his way to the Moon on some routine business which should have included Ella Bradley and a number of burning questions. Now he was back. There was something wrong, really wrong, and de Kuyper wasn't telling her. Not leveling with her at all.

There was, of course, always the phial. Her fingers caressed it as if it were a pet. Always that. The security officer might tell her something, by the very purpose of her visit.

She moved stiffly to her desk and sat behind it, smoothing her lab smock, envisioning a blue-clad, blue-jawed bull of a man with UN credentials ambling down the hall . . .

Yesilkov had monitoring electronics in her briefcase, radio-linked to a button secured behind her ear by the post of the pierced-ear stud whose back it formed. Couldn't risk a visible wire in these circumstances.

A shame, because there was too much metal paneling for the radio transmitter to function beyond the office's walls. Or else she could have been talking to—or at least listening to—Yates the entire time. As things stood, she was storing the data her system was recording on magnetic cassettes which digitized everything she said and heard. When

Spenser half rose from behind her desk in greeting, Yesilkov fingered her right ear, enabling the discriminatory voice-signature mode to isolate Spenser's voice.

From now on, everything the fiftyish, horse-faced lady doctor said would be scrutinized mechanically for stress, as well as recorded verbatim. Yesilkov would hear a beeping that increased in frequency when and as the respondent's voice-stress heightened.

Later she and Yates would go over the tape. "Lieutenant Yesilkov," she said, approaching Spenser's desk with her hand outstretched.

"Yes, I assumed . . . I mean, that foolish boy at the desk gave me to understand you were a man, Lieutenant—if I seem startled, that's why."

Beep. Beep, beep. Beep beep beep. Beepbeepbeep. Beep, beep. Beep. Beep, whispered the monitor in Yesilkov's ear as Spenser spoke. *Startled, I guess, lady. That middle group was an outright lie. Whatcha got to lie about, this early on?* Thinking about it as she took the chair before the desk, beside which a pile of files was strewn, Yesilkov realized that Spenser had lied about the receptionist giving her the impression that Yesilkov was a man. *Off to a great start, Dr. Spenser.* And, aloud: "Happens all the time, Doctor. No sweat." Yesilkov settled the blue attache case on her knees and rested her elbows on it.

"What can I do for you, Lieutenant Yesilkov?" Spenser's lined, heavy face was emotionless. "From the UN, I was told. Have you credentials?"

This time the telltale in Yesilkov's ear only beeped once, immediately following Spenser's enunciation of UN.

Yesilkov reached for the chain around her neck and drew it out from under her blouse to flash the poly-card hanging from it. If Spenser wanted to examine it more closely, she'd have to ask. Then she might realize that Yesilkov's UN Directorate of Security, Patrol Division, Company Four credentials didn't entitle her to any special treatment—or give her any real authority—on Sky Devon, a British protectorate. But most people didn't understand international law as it pertained to UN signatories that well. "UN, lunar colony," Yesilkov said, watching Spenser's face.

The horsey jaw didn't twitch, but lips stretched closed over a sufficient overbite to pock the woman's chin with the effort. And the telltale in Yesilkov's ear went *beepbeep-beep* as Spenser said, "Really. I wonder what it is you think I can do for you, Lieutenant Yetsiloff?"

"Just some routine questions about yer work—we had a recent outbreak of disease, y'll have heard. Lot of our food comes from—"

"Nothing," said Spenser sharply, while in Yesilkov's ear the monitor brayed an unbroken *beepbeepbeep-beeeeeeeep*, "that came from Sky Devon could have precipitated the sort of illness you're talking about." Spenser's nervous fingers found a wisp of graying hair escaped from its clip and tugged on it.

Yesilkov said, "Oh yeah? That so?"

"Yes." *Beep.* "It's so—nothing that could be carried by pork, or by grains or fruits or vegetables—not botulism or ptomaine or even salmonella"—Spenser grinned as if she'd made a joke, which was lost on Yesilkov—"has symptoms such as the media described as present on the Moon during that outbreak. Which, I've heard, has now subsided."

Except for the single, lonely pulse at the beginning of Spenser's reply, the telltale remained silent. A little truth, for what that was worth. Yesilkov shifted in her seat and steadied the attache case on her lap. A much more precise, much more expensive, sophisticated, and dedicated piece of lie-detection equipment known as Sonya Yesilkov was monitoring Dr. Kathleen Spenser, and redlining.

This weird old bag was in this up to her whiskery chin. All Yesilkov had to do now was prove it—get sufficient beeps on her tape to justify bringing the woman in for questioning. So she needed samples of nonstressed responses—clear, truthful statements as controls. She said, "That's good to know, Dr. Spenser—it'd wreak havoc with our budget to have to import from Earth. Nobody wants to quarantine Sky Devon's agrigoodies—synthetics don't taste that good yet, and Earth-boosted stuff's too expensive for the rank and file. What we've got here, then, is a routine enquiry. Could you tell me a little about your boss, Doctor, uh . . ." An inquiring stare.

"Director, not Doctor, Sutcliffe-Bowles? Yes, indeed, what would you like to—"

No beeps. "Y'er kiddin'? That's his name? I thought it was a computer screwup. Yeah then, I'd like to know how you think—"

Behind Yesilkov the air-conditioning duct high in the wall seemed to burp. Then a blower somewhere behind its grate speeded up audibly.

"Drat. That thing's so noisy, Lieutenant, that sometimes I wish—"

Spenser's apology turned into a gasp and then a strangled cry as a hollow bang sounded, followed by a susurrus of sound and billows of gas that filled the room with haze in moments.

Yesilkov was on her feet, attache case clutched under her arm, by the time Spenser had risen, an amazed look on her face as she craned her neck toward the duct's grating.

Then Spenser fell, inelegantly and flaccid, facedown across her desk.

Free hand grabbing for her stunner, Yesilkov dove for the floor, where the air should be better, thinking to crawl to the door. But by the time she landed on her knees, Yesilkov was losing control of her limbs. The stunner wouldn't stay in her clumsy fingers, and the attache case was skidding out of her grasp. Her knees felt like jello melting in the sun.

She balanced herself on her hands and knees for an instant, determined to reclaim the stunner, the case, and make it to the door. Then she forgot what she was trying to do, as pink peppermint clouds enveloped her mind, already miles away from the unresisting body that lay motionless on the floor of Spenser's office.

Behind Spenser's desk, unbeknownst to the two unconscious women, a wall panel shifted, then slid aside.

Jan de Kuyper stepped through the detached wall panel into Spenser's office wearing nose filters and an unpleasant smile. In his left hand was a plasma gun. In his right he held a roll of tape, the kind used for strapping payloads to vacuum jeeps.

Carefully he approached Kathleen Spenser, who was

sprawled over her desktop with her hand cupping the crystal phial she wore like a religious medal around her neck. Our Lady of Pestilential Roulette . . . The phial, however, wasn't broken. Not even cracked. The hand curled around it had cushioned it from the impact as Spenser collapsed. That was good news.

The Afrikaner considered removing the phial, but try as might, he couldn't steel himself to touch it. With a grimace, he contented himself with a kick at the unconscious, but still unpleasant, female before he turned to her companion.

Binding the blond security officer as he had her male traveling companion who now lay, trussed and stunned, near the air lock where de Kuyper had left him in a maintenance closet, de Kuyper noticed the chain around her neck. It was the nature of the chain—a string of tiny metal beads— that made him pull it from her blouse to see if anything hung from it.

What he found there—the credentials of one Lieutenant Sonya Yesilkov, UN Directorate of Security—dovetailed with what he'd learned from Yates when he'd pulled the unconscious man's wallet. Sort of. What were these two up to? Yates was Lunar Entry Division, Yesilkov from Patrol Company Four . . . neither were authorized hitters in this ballpark—at least not by their credentials they weren't.

With a growl of frustration, de Kuyper shelved speculation. He continued binding Yesilkov until she was securely trussed, then made his way through the volatile mist that filled the office until, at Spenser's desk, he could slap his collaborator with an antidote injector.

Spenser would not be pleased when she awoke, not with her terrible headache or de Kuyper's improvised solution to their mutual difficulty. But then, Spenser was the least of his worries.

Yates and Yesilkov had been with Bradley at the lunar docking tube. Bradley should have been in van Zell's hands. Piet van Zell had left a message on de Kuyper's machine, but it told him nothing more than what he'd learned on his own—that the attempt to abduct Bradley had ended in failure.

Something would have to be done about van Zell and his

men. Done fast. If it weren't already too late. And something
would have to be done about this woman, Yesilkov, and
Yates. It was obvious by their presence here that they knew
too much.

Jan de Kuyper was beginning to sweat as he dragged the
bound lieutenant toward the gaping hole in the office wall.
It wasn't so much that he knew he was going to kill both
Yesilkov and Yates, it was that he'd have to report this
problem if he couldn't solve it. And that might imperil the
Plan. He didn't like the thought of what reporting even a
partial failure might mean, not only to the Plan, but to his
own future.

Right now his choices were too limited. He was feeling
an operational claustrophobia he knew could be deadly. So
he would continue to act until he reached a point where any
report he made would be more hopeful, more survivable.

To reach that point he needed to get Yates in here before
the big man was discovered, interrogate the pair with
Spenser's help, and dispose of them. Before that he had to
keep Spenser from doing anything foolish when she'd re-
covered sufficiently to be angry.

He straightened from the trussed lieutenant, moved to the
stirring woman sprawled across her desktop, and began rubbing Spenser's wrists. He needed the doctor awake and
cooperative.

In order to get Yates in here, Spenser must help him clear
the lab of regular personnel. Only then could he go about
his business: finding out how badly van Zell had screwed
up, and what must be done to preserve the Plan and his
own life.

Chapter 23

BRADLEY'S MOVE

In Ella Bradley's apartment the phone only rang once before she snatched the handset from its cradle. "Yes?"

"Dr. Bradley, please," said a staticky voice.

"This is she." Some secretary, from some distance. Ella was disappointed because none of the priority calls she'd been expecting should have started this way.

". . . from NYU main office at Washington Square. Deputy McLeod's assistant has been in touch with us concerning your request for background data on one Rodney Beaton."

The hostility in the voice on the other end of the line came through, despite transmission quality so bad that Ella was unable to tell if the caller was male or female. Whichever, this was the owner of the tail Taylor'd had his people tweak for her, calling personally—and at no little expense—because that tail *had* been tweaked.

Bless Taylor and his hallowed connections! At last she was going to get the dope on Beaton. Next to a call from McLeod himself, or from Yates and Yesilkov, it was the best thing that could have happened to her right now.

But she'd ignored the name of the speaker when it had been given. She'd have to wait for an opportunity to ask for a repetition. . . . "Yes," she said. "I've been waiting for that file. If you'll just hold on, I'll set my equipment up to take a dump, and you can upload it to me."

The signal delay in Earth/Moon communications always made it seem that one party or the other had a hidden agenda; it made honest conversations fill with awkward pauses, so Ella didn't at once realize that there was an actual hesitation on the part of the person on the other end of her downlink.

Until that person said, "Well, that's it, you see. We can't give you that data because we can't get it. Not right now, not just yet."

Pause.

"What do you mean? I'm cleared for anything that could be in this Beaton's file. And surely Deputy McLeod's office instructed you that this is a priority matter."

Pause.

"Be that as it may, Dr. Bradley," said the other party stiffly, "when we followed up on your request—which we did with all speed—we were told by Sky Devon that it was to be handled by a Dr. Spenser. Now it seems that there's been an accident at this Spenser's lab and no data's going to download from there any time soon. We'd appreciate it if you'd relay to USIA your personal assurances that this office has been cooperative to the extent of its ability."

In the ensuing pause Ella realized that this was the reason for the call: NYU wanted off the hook. But it was the rest of what the New Yorker had said that bothered her.

"What kind of accident?" she demanded.

And the pause before the response came back was a lifetime long: "We don't know, exactly. We don't have a need to know. I doubt it's anything too catastrophic, but whatever it is, it's going to take time to iron out. You will forward our apologies to your friends in Washington and make it clear that no one at NYU was less than helpful? After all, you're on our staff, not theirs."

That stung. This wasn't a flunky, not if the person dared to make that kind of crack. Ella said, "Just give me your name again, friend, and I'll do that," before she realized she was talking to dead air.

Hung up on her, whoever-it-was had. She slammed down the phone and slid sideways on the couch, one arm over her eyes. Damned bureaucrats. But she wasn't as angry as she was concerned.

She should have heard from Yates by now. Yesilkov might not have called, but Yates would have, if he could. She was almost sure of it. And an accident right where they were going . . . it was too pat, like so much of this chaotic interval, just too damned coincidentally convenient for someone—the same someone who had her kidnapped, she was willing to bet.

She hadn't told McLeod about the kidnap attempt, because he'd tell her to chuck her job and take the next shuttle to Earth. Or put her under such tight security that the men stationed in shifts outside her door would seem more like freedom than constraint, in retrospect.

At least it was only one man at a time. She could book a shuttle from here, then make the security guard trail her to the women's gym, where she'd shaken the last one when she'd needed to. A background in the third world didn't hurt when push came to shove.

Ella Bradley sat bolt upright, realizing where her train of thought was taking her. Was she really going to go running after Sam Yates like some high school girl, because he hadn't called her?

Not because he hadn't called her—because he might not be able to call her. Yates and Yesilkov might be Security, but they didn't seem to be able to look more than one step ahead. That lack of imagination could be fatal, if there really was some conspiracy, called the Plan, into which time and money had been put by powerful people.

Two beat cops against a high-level plot to eradicate certain genetic strains from humankind? It just wasn't plausible that they could win, but she hadn't been able to convince either security officer of that. They didn't have her sort of experience with totalitarian thinking, revolutionaries and counter-revolutionaries. They also didn't have her kind of friends.

The sensible thing to do was what she'd wanted to do all along: bring higher authority in on this, get backup, alert someone who could follow through in case Yesilkov, Yates, and she couldn't singlehandedly save the world. That was what she'd said. It should have done the trick. It would have, if either Yesilkov or Yates could admit to what was going on and what they were trying to do.

Yates had told her he wasn't in the world-saving business, just in the Yates-saving business.

Yesilkov had rolled her eyes skyward and muttered about conspiracy theorists.

Now they were probably sorry. Now it was up to her. She picked up the phone, dialed a coded downlink, got a busy signal, and left a priority redial. Then she got together an overnight case, and stuffed into it the stunner she'd found when she moved the couch to clean this morning, a stunner that must have been there since the kidnap attempt. Not a good commentary on the effectiveness of Yates' and Yesilkov's people, but they weren't trained for this sort of thing.

Neither was Ella Bradley, officially. But she'd been around covert actions in Africa, and she had friends who *were* trained to deal with exactly this sort of exigency. Friends who didn't think she was paranoid—or no more paranoid than was necessary to get along in the world they'd chosen to frequent, the world of geopolitical struggle that had managed to export itself even into space.

You couldn't hang out on the slideways or watch the UN dignitaries in their cars here and not realize that it was just a little Earth up here, no better, no worse, and certainly no less factionalized.

Yates would never forgive her, but she was going to put Taylor in the picture. Swear him to secrecy, of course, but let him know where she was going, and why. Taylor McLeod wouldn't forbid her; he knew her too well for that. He'd give her some help if she asked for it, though. And he'd make sure that if something happened to her, what she and Yates and Yesilkov knew didn't die with them.

That was the most important thing, the thing she couldn't seem to make the security officers understand. All they could think about was the effect of certain incidents on their own careers. They couldn't believe there was anyone they could trust with this. They couldn't see the larger picture.

But Ella could. And Taylor McLeod could.

She thumbed the dialer on her handset, and when the ticket agent answered, booked herself on a shuttle flight to Sky Devon.

It left in three hours. That gave her plenty of time to talk to Taylor, or record a message for him if she couldn't. It also gave her enough time to saunter down to the gym and slip the bodyguard's surveillance. If she was going to need help on Sky Devon, it wasn't the sort that Yesilkov's patrol officers were trained to provide.

Chapter 24

DAMAGE CONTROL

It seemed somehow appropriate to Kathleen Spenser that when she entered Director Sutcliffe-Bowles' office, speakers were blaring Wagner's Naziesque mysticism from the Ring cycle. Wagner would have been right at home with the Plan.

Sutcliffe-Bowles swung his chair around and tapped the remote on its arm which lowered the volume. Abruptly there was silence, a stagey, ominous silence in which Sutcliffe-Bowles glared at her, his normally pink and pudgy cheeks reddening even more.

All planned, she realized, for effect—the overblown, self-important music full of braying power; the huge executive chair turned away from her when she entered; the swiveling and the ensuing silence in which the director glared at her like some great horned owl wearing rouge.

"Damage report, Kathie, is that what this is?" Sutcliffe-Bowles finally said when she didn't react in any discernable fashion.

She was standing before the director's composite desk, her hands dangling at her sides so that her fingers could have brushed the desktop. "Damage *control*," she corrected firmly. "Damage limit*ation*. I reported a possible—by no means certain—release of microorganisms in my work area. Clearing and sealing the lab is simply a precaution, Director."

"Hrmph," said this man who ought to be wearing tweed as he took tea in some Stratford-on-Avon garden, not sitting behind a New British Empire graphite desk in Sky Devon, getting ready to take her to task with all the insufferable tact of his kind. "What, Kathie, do you perceive as the difference? After all, the lab is . . . sensitive. We're looking at a scandal here, if word—''

"Sir," said Spenser, suddenly experiencing a secondary onslaught of symptoms she'd thought she'd shaken off. " 'Word,' as you say, won't be a problem. Unless someone on your staff gossips, we've got it well in hand. I'm working with Maintenance, under the table, to sterilize the area *without* a scandal.'' The symptoms shouldn't be recurring, and that made them worse: she was dizzy again, a legacy of the gas and the antidote. She was dizzy enough that she'd interrupted Sutcliffe-Bowles in mid-sentence.

And that, as much as her veiled threat that any leaks and subsequent embarrassment would bring scrutiny upon his office, made Sutcliffe-Bowles stare as if he'd never seen Kathleen Spenser before.

She didn't have time for this fool, not the way she was feeling. It was all she could do to keep her hand from going to her forehead, or to the desk where she could lean for support. She didn't know that her shoulders hunched or her neck outthrust as she stared back, but they did.

Very slowly and very precisely, she enunciated, "So, Director, if you wish to keep this incident from turning into a disaster which comes home to roost, I suggest you get about the process of issuing a gag order that will muzzle your staff. If one word of this leaks to the press, you're going to be explaining how it happened for the rest of your life.''

Sutcliffe-Bowles knew what Spenser *wasn't* saying: on a space habitat like Devon, fear of contamination was second only to fear of depressurization. After what had recently happened on the Moon, people were even more skittish. Sky Devon needed its research facilities to function and to prosper. The agrihabitat ran on the products of its labs as much as its pens and tanks: without faith in its products, Sky Devon would be a multibillion-pound ghost town in months.

The color drained from Sutcliffe-Bowles' face as Spenser watched with light-headed satisfaction. Then the director said, his words clumsy because terror had dried the spittle in his mouth, "Kathleen, I want your personal assurances that this matter can be handled without . . . publicity. That there's nothing here that you're not telling me. Nothing . . ." Sutcliffe-Bowles sat back, his pupils dilating as she watched.

"Nothing virulent, you mean?" she said sharply, unable to contain herself. For the first time she had this miserable, posturing, inbred aristocrat where she wanted him. "Nothing life threatening, like they had on the Moon? I can assure you, Director, that it's nothing like they had there. And if you do your job, it won't threaten *your* life, your lifestyle, or your livelihood, which is all you're worried about. But I'll need your full cooperation. . . ."

"You'll have it. You have it now," Sutcliffe-Bowles promised, meek as even Spenser could wish.

"Fine," she said with a curt nod. "I'll be back when I have something further to report. Meanwhile, keep your people out of my way and your qualms to yourself."

There was nothing like the possibility of an epidemic to put the fear of God in people, even people like Sutcliffe-Bowles.

Chapter 25

PRISONERS

Jan de Kuyper, hauling the big security officer into the "abandoned" lab, was puffing with the strain. Yates was a big man, that was all; that, and all the stress and the degree to which de Kuyper's muscle tone had degenerated in low gravity.

That was all it was, he assured himself, not wanting to think about the other reasons he might be short of breath. If he was coming down with something, if the burning in his lungs meant anything more ominous than simple battle fatigue, de Kuyper was going to kill Kathleen Spenser very slowly, with his own hands.

If the woman had booby-trapped him somehow, the way she'd booby-trapped herself with that damned phial she wore around her neck, she wouldn't live to gloat.

Gloom was settling over de Kuyper as the situation became more complex. Not fear of failure, but simple pragmatic distaste for the unavoidable dangers ahead, some of which weren't even clear. When he'd done with this lot, he still had Piet van Zell and his bumblers to deal with. The Plan left no room for fuckups, or for fucker-uppers.

With one final jerk on the unresisting dead weight of the man he'd been dragging into the lab, de Kuyper let the body go. Supervisor Samuel Yates' head hit the floor with a satisfying thump.

Over at the air locks one of Spenser's flunkies closed the doors. Having done that, he then begged to leave. There was sweat on the man's thinning pate and sparkling beads of it on his brow. He was a doctor, someone Spenser had detailed to this duty, someone she either suborned or otherwise controlled. But the look on the man's face said that he'd nearly reached his limit.

Scornfully de Kuyper said, "Yes, go on. Go. Go to your quarters. Spenser will contact you." Jan de Kuyper had no limit to reach. He had only the Plan and his determination to stand on the veldt, free to roam as far as his eye could see, and never encounter a nigger with a gun.

Once Spenser's boy had gone, de Kuyper made a mental note to make sure the flunky didn't outlive his usefulness. Then he turned to Yates, still unconscious. He manhandled the trussed prisoner into Spenser's office and slapped the lock plate behind him.

Now it was just de Kuyper and these fish he'd given up Ella Bradley to catch. One way or another he was going to make the trade-off worth his while.

Before he dragged Yates any farther, de Kuyper checked to see that everything was as he had left it. It was. Yesilkov was still insensible, lying on the floor in disarray. He lifted both her eyelids and stuck his hand between her legs, probing with his finger to make sure. If she were faking, the intrusive touch would have startled some reaction out of her. For a moment longer than was necessary, he probed there at the woman's crotch.

Then he rose, grinning. Touching the woman had given him an idea. But first he must make sure they wouldn't be disturbed. He checked the panel he'd detached from the wall behind Spenser's desk, even sliding behind it. All clear.

He rummaged through the desk, making certain that no recording equipment was on, no intercom engaged. Then and only then did he drag the sedated Yates to a spot opposite Yesilkov, propping the man's unresisting body against Spenser's desk.

Normally for this kind of interrogation one positioned a light to shine in the captive's eyes—as much for psychological effect as to prevent him from identifying you. You only worried that he might identify you if you were still considering the possibility that the captive might survive.

But de Kuyper was not considering that possibilty. He wanted Yates to realize this. And he wanted Yates to have a good view of Yesilkov, in case the woman proved to be an avenue of control over the man. You never could tell what might work.

Jan de Kuyper didn't care what he had to do to find out what he needed to know. He simply needed to know it. Having a little fun with Yesilkov at Yates' expense would be amusing, but it wasn't uppermost in his mind. It was merely easier than beating the information out of the two of them.

Content with his plan, he bent over Yates and slapped the big man with an antidote injector. Then he rolled Spenser's wheeled armchair over to a spot between the two bound captives on the floor and settled down to wait.

He watched Yates carefully, committing to memory the different states of the man's face. The planes of it in relaxation would change drastically as Yates came to consciousness. The onslaught of realization would tighten muscles, and by that means de Kuyper would have a referent for the helpless fear he meant to engender.

Waiting watchfully to see the facial expression that he must recreate in Yates before he could believe that anything confessed was the truth, de Kuyper estimated dreamily that in other circumstances the two men might have been friends. Yates was pale, blond, some combination of Norse and Slavic bloodlines, or perhaps German. The high, wide cheekbones, the protruding ridge over slightly slanted eyes, the Netherlands nose—none of these softened the Teutonic mouth and chin sufficiently for de Kuyper to be fooled. This man was of good blood, and hard nature.

In other circumstances, a compatriot. Now, an enemy not to be underestimated. Jan de Kuyper had dragged Yates too far not to have judged the power in the barrel chest of his captive, or in those long limbs so recently arrived from Earth. This man still had his Downside strength.

But de Kuyper had been very careful with Yates' bonds, even injecting him a second time when he'd gone back for the supervisor, whom he'd stashed near the air lock. Yates' credentials said only that he was UN Security, Entry Division. But there had to be something more, or Yates wouldn't have been here.

Therefore, those credentials were only cover. Yates was

more than he appeared. An agent of the opposition, clearly. But which faction of the opposition? From what office? What government? How many others of his kind, back on Earth or the Moon, knew he was here? And what kind of forces would come after him, looking for their agent and revenge upon his attackers, once Yates was declared missing in action? How long would that take? How—

"You work for Spenser," said Sam Yates with some difficulty, his enunciation slurred and his voice scratchy.

Jan de Kuyper took a taser from his belt and sat forward in his chair, elbows planted firmly on his knees. Playing with the taser so that Yates' eyes couldn't help but fix on it, he answered lazily, "Ah, we're awake, goodfellow? About time. Look around you, take your time. What do you see?"

Yates' eyes never left the taser, never flickered to Yesilkov's prostrate form. Well, Yates knew she was there; he could not have failed to notice her.

The security officer said, "I see some fool who works for Spenser. Spenser's ass is grass, buddy, whether I call the shots myself or not. It's too late—"

"I do not work for Spenser." From de Kuyper's mouth, the words roared unbidden. He was furious that this man should assume he would be in the employ of that prune-faced spinster whose female parts were probably the dark lair of spiders, if anything at all. "I 'work' for no one, only the Plan, the return to Earth of my people, and an Africa cleared for settlement by *human* beings. Spenser is nothing, a cog, a crazy woman. Only a crazy woman would wear around her neck a phial of virus. A bead that, if she jerks it off its chain, will be shattered by electrical means. And then, for the next ten minutes, the virus is lethal to any man—" And de Kuyper caught himself then, shutting his mouth with an audible snap of his jaws.

Spenser is crazy, goodfellow. And so are we all. He wondered what had prompted him to say those things to Yates, and then realized it was because Yates must comprehend how desperate the situation was—how desperate for all of them.

De Kuyper knew now he'd made a mistake: Yates must

think that his life hung in the balance, as well as the woman's. He must be given the idea that he might survive. He must . . .

Before de Kuyper could reopen the conversation, Yates said, "Fine, you don't work for Spenser," and de Kuyper saw there the facial expression he'd been waiting for: Yates looked exactly as he had when he'd first come to consciousness.

"I will ask the questions," said de Kuyper flatly. "You will answer them." He stood up, still holding the taser whose poles shot forty thousand painful volts through any flesh they touched, and approached Yesilkov.

Beside the bound woman on the floor was her briefcase, open. She'd been fumbling with it before the gas took hold. Bending down to examine it as he hadn't had time to do previously, de Kuyper forgot momentarily about Yates.

"Wait!" said the security officer urgently. "Look, let's talk about this."

Jan de Kuyper realized that Yates had thought the Afrikaner was bending over Yesilkov to apply the taser. Yates wasn't aware, then, that the woman was still doped and unconscious.

Interesting. Without showing that Yates' words had had any effect, de Kuyper continued his motion, hunkering down between the woman and her briefcase. He fingered the case and then looked over his shoulder at his prisoner. "Who are you, really, Supervisor Yates? On whose behalf are you here?" He fingered the Security seals on Yesilkov's briefcase. "I will find out eventually." He reached into her blouse pocket and came up with a knife whose blade he snapped out, still looking at Yates. "Speak."

"I don't know what you mean," said Yates levelly, a crosshatch forming over the bridge of his nose. "I'm Entry, she's—

"I'm checking on you, back where you came from. You'll be explaining many things to me, other things, also. Do this before, and not after, the goodlady suffers in your place."

When Yates only stared at him, de Kuyper reached down with his knife hand and began cutting away at Yesilkov's pants. When he'd slit the crotch seam and slid the knife up and around, exposing the woman's upper thighs and pubic hair and soft belly, Yates said, "Wait a minute, man."

But by then the game was getting interesting and de Kuyper was busy trying to decide whether he'd use an antidote injector to wake the woman or whether the taser, judiciously applied, would be sufficient to the task.

Chapter 26

LADIES FIRST

Ella Bradley had never been to Sky Devon before. If it hadn't been for the nice young man who met her at the docking hub and said, "Ting sent me to help out," she'd never have found her way to her destination.

Ting was a nickname Taylor McLeod hated, one that had been given him in childhood by his parents, a derivative of Huntington, his middle name. When she'd met his family one Thanksgiving, when Taylor had brought her home to Bedford, she'd found out about the nickname and teased him unmercifully: the only people who dared to call him that to his face were his black nanny and his DAR-president aunt from Atlanta.

So the use of his nickname in this place that smelled of pig feces and worse was better than any standard code word they might have determined between them on the groundlink and that might have been overheard. It was absolute identification. Bless Taylor's quick thinking. His young man was perfectly mannered, even-featured, short-haired, impeccably groomed, and more importantly, devoid of questions.

"Anything you need, Doctor, we'll be happy to provide. Anything," said the fellow, who gave her a business card on the back of which he wrote priority com numbers.

Meeting the eyes of the young man she assumed was USIA, she found only calm competence. And a cool amusement, coupled with a genteel hardness one saw in a certain type of man who worked for Taylor.

It was entirely possible that this thirtyish fellow who'd whisked her through customs without the opening of even her purse was not USIA, but something more sinister. One didn't ask. One assumed that a helper of this sort was exactly the right man for the job.

The single job she'd asked of the fellow was to escort her to one Dr. Kathleen Spenser's apartment.

"That's it there, the third door on your left," said the fellow whose card said Peck Smith and who had only the tiniest trace of an Oxford accent. "You're certain there's nothing more we can do?"

"Not unless you can let me in the lady's door if she's not home, so that I don't have to wait in the hall." It was a joke, said with a smile.

"My pleasure," said Taylor McLeod's man, with a smile of his own. Then, after peering elaborately in both directions and placing a finger to his lips for silence, he strode up to Spenser's door, knocked, waited a minute, and bent to the lock.

"Voilà," he said with a hushed flourish as he pushed it open.

In less difficult circumstances Ella might have giggled, or thrown her arms around the man's neck in joyous thanks. As it was, she merely slipped by him and whispered, because she was illegally entering someone else's premises, "Thank you, Smith. I'll tell Ting what a help you've been."

"I won't wait, then. If you need anything else, or just want some company, punch my number. We're here to serve." He winked and swung off down the hall and around the corner before Ella had enough presence of mind to get out of the other woman's doorway and close the door firmly behind her.

God, what was she doing here? *Never mind, Bradley; don't answer that.* She knew exactly what she was doing. What disquieted her was that young Peck Smith seemed to know, too, and didn't care. Or did care, rather, but cared to aid and abet. Things would never again be quite the same between Taylor McLeod and herself. Not now that she knew more than she'd ever have wanted confirmed about his work. . . .

For there to be the awkward moment she was envisioning between them, she'd have to survive this insanity she had in mind. She could, she supposed, have detailed the fine young man Taylor had loaned her to do the dirty work for her. He would have been glad to oblige, without a blinked eye or even a hesitation.

But she didn't want to betray Yates' confidence any more than she already had. Yates and Yesilkov were adamant that no one be brought in to this. If she called Peck Smith again, it would be to get any or all of their party out of jail, or off Sky Devon sans hot pursuit.

It was only for such exigencies that McLeod had loaned her the man. They'd discussed it obliquely, and the bounds of their agreement were clear: she would do what she thought necessary, and only if she failed would McLeod take direct action on his own. In return for this admittedly chancy hesitation on his part, she was to come to him directly with specifics, once she learned them.

McLeod's voice had been dry and precise as he'd said over the coded Earth/Moon link, "Of course, what matters to us ultimately is *who*. Some proof of what, where, when, and why would be nice, certainly, but I doubt this thing will go public . . . at least not through my office. We would, however, appreciate—"

"The culprits, yes. Well, I wouldn't know what to do with them if I had them," she'd said. "Yesilkov and Yates, however, might have some objections."

A chuckle had come up from Earth. "I have a feeling your friends are going to find themselves well out of their depths, and soon. Not with the culprits, as you call them, but with the people behind them—the men that pay the bills."

"You'll take Yates and Yesilkov into consideration, then?"

"I have no choice. They're in this up to their collar tabs. I'll guarantee their anonymity if they allow me room to move, but you'll have to reach them and explain. A trail of mayhem won't be easy to cover, and that's what those types tend to do. That's why I'm not arguing with you—I need you to establish some viable guidelines, a chain of command."

You need me? How lovely. You need someone on the scene, and I'm it. It's almost romantic, nearly exciting, she'd heard herself thinking. It wasn't either, of course, but neither was it excessively foolhardy in Taylor McLeod's opinion. Which in itself was strange; she'd made him promise before she filled him in not to argue about her participation, because she'd been nearly sure he would. Whatever McLeod perceived in this as advantageous to himself, it was sufficient to keep him from telling her not to go.

But she'd underestimated the thoughtful, low-key man on the other end of her com line. Or the seriousness with which he took all this business about the Plan and some Club and the viruses that could be tailored to suit and unleashed on a timetable.

Whatever, she now had "All my support, everything we can do to help. Just ask. And my best wishes. Do be careful, Elinor. If it wouldn't take too long despite every string I can pull, I'd ask you to wait for me. But it would, and I can't."

There had been a longer pause than the number of nanoseconds between Earth and Moon could account for, before she said, "Taylor, you're wonderful."

Again the chuckle. "You're pretty wonderful yourself. Go give 'em, hell, Dr. Bradley. And don't worry about picking up the pieces—that's what my men are for."

She'd rung off, and realized that her heart was pounding. It was rather like the old days in North Africa, when there'd been a clear division between right and wrong and she'd exceeded her brief, on occasion, because the real world has nothing to do with channels and paper flow and command trees.

If she hadn't known McLeod from those days, she wouldn't be standing here now, inside Kathleen Spenser's Sky Devon apartment, lurking in the dark like a mugger.

But she was. Waiting, she began to have second thoughts. She shouldn't be here. This wasn't helping to smuggle a defector across the Algerian border or helping to get an ANC dissident out of a South African jail. This was a one-on-one confrontation with a desperate enemy; it had nothing to do with what color one's passport was or how many friendlies in convenient embassies or film crews one knew.

This could be dangerous. She should have asked Peck

Smith to stay. But what she had in mind wasn't something she really wanted anyone to see, especially not someone who was being daring and modern and egalitarian by dropping the hyphen from his name.

She could have had Peck Smith's help; she'd known that once he'd picked Spenser's lock for her. But then she'd been thinking that the man would, of necessity, have had to file a report, if only verbally to McLeod.

And she didn't want Taylor McLeod to know that she'd brought proscribed substances in the form of truth drugs, as well as the needle stunner, through customs. She especially didn't want him to know what she intended to do with them. It just wasn't ladylike, and like the darker side of his own work, it ought not to be discussed or even acknowledged between them.

Just as she was beginning to lose her resolve and thinking that she might call Peck Smith, that this was no time to worry about what Taylor thought of her, she heard a sound outside the apartment door.

She pushed herself back against the wall as if she could melt into it, the stunner grasped tightly in one sweaty hand. For the first time in what seemed like hours, she thought about Sam Yates, Yesilkov, and the poor dead people from Le Moulin Rouge.

Dead Arabs—those she'd seen, and the seemingly countless corollary casualties that had come after. All a test, if what Yesilkov had learned from Piet van Zell could be believed.

All this woman's handiwork, if the person now opening this door was indeed Kathleen Spenser. And all the frustration in Ella Bradley, who'd joined the Peace Corps and later the UN, and finally NYU because of her humanitarian bent and a genuine desire to promote equality and understanding where equality was impossible—all that frustration surfaced as the person came through the door and hit the light switch.

It was Kathleen Spenser; the face matched the image Yates had shown her in his holotank. She was alone. As the other woman started to close the door, Ella Bradley stepped away from the wall, out from behind the door, and said: "Please stand very still. I'll close the door. You drop your pocketbook and hold your hands away from your body. I want to know where Yates and Yesilkov are, and I want to know now.''

''What the hell?'' said the doctor named Spenser, one hand reaching for her throat.

Spasmodically, at the other woman's movement, Ella Bradley's finger squeezed the trigger of the stunner, and with a little cry, Kathleen Spenser toppled backward.

Chapter 27

HEAD GAMES

Sam Yates didn't at first remember, as he awoke, what was wrong. He couldn't roll over; his arms and legs were tangled up in his bedcovers. Yeah, that must be it, because he was cold too. Naked and cold.

And then he did remember, and lunged against his bonds, driving the raw flesh at his elbows, wrists, and ankles against the vacuum tape that restrained them. It hurt like hell.

He opened his eyes, hoping against hope he was coming out of the worst drunk of his life in some nice padded holding cell somewhere. Hoping that what he remembered wasn't true.

But it was. There, naked and tied to the chair opposite him, was Yesilkov, her head thrown back, livid bruises and taser burns on her bare breasts and belly. He called her name, but it came out from behind his taped lips as nothing more than an animal moan.

Their interrogator was concentrating on Yesilkov now. Yates could see her flesh quiver as de Kuyper moved close. Yesilkov's body was trying to cringe from the taser and the knife the Afrikaner held, but she'd been bound by an expert.

A practiced interrogator such as de Kuyper could bring a stronger personality than Yesilkov's under his control.

Yates struggled wildly, but managed only to rock his chair slightly. This got Yesilkov's attention, but not de Kuyper's.

The big Afrikaner slapped the woman's cheek with a backhanded motion that sent sympathetic trauma down the side of Yates' face and into his aching neck.

Sonya Yesilkov sobbed once, then straightened, looking

not at de Kuyper but at Yates, defiant, her lips puffy but tightly closed.

They'd been lying there on the floor and de Kuyper had been cutting at Yesilkov's crotch and Yates had tried to get the man to stop. . . . He closed his eyes, remembering how he'd shouted for de Kuyper to stop.

And how he'd told Yesilkov, "Don't tell him anything. He's just going to kill us anyhow, or he'd be more careful. Man's going to let you go, he doesn't slice your clothes up—"

Smack went de Kuyper's backhand, but it had gotten that taser away from Yesilkov's quivering inner thighs. For the moment.

He hadn't saved them anything—nothing real important, at least. Their clothes were now piled neatly on Spenser's desk, the only positive result of Yates' attempt to draw de Kuyper's attention from Yesilkov to himself.

In answer to Yates, Jan de Kuyper had pulled on his nose ruminatively and said, "You're wrong, Supervisor—I'll let you go, both of you, as soon as you tell me what I want to know." And he'd grinned then, as he came forward with a knockout ampule Yates couldn't avoid.

Once it pierced his skin, the room began to spin. He'd been barely aware of de Kuyper explaining to Sonya that if she were a good girl and took her own clothes off without any false moves, de Kuyper might let her strip Yates for him.

So that was how Yates had come to be tied to this chair. Adrenaline goosed him as he realized that he had no way of determining what, if anything, Yesilkov had divulged to de Kuyper. Like he had no way of stopping the torture progressing before his eyes.

Keep 'em closed as long as you can, he warned himself. But even through his tight-shut lids he fancied he could see Yesilkov's flesh as it tried to flinch away from the taser shocking her genitals.

Maybe Yesilkov hadn't said anything. Or maybe de Kuyper wasn't satisfied with what she'd told him. The Afrikaner wasn't going to buy the fact that Yates and Yesilkov were here without any sort of official backing—no brief, no portfolio, no support structure on Sky Devon. Any more than he'd buy that Yates was exactly what his credentials said—Entry, nothing heavier. Not from some acronymous government organization or rival terrorist group. It wasn't sensible, so de Kuyper was going to keep digging until he forced the information he wanted to hear from Yesilkov.

Or from Yates. Yates' eyes snapped open of their own accord. Now he understood why Yesilkov looked like that. The Afrikaner wasn't going to give up until he heard what he wanted to hear, and Yesilkov didn't know what to tell him.

Yates was going to volunteer. He thrashed as noisily as he could in his chair, suddenly conscious of his own nakedness and vulnerability.

A few feet away Yesilkov was emitting strangled screams as the taser shocked her. Her knees, Yates now noticed, were taped to the arms of the chair to keep them open.

When de Kuyper finally turned to Sam Yates, the security man wasn't even aware that he was yelling through his gag at the top of his lungs.

He just wanted to make it stop, to deflect the Afrikaner to another target besides Yesilkov, who wouldn't be in this if it weren't for him.

He no longer harbored any illusions about the two of them surviving this interrogation. You didn't do to a prisoner what de Kuyper was doing to Yesilkov unless you were going to imprison or kill that individual out of hand. And de Kuyper couldn't have facilities on Sky Devon to keep Yesilkov in this condition semipermanently.

This sort of thing only happened to people who "disappeared," in the time-honored usage of the word.

And de Kuyper, now stalking over to him with a pink-stained knife in one hand and the taser in the other, was having too much fun with Yesilkov to let up any time soon. Not soon enough for her to survive.

Yates was ready and willing to make a deal. He tried to shout his intention to de Kuyper, but he couldn't form words with his lips taped.

The arid eyes of the Afrikaner met his and the big man said, "So? Nice of you to join us, whoever you are. I've been hoping you would. Do you know, by any chance, what would be the result if you and Yesilkov were"—he smiled a carnivore's smile—"connected, let's say, when the taser touched her wet cunt? By means of your tongue, perhaps, or your lips? Or some other part of you?"

Jan de Kuyper was fondling the taser at eye level, and Sam Yates couldn't help but fix on it. His eyes were fastened to it as if someone had taped them to the taser with the same viciously adhesive material that bound his elbow, wrists and ankles.

As de Kuyper lowered the taser toward Yates' crotch, very slowly and deliberately, Yates shouted again: "I'll tell you anything you want to know, damn it. Just stop!"

Yates thought it was incomprehensible, but it must not have been, for de Kuyper chuckled like a gagging cat and said, "I know you will, I know you will—when I get through with you, you'll do anything I say. And you will not dare to lie."

Inexorably the taser came closer, and Yates craned his neck, forcing himself back against the chair he was tied to, every inch of him desperate to escape, while in the background, out of sight and nearly out of mind, Yesilkov sobbed softly.

Chapter 28

BACK CHANNEL

The plastic body of the needle stunner was as warm as Ella Bradley's hand, but its weight kept forcing her to remember that she held it. Batteries, high frequency oscillator and coils to charge and spit out the bipolar needles . . . the needles themselves.

She couldn't remember anything hurting her as much as the needles that knocked her down in her own apartment. White pain fluctuating from her abdomen had made her legs numb and her arms thrash. She would have screamed as the bearded Afrikaner bent toward her with the drug injector, but her shuddering chest could not pass enough air through her vocal cords to make the sounds.

Ella shuddered again. Her mind slipped back to the present, where her left hand reached forward with a lamp glowing deep amber, and her right foot was poised to step over a trio of heavy conduits blackened with the slime that migrated to the lowest levels of Sky Devon. She took the step.

The man who had shot her was dead. His companions were dead. And the two people whom Ella Bradley had involved in this . . . terror, were going to die if she froze or failed.

Her mind threw her the image of Sonya Yesilkov, spread-eagled on a laboratory table—her bloody scalp in the hands of a bearded man, and Dr. Spenser peering attentively at the twenty feet of intestine she had uncoiled from Yesilkov's belly.

The vision was bad enough without the instinctive flush of pleasure that followed it. Ella's face prickled with embarrassment—though no one could have seen the inside of her mind, and she knew perfectly well that it was the sort of thought that occurred to even the most civilized people.

Under certain conditions of rivalry.

She *really* didn't want to think about that. Which was good, because the confused emotions gave her the energy that she needed to clamber through the dark recesses of Sky Devon under an apparent gravity much higher than that of the Moon.

She was not especially frightened by what would happen when she reached her destination, because she hadn't been able to imagine that scene in terms even she could believe were realistic.

The hope to which Ella clung was that she could not possibly fail to find the Pest Control Research Laboratory if she continued to grope in the proper direction through the bilges of Sky Devon. She had gotten to the proper segment, number 9; and she had found the access door beneath the transit platform and opened it with the mechanical key—stamped MAINT.—which Spenser had surrendered to her.

But the hundred meters or so that she had to grope along the habitat's lowest level was much farther in reality than she had expected it to be.

The huge ducts to either side of Ella channeled her progress as surely as the walls of a tunnel. One of them was silent, but the other coughed and rattled hugely at regular intervals. She guessed that it shifted solid material—produce, judging from the duct's size and the fact that its contents were not being moved in a water suspension, as wastes would be.

She could not miss the lab in this linear waste of darkness, stale air, and the effluvia which dripped down from even the most rigidly-attended activities on the higher levels. She had to believe in the certainty of success, or she would hunch down into a fetal ball and let the terrible memories cover her.

Because the darkness was so complete, what Ella first saw in front of her was the reflection of her glow lamp rather than the looming wall on which the daub of yellow light appeared. She thrust the needle stunner out in front of her but did not fire. The motion was instinctive, but the reasoning portion of the anthropologist's mind analyzed it as soon as momentary paralysis passed. She was using the gun as a hard object with which to fend off whatever was approaching in the darkness—

And nothing was approaching. She had reached the wall of the laboratory, her destination.

Something thundered like an express train through the duct to Ella's right as she paused to examine the wall of aluminum sheet/glass sponge sandwich. She had brought the tiny glow lamp in fear that a brighter light would expose her to workers on their ordinary duties, as well to de Kuyper and others of Spenser's associates. She had not expected the bottom level of the habitat to be so unpopulated.

And she could not have conceived anyplace being this dark.

The glow lamp showed nothing, not even shapes, more than arm's length from its bioluminescent surface, so it was only by sidling across the face of the wall that Ella could examine it.

Many of the smaller ducts and conduits that had made her footing doubtful disappeared into the barrier. One torso-thick pipe was painted blue. The coding meant nothing to her, nothing certain to anyone from outside Sky Devon—but the access plate near the wall had not been dogged down properly after the last time it was removed. A draft of air, clean-smelling and rather warm in this environment, drew her attention to the line.

The handle attached to the panel beneath looked so normal in the context that Ella did not immediately realize that it was what she was searching for. She touched it—bent tube stock, the ends flattened and glued to the paneling—and tugged it gingerly toward her with the hand that held the light.

Nothing moved.

Idiot! There had to be a catch, a fastener.

A simple draw bolt was mounted a few centimeters under the handle. Ella slid it open; set her glow lamp on the floor with a delicacy instinctive even in these circumstances; and poised, her left hand on the handle, and the needle stunner held vertically beside her right cheek.

She had to remember that the gun *shot* things out—that it wasn't simply a bludgeon of dense plastic. She *knew* how to use the stunner properly, if not expertly; but if the wrong reflexes took over in a crisis, she would fail.

Also, she would die.

Ella squeezed her eyes shut, then opened them and tugged at the door handle with all her strength. The lower edge of the panel scrunched slightly, but it pivoted outward without serious binding. De Kuyper was an expert craftsman, and he had used as much skill in executing this project of his own as he would have if it were part of his regular employment.

The other side of the opening was an office. The muted lights in the molding were on automatically because a human being was in the room. The effect on Ella's dark-adapted eyes was equivalent to stepping from a cave into sunlight.

She sneezed.

"Mmmh!" grunted Sam Yates in response.

The big security man was seated in the chair within arm's reach of Ella as she pointed the stunner through the opening with an earnestness meant to atone for her initial stumble.

Yates had been stripped, and no effort of which his muscles were capable had been sufficient to affect his bonds. The Afrikaner had immobilized his prisoners with cargo tape, designed to strap payloads onto the barges which ferried produce from Sky Devon across the human universe.

Nor had de Kuyper made the amateur's mistake of using a piece of furniture as an integral part of the bonds. Yates' ankles were taped together, his wrists were taped together and a third length of tape connected his wrists and ankles. Only then was a loop thrown around his torso and the chair back to anchor him there. Even if the security man had been able to dismantle the chair, he would have been no closer to freedom or mobility.

Yesilkov was similarly strapped into the visitors' chair across the desk.

The office door was open. Through it Ella saw the corner of a laboratory bench and banks of data processing equipment against the wall beyond. She could not see or hear anyone else in the lab, but the lights were on. Clumsily—her eyes were glued on the doorway and her right arm held the stunner out as stiffly as a girder—she stepped through the square opening into Spenser's office.

Ella's fingernails were long enough to be awkward when she keyed data into her computers, but now they lifted the end of the tape over Yates' mouth enough to give her fingers purchase.

She'd had first-aid training years before in the belief that anyone who planned to study nonstandard human societies had better not count on the medical facilities taken for granted by those who remained in the more civilized areas of Earth. It stood her in good stead now as she jerked the tape away with a single crisp motion that isolated the pain instead of spreading it excruciatingly across a cautious pull.

It was only after the motion was complete that she realized what would have happened if the prisoner's mouth were closed by the same cargo tape that bound his limbs. Adhesive meant to anchor pallets of cargo against rocket thrust would have lifted the skin from Yates' face.

There wasn't any problem. The prisoners would have been useless to de Kuyper if he could not free them to talk himself; and no one talks usefully when his mouth gurgles with blood from his flayed lips.

"He's out there," Yates whispered, gesturing toward the lab with a toss of his head. "He's waiting by the air lock to let Spenser in."

"She's not coming," Ella said grimly as she reached toward the strap holding the security man's ankles together.

The anthropologist had expected her fellows to be tied, not taped, but she knew there was no likelihood she could quickly unknot ropes a strong man had tied. The steak knife she carried in her purse was perfectly satisfactory for her present need.

The button on the handle was awkward, because her left hand wasn't practiced with the tool. Nonetheless, she pressed the button on the side of the handle with her index finger so that the blade snicked out from between its ceramic guards, giving its edge a sharpening touch as it did so.

Ella sawed, her tongue set grimly, and lurched against

Yates as the tough reinforcements finally parted beneath her blade.

"The wrists," said the security man in a low voice; but instead, Ella cut away in two quick passes the strap holding Yates to the chair. She was afraid to cut close to the man when she knew she was clumsy. The tape required more effort to cut than the prisoner's flesh would if she slipped.

The captives' clothing was stacked on a corner of the desk with a neatness that seemed typical of de Kuyper. Maybe she would feel less awkward when her companions were dressed again. . . .

Yates determinedly stretched his arms out behind him. "My *wrists*," he repeated.

"*Mmmm!*" said Sonya Yesilkov as the Afrikaner walked back into the office.

De Kuyper was even more startled than Ella Bradley, for she at least had known consciously that the Afrikaner was nearby. He had the better reflexes for the situation, though. He launched himself without hesitation toward the startled woman.

The knife he had brought into the office for other purposes was open in his hand, while Ella's fingers could neither swing the stunner on target nor squeeze its trigger.

Sonya Yesilkov thrust herself and the chair to which she was strapped, pushing against the desk with her bare toes. Her shoulder slammed de Kuyper in the stomach as he started to leap the desk.

"*Shoot! Shoot!*" screamed Yates, rising to lift his bound arms off the chair back. He teetered, unable to spread his legs.

Ella braced herself, staring at the gun with both eyes. It expanded into a black blur. All sound paused. There was only motion and stray color beyond the fuzzy outline of the weapon. She shot at empty air, and the world locked into normal focus again.

Yesilkov had tangled the Afrikaner with her legs and those of the chair. The two of them crashed into the front of the desk and both fell to the floor.

She couldn't hold him. De Kuyper pushed himself away

with three limbs and stabbed with the knife in his right hand, a motion as instinctive as the disemboweling stroke a leopard makes with its clawed hind legs.

The point sank a half-inch deep in the plastic chair back and stuck there. De Kuyper rose with his teeth bared in savage intention. The needle that Ella Bradley triggered by sheer willpower snapped into the shell of the Afrikaner's right ear.

Nerve spasms flung de Kuyper across the room. The instant effect was that of being slapped in the head by a heavyweight boxer.

Slapped, not punched. There were too few nerve endings in the skin and cartilage where the needle glittered to transmit the full paralyzing charge that a solid hit could deliver.

Ella squeezed the trigger again and shot three more needles out the empty doorway.

Yesilkov was making smothered squalls like those of a cat in a bag. She could see there was no one in the doorway through which the needles sparked, but the desk blocked her sight of her fellows. She couldn't even twist her head far enough to see de Kuyper behind her.

"*Mmmm!*"

She didn't know about the knife sticking into the chair back that had saved her life; but anyway, that was the risk you took when you jumped an armed man.

"At *him!*" Yates cried. He was unable to hold his balance any longer, but he managed to teeter across the top of the desk instead of falling onto the floor in back of it.

Ella swung the gun with a forcefulness more fitting for an eight-kilo hammer. She fired again. The needle shattered in a purple nimbus on a filing cabinet along the sidewall.

Jan de Kuyper was half blind, and the pain that wracked the side of his head was no less real for being superficial. He *knew* needle stunners and knew that the effect would wear off in another ten or twenty seconds.

But he also knew that he was cold meat if he tried to grapple with the shooter immediately—even with a clown like the frozen-faced woman he saw through curtains of dazzling pain. He bolted for the door to the lab.

Yesilkov kicked at the Afrikaner as he jumped past her,

but her bare feet only brushed his pants's leg. "Mmh!" she grunted as Yates shouted, "That's right, that's—"

De Kuyper leaped out of the office. Ella Bradley's arm traversed like a gun turret while her index finger squeezed down on the trigger and needles clicked and bounced at waist height from the front wall. It was the same motion that Steeks had used to paralyze her while she struggled in her apartment.

The momentary hesitation when de Kuyper changed the direction of his flight meant that a needle buried itself near the base of the Afrikaner's spine even as he slid for cover behind the laboratory bench.

"You *got* him!" Yates shouted, sprawling across the desk like a hog trussed for slaughter. "My hands! Free my hands!"

Ella hadn't dropped the steak knife, though for a moment she didn't remember that or even remember that the tool existed. De Kuyper was howling somewhere out of sight. She did not know whether the thump of equipment she heard meant the Afrikaner was getting a weapon of his own or just thrashing wildly.

Deliberately, because the seconds of panic had burned away all ordinary fear and left Ella's intellect in full control, she set the stunner down on the desktop and switched the knife to her right hand—the blade snicked in and out of its guards as her right thumb replaced her left index finger on the button.

It was more important that she free the security man quickly and safely than that she stare over the sights of a gun she didn't understand toward an empty door through which a killer would return when he was ready.

Her blade slid through the cargo tape with a rustling the razor edge would make in gristle.

"Here," she said, placing the stunner firmly in Yates' hand before the big man was even sure that his wrists were free. "But don't move until I've got your ankles."

She bent to her next task while Yates braced himself on his side, a position as awkward as it was ridiculous for the naked gunman.

"There!" said Ella, and the security man pivoted off the

desk in a motion made easier by the muscles that still had
much of the tone they had gotten in Earth gravity. Ella
stepped around the piece of built-in furniture and reached
the sprawled police lieutenant as Sam Yates fired at the
Afrikaner, who had just wormed his way into sight.

De Kuyper fired back with a plasma discharger.

Sam Yates' needle spattered harmlessly on the dense glass
of the laboratory bench, but perhaps the wicked sound of
it startled the Afrikaner into squeezing his own trigger a
millisecond early. Yates' hair stood up and his bare left side
prickled in an echo of injuries still unhealed, but it was the
back wall of the office and not his torso that exploded in a
ball of flame.

Ella moved with programmed precision. She slashed the
strap between Yesilkov's wrists and ankles, then freed the
wrists from one another. The desktop protected both women
from the globe of vaporized glass and metal, but the anthropologist's knife hand did not even twitch at the flash
and bang.

She was fully committed to her task. By focusing herself
completely within that compartment of her mind—doing
something that was necessary and which she understood—
the anthropologist could relegate all other occurrences into
things glimpsed in the news from distant countries.

Ella reached for the security lieutenant's ankles. Before
she could sever the tape there, Yesilkov kicked with both
feet together and slammed the office door onto another
plasma bolt. The panel was two sheets of thin titanium,
hollow within except for the struts from corner to corner to
stiffen it. The outer panel vaporized. The inner bulged and
bounced back on its hinges as if kicked by someone hugely
stonger than a human.

Yesilkov snatched the steak knife away from Ella and cut
her own legs free. The chair was still strapped to her back,
and her mouth was taped.

Sam Yates had dived out of the doorway in reaction to
the first plasma bolt, though it was past him and crashing
coruscance on the far wall before his brain told his body to
move. The fireball congealed, some of it across his back
and shoulders. When he hit the floor beside the two women,

the sheet of redeposited glass shivered off again in flakes and shards as his muscles flexed.

They weren't going to win a slugfest against a plasma discharger in the hands of a man who knew how to use it. The gun frightened Yates, and the aging, incredibly tough Afrikaner who wielded it scared the security man even more. De Kuyper had taken a couple stun needles. From the broken-backed way he squirmed out from behind the bench, his legs were probably paralyzed.

He was still going to cook the three of 'em alive if they hung around much longer.

Yesilkov was freeing herself from the chair. Ella Bradley hunched over something between the desk and the filing cabinets.

"Come *on* and keep *low*!" Yates said as he kicked the lower edge of the door to close it again.

The titanium glowed white where it bulged, radiating heat fiercely into the office, but the sheet a meter below the plasma's impact was still at room temperature. Much of the outer door panel was gone, but the hollow core and titanium's high melting point preserved the inner surface as a barrier against another shot.

Which enveloped the front of the office as the trio, protected by the desk, crawled toward the opening in the rear wall.

"*Run!*" screamed Sam Yates to his companions as he stood and fired his needle stunner back through the inferno of burned air and burning metal.

The top half of the door was gone, and beside it a meter-wide semicircle of the wall. Carpeting had melted, and the wall finish had become hot enough to sparkle with low, sooty flames. Where the door had been, brown gases and heat waves turned the air into a translucent curtain through which the lab bench was a wobbly shadow and the gunman beside it invisible.

But the incandescent bore of the plasma discharger was a glaring point of aim for the security man. He snapped toward it the three needles remaining in his weapon's magazine.

Jumping bolt upright had been crazy—he could have

peered over the desktop and fired with as much effect. It'd seemed the right thing to do at the time.

All Sam Yates could think about now was the way his bare cock swung in the air with *nothing* between it and the next jet of plasma.

"Run!" he repeated at a higher pitch than before as he turned, ducking toward the gap where de Kuyper's first shot had widened the opening of the hinged panel. The two women, the *idiots*, had halted just the other side of the wall.

Yesilkov had jumped past when Ella Bradley shifted her bundle, before she swung her leg up and through the hidden door. The plasma bolt didn't penetrate far, but its energy had devoured part of the air duct that served the office. The individual fan, most of its motor, and the associated resistance heaters were gone. They'd protected the resin-cased packet with a data window and a caged button lying behind them in the duct.

When the security lieutenant paused in the doorway, Ella bumped past her more firmly than necessary. "What are you *doing*?" she cried to the naked woman.

"Look!" said Yesilkov, but it didn't look like anything even when Yesilkov flipped the cage away from the packet's button and the window began to flash the digits 30 in red light.

"Run!" Sam Yates was saying as he bowled into them. He grabbed Ella's upper arm fiercely and dropped the stunner in order to reach for the blond woman.

Yesilkov swayed away from the big man long enough to slap the button with her palm. The digits switched to 29 as Yates propelled the three of them into the darkness. Unlike the women, his muscles still regarded a half G as low gravity.

"Maybe I hit—" Yates said, and the room behind them blazed with a plasma bolt which disproved the hope before he had time to fully utter it. This time the blast was echoed by high-voltage arcs. The Afrikaner had hit the desk, and the power lines feeding its circuits were shorting across the fireball of conductive ions.

The security man sprawled, throwing his companions down to either side of him. The plasma bolts had been so dazzlingly bright that the light from the office behind them did them no good.

When they fell, Ella freed herself from a grip that was as needless as it was insulting. She slipped to one knee again immediately—the conduits had tripped them the first time—but she struggled up determinedly and stayed half a step ahead of her companions. They would all be filthy when they reached the access shaft, but that shouldn't be a crucial problem.

Not like being stark naked would have been.

"I have . . . your clothes," she said, breaking the sentence when she almost lost her footing.

Yates jostled into her, keeping the anthropologist upright by accident as they stumbled along. "Huh?" he said.

As Ella opened her mouth to speak, the blond woman fell with a greasy smack and a shouted curse that proved she'd pulled the tape away from her mouth. "No, *run*," she said, leaping to her feet before the man could help her. "He'd demo-charged Spenser's office, and I just pushed the timer. Maybe"—another bellowed curse—"maybe the bastard'll be inside when it—"

"Here's—" Ella began. Her eyes had readapted enough that the door at the base of the access shaft was a lighted rectangle, though it didn't illuminate the few meters between itself and the escapees.

There was a thump. Air slammed the trio down as it rushed back the way they had fled.

The lower level of Sky Devon blazed with deep red light so intense that it covered the volcanic explosion that gave it birth.

Jan de Kuyper's instructions were to ensure the destruction not only of the project director but of every bit of equipment, data, and virus pertaining to the project as soon as the Club had what it needed. The Afrikaner had never been one to underperform a task of that sort.

The directed charges placed around the walls and in the ceiling of the sealed laboratory compressed everything within into a ball of superheated gas. The blast with which the gas reexpanded ripped a hole into the sunlit level above and seared the backs of the three escapees even though they were lying flat and a hundred meters away.

"God," said Sam Yates.

At first Ella thought he had whispered, but she realized that only a shout could have been heard through the ringing of her ears. "Your clothes," she said. "We have to get away from here."

There was light again, through the bulged roof and from insulation and organic matter smoldering closer to the center of the explosion.

"God," repeated Sam Yates as he and Yesilkov numbly began to dress over the tags of cargo tape that still clung to them.

Ella wished she had something to do with her hands also. It would have taken her mind off what she was sure was the smell of Jan de Kuyper, incinerated by the blast he had prepared himself.

Chapter 29

A LITTLE HELP FROM
MY FRIENDS

"God," Yates said again, this time with a pejorative tinge to his voice.

They'd been moving fast, away from the explosion in no certain direction, here where none of them knew their way around. Yesilkov had patched up the torn crotch of her pants with scraps of cargo tape.

Ella didn't care to know how those pants had gotten that way—what she'd seen of Yesilkov's condition had been more than sufficiently abhorrent.

Appalling, really, this whole thing was. And now when she'd only said to Sam, "I've got a friend up here—Taylor does—who'll get us fresh clothes and out without asking—" Yates had interrupted with that cold disgusted look that shot between him and Yesilkov, a disparaging shake of his head, and the single spoken word.

"God," he said again, leaning against a corridor wall, his chest heaving and sweat running down his flaring jaw, "that's all we need—your friends. Who the fuck's Taylor, anyway?"

"Taylor McLeod," Yesilkov said before Ella could respond, a derisive, I-told-you-we-couldn't-trust-her implication in her voice. Yesilkov, too, was winded. Her chest was heaving. Her breasts didn't seem so saggy with her uniform shirt over them. But the bruises Ella had seen there seemed to shine through the intervening cloth, somehow.

"That's right," Ella blurted defensively. "A little help from my friends won't hurt. We obviously need all the help we can get. We're somewhere—none of us know exactly where—in Sky Devon's corridor system, and we don't know

even where we're going; there's just been an explosion to
which we're party. Spenser is—''

"I don't know 'bout you, honey, but Spenser's where
I'm goin'. Now." Yesilkov straightened with a wince as
her hands went to her hips.

Sam Yates was still watching Ella in the indirectly lit
corridor as if the light were too bright for his eyes. Ella
said "Sam . . ." pleadingly, hoping for understanding.
"McLeod just detailed a man to me, somebody with some
clout here. All he wants in return is—''

"Not now, Bradley, okay?" Yates told her, and then
reached out to touch Yesilkov's shoulder. "You all right,
Sonya? You up to this?"

Ella had no idea what "this" the two of them were discussing, but it was serious.

"I'm okay, Sam. No sweat. I'll meet you back at the
colony when I'm done. But I don't want *her* smarmy friends
'helping' me or feeling they've got the right to debrief me
afterward. I—''

"Ella, tell me you didn't fill this guy in on us."

"I didn't, Sam, honestly I—'' Why did she feel so defen-
sive? She'd just been trying to help, to save their lives. She
had saved their lives, damn it, and they were treating her
as if she'd betrayed them.

Yates didn't even give her time to finish her sentence.
"Go on, Sonya, go."

"Right, don't worry about hardware—I'll use what's at
hand," Yesilkov responded, her fingers going to her shoulder to clutch Yates' there.

Ella Bradley averted her eyes; if the two of them were
going to embrace, she didn't have to watch it. A hot flush
crawled up her neck: here she was, in the middle of chaos,
in the aftermath of an explosion that could very well have
killed them, and what bothered her the most was whether
Sam Yates was going to kiss that Slavic cow.

Whether they did or not, she didn't see. She did see
Yesilkov swing off down the corridor as if she knew where
she was going—how to get to Spenser's from here.

And Yates was saying, "Now, let's talk about this 'friend'
of Taylor McLeod's—who he is, how much he knows, how

much McLeod knows.'' There was a severity in his voice
that made Ella retreat three paces, until her back hit the
corridor wall.

''Sam Yates,'' she said, blinking back surprising tears,
''how dare you talk to me this way? Taylor only wants to
know who's at the bottom of this—who's calling the shots.
He thinks you'll be out of your depth with them. And we
need somebody . . . to clean up after the mess you make,
at the very least. You run around killing people and having
firefights and blowing up labs, and then it's me who's out
of line.'' She covered her mouth with her hand and shook
her head, suddenly wordless.

''I should have expected this. You think like a bureaucrat,
an organizational type. You are one. Come on, we're going
back to the Moon. Hopefully without checking in with your
'friend,' whoever—''

''Peck Smith.''

''Of course.'' Yates was even more severe. ''Is that 'Lord
Pecker-Smith,' or will a simple 'sir' do?'' He took her
roughly by the arm and propelled her down the corridor in
Yesilkov's wake.

The other woman was nowhere in sight, and that realization prompted Ella to say, ''Yesilkov's going to Spenser's,
is that so? Why? Spenser's surely on her guard now. We—I
broke in there, used a stunner on her, I—''

''You what?'' Yates laughed out loud. Then sobered.
''We'll be on that shuttle too long to risk Kathleen Spenser
finding out we're passengers—we'd be sitting ducks.''
Around the corner ahead, Ella sighted a lift whose indicator
lights were lit. By its doors was an information routing
plaque, the sort that said YOU ARE HERE beside a blinking
light.

''You didn't answer me, about this Peck-Smith.'' Yates
crossed his arms once he'd hit the elevator's call button.

''You didn't answer me about Spenser. That makes us
even.''

''Oh yeah, I did,'' said Sam Yates with a level stare that
chilled Ella to the bone. ''When we get to a phone, maybe
you ask your hotshot friend to get us a priority booking on
the next Moon-bound shuttle, and an open return ticket for

Yesilkov, so's she doesn't get stuck here if things get complicated. Or doesn't your friendship extend that far?''

Ella Bradley faced Sam Yates squarely. ''If I understand you, what you're implying . . . What do you want me to say to them: this woman Yesilkov's going to commit a felony and we'd like her not to be bothered about it?''

''Yeah, that'll do. Or diplomatic immunity, some shit like that—only if it's necessary, of course. You said that's what Peck-Smith is for—cleanup.''

Not after cold-blooded murderers. But she couldn't say that. With a sick feeling in her stomach, she answered, ''I'll call him and say that it's imperative that your Lieutenant Yesilkov not be detained in any way—not questioned or searched. That's all I'm willing to do.'' She crossed her own arms. She certainly wasn't going on record as an accessory to murder. Taylor wouldn't approve. It just wasn't the way these things were done.

In the main docking hub she'd make the call. Like this corridor, it would be nearly deserted: the explosion had invoked emergency procedures. People were staying away from areas that might be dangerous. She ought to do that herself.

She would have, except that anyplace Sam Yates was could become a danger zone on a moment's notice. She was no safer here with him than she'd been back in the lab with de Kuyper, or than she'd be when she settled into her shuttle seat for the journey back to the Moon.

Chapter 30

COLLISION COURSE

Karel Pretorius rounded the corner into the corridor leading to Kathleen Spenser's apartment with all the savoir faire he'd have displayed were he about to face the Club in all its muscular glory.

He wasn't unaware that Spenser's lab had exploded—it was the talk of the docking hub. As soon as he'd stepped off the inbound shuttle, he'd stepped into a circus of emergency procedures that wouldn't keep a gnat safe on the veldt: nervous security guards; women in fire-retardant suits; civilians gripping emergency breathing apparatus in sweaty hands. As if a nose-mouth unit with an hour's worth of air would save you if Sky Devon puked its life-support into vacuum.

Pretorius was angry, and his stride was quick because of it. He'd come to get the virus for Earth release—*the* virus: not the Arab-killing test batch, but the real thing, the virus that used sickle-cell tendencies as its beachhead; the virus that would free all of Africa of its plague of blacks.

Nothing could be allowed to abort this project. He was withholding judgment until he found out how badly the timetable had been disarrayed by the lab explosion. There was still a chance that the entire matter wasn't a blunder— just Spenser covering her tracks in a ridiculously over-powered fashion. If so, the woman had outlived her useful-ness.

Spenser had done that in any case, he admitted to himself as he reached her door and knocked loudly.

In less than a minute the door opened and Pretorius was

facing not Spenser, but a man—a man in a smock, with a harried look on his face.

"Who're you?"

"Out of my way," Pretorius said, and shouldered by the smaller man in the blue smock.

The force of Pretorius's shoulder physically displaced the lab-coated fellow, and he staggered backward.

There, beyond the man, was Spenser, sitting cross-legged amid the litter of some struggle, dabbing at her nose with a bloody cloth.

Pretorius hardly heard the door close behind him. His quick eyes sorted through the mess and saw strips of cloth, as if Spenser had been bound by—

From behind the smaller man grabbed him by the arm and tried to spin him around. "I said, who are you?" It was not the lab-coat's tone, but his projectile weapon, a Hi-Power that was probably loaded with rubber bullets, that got Pretorius' attention.

Rubber bullets of the sort used on space habitats were deadly.

He said in a rumbling, languid tone meant to diffuse the tension in the other man, "I'm Karel Pretorius, a business associate of Kathleen's."

"Business, my ass," retorted the lab-coat. "You don't know me, I'm just a hired hand, right? Well, you'd better take a good look, friend. I'm the only person left on this project with a shred of—"

Pretorius, as the other man spoke, had reached into his coat pocket. He fired without withdrawing his weapon, a composite kinetic-kill revolver with no metal parts that shot poisoned projectiles illegal under all international conventions, but undetectable by conventional security means.

The lab-coat clutched his gut, even as the report echoed in the small apartment, and crumpled.

Pretorius didn't even wait to make sure he was dead. He turned immediately to Spenser and said, "I assume the Plan is not impaired by what's happened in the lab?" as if he hadn't just killed a man while she watched.

Spenser scrambled awkwardly to a standing position, still dabbing her nose as she screamed, *"Plan! Plan! What Plan?*

There *is* no Plan, not anymore, you racist jackass! It's failed utterly, you fool. Don't you know the lab blew up? Don't you appreciate what that means? I—''

Pretorius didn't wait to hear more. He shot the woman where she stood, again through his coat pocket, and turned to leave.

Somehow, he hadn't heard the door open. So he was shocked when he saw the pale-haired female security guard standing there with a man in expensive civilian clothes who looked unruffled by what the two must just have seen.

Confronted with two possible, and possibly capable, antagonists he hadn't been expecting, Pretorius instinctively started to drag his composite pistol from the pocket of his jacket.

It fouled.

He heard the woman say, "I hope you've seen enough, Smith. I'm makin' my own call."

And then he saw that the woman was wresting a security revolver from the man's hand and pointing it. . . .

Karel Pretorius was still trying to free his pistol from his pocket, or the snagged hammer from the lining of the coat, when a bullet smashed into his forehead, making further effort useless. His dying spasm caused the hammer to come down on the firing pin of his gun, and it went off despite the silk caught on the hammer. The shot discharged into his foot, but Karel Pretorius didn't feel a thing. He was already dead.

PART FOUR

Chapter 31

CRISIS COMMITTEE

"An' then ol' Pecker tells me he don't mind me takin' the original, if y' please, so long's he's got a copy of Pretorius' list to shoot Downside to McLeod's office." Yesilkov grimaced and shook her head, easing gingerly down into one of the chairs opposite the holotank in Yates' office. "Wasn't nothin' I could do about it, Sam, after *she* brought them in on this."

Yesilkov glared archly at Ella Bradley, over by Yates' desk, and Yates couldn't help but follow the security lieutenant's gaze. *Hell of a note, having this case "followed" by the brie-and-Chablis spook set*. Out loud he said, "Well, we weren't complaining when we needed them. I bet you weren't, Sonya, when he handed you that gun at Spenser's, or a ticket out of there right after, no questions asked."

It sounded good, but even Yates didn't believe it. Bradley had complicated things mightily by bringing in her school-tie buddies. The way it made Yesilkov and him feel wasn't the least of it.

And Bradley knew that. She was drifting around Yates' desk, her fingers trailing over its surface as if she were saying good-bye to it. She'd been too quiet, had Bradley, all the way back from Sky Devon. And until Yesilkov walked throught that door, bristly and mean, Bradley had been in some sort of black funk where Yates couldn't seem to reach her.

He really wished Ella would say something—anything. Come to her own defense, to her friends'. Chew Yesilkov out. Whatever. She didn't, though. She just watched her fingers stir the papers on Yates' desk.

Maybe the mess in Spenser's lab got to her worse than I thought. Or Spenser herself . . . It could well have been that, he admitted. And he couldn't blame Ella: they'd gone after Spenser in cold blood, and gotten her. And Ella's precious friend had *helped*. Done a damn fine job of helping. No, he didn't blame her, no matter the repercussions of letting a man like Taylor McLeod have something on you—have a file on you which meant that if he ever asked you to jump, you couldn't even argue about how high.

Water under the bridge, Yates told himself. And he really didn't think it was Ella's fault—she'd done what she thought was right.

But Yesilkov did. "So it's about them and their damned copy," said the security lieutenant when no one else broke the lengthening pause. "I want little Miss Connections here to get on the line to her boyfriend and make sure they don't 'help' us right out of the game. Or into our graves."

"Something Peck Smith said," Ella Bradley spoke suddenly, her voice devoid of inflection, "must have given you the wrong idea, Lieutenant. McLeod hasn't even moved up his return flight—he's not due back for another week. I had a message from him on my answering machine to that effect. So you're jumping to conclusions."

"Yeah, what kinda conclusions?" Yesilkov was rod straight in her chair.

"That his office," Yates put in, uncomfortable enough with the tension to admit he'd better try to defuse it, "will interfere. My guess is, they're happy enough to let us take the weight. They won't come in again unless they're asked—by Bradley. That right, Ella?"

"That's right." This time there was a slightly rising inflection underscoring Ella's words. Her chin raised, she sat primly on the corner of Yates' desk. "I'm sure they'd prefer that you forget Mr. Peck Smith, or that Taylor's office was involved in any way. I know *I* would."

Yesilkov made a face and crossed one booted ankle over her other knee. "Right-o, sport. It's forgotten."

"Come on, you two," said Yates with a sigh. "Sonya, if you'll haul out the damn laundry list that's got you so riled up, maybe we can get down to work." Whatever was on that list, it had caused Smith, as McLeod's representative, to back off while at the same time being uncharacteristically forthcoming. It wasn't usual, from what Yates knew of spooks, for them to get specific about sensitive data they acquired. Or to let other people walk away with that data, to take whatever action those outsiders chose.

Yates had a distinct hunch that if Ella Bradley hadn't been in this up to her pretty neck, neither he nor Yesilkov would have gotten out of Sky Devon alive.

A sidelong glimpse of Ella told him nothing but that the NYU anthropologist was still uneasy. She'd been like that ever since they'd gotten home, though. It wasn't anything Yesilkov had said. . . .

The lieutenant pulled a folded piece of paper out of her breast pocket and leaned forward. The movement of her hand to her breast, the widely crossed legs which gave him a view of her inner thighs, and the slight wince as Yesilkov leaned forward to hand him the piece of paper that she and Peck Smith had found in Karel Pretorius' pocket when they searched the corpse—all of these reminded him of Yesilkov taped to the chair in Spenser's lab while de Kuyper . . .

Yates ran a hand over his jaw before he took the paper Sonya Yesilkov held out with something like wry pride.

He understood how she felt. It had cost them enough. They'd gotten lucky. If the slip of paper hadn't happened to be in Pretorius' pocket, the search for the Club would have dead-ended as soon as Sonya pulled the trigger.

It was bothering the hell out of him, in retrospect, that Peck Smith hadn't tried to stop her from doing that. He'd asked Sonya about it, and she'd said it was her judgment call, and none of Smith's business.

But their eyes had met, and he saw in Yesilkov's a mirror of his own doubts: why hadn't Smith tried to stop Yesilkov from killing their only remaining link to the conspirators?

Nobody had an answer for that one, and all three of them were still alive, so maybe Yates was paranoid. Or maybe, if McLeod's USIA office covered what Yates thought it did, McLeod wanted a quiet resolution to this thing more than he wanted the instigators. For all Yates could prove, McLeod and his peers might have known about the Plan and the Club all along, and just hadn't found a diplomatic way to stop it. Which Yates and Yesilkov had neatly provided, being low types whose actions couldn't be predicted.

So maybe it didn't matter to McLeod and his people whether there was a living link to the Club—maybe what Yates and the two women had done was perceived to be sufficiently disturbing to cause the Club to table the Plan.

Or maybe Taylor McLeod's office didn't really give a damn, beyond protecting a personal friend—Ella Bradley. *God knows, I've seen that before—government types sitting back and letting something illegal and immoral happen because there wasn't a polite way to stop it, and the victims weren't a valuable constituency.*

Yates shelved supposition with an effort—all it was doing was giving him gooseflesh. But he got that way every time he looked at Bradley, who was so damned controlled and seemed almost hostile.

He unfolded the paper Yesilkov handed him. It was the original, in Pretorius' spidery hand, dotted with food stains and feathered at the fold marks. And then he whistled. And blinked. And read the list again. And wondered if maybe he hadn't been a little hard on McLeod's man Peck, and Ella, and even the guy he'd never met whose suit he still had.

"These are some heavyweight players," he said, his voice scratchy.

"Tell me somethin' I don't know," said Yesilkov from her chair.

"Let me see," said Ella from the desk.

Yates was beside the holotank without remembering how he'd come there. He leaned one elbow against it and said, "Come take a look. We might be glad we've got those friends of yours. . . ."

"Yeah, they'll send us fruit baskets once a month the whole time we're in Leavenworth. Or maybe it'll be the prison asteroids. . ." Yesilkov bared her teeth at him cynically.

Bradley hadn't moved from her perch on his desk, so Yates took a chance and read the names out loud. His office was pretty secure—if it wasn't, they were screwed whether he read the names or not. And he wanted to somehow burn the list into reality, make himself believe it by speaking the names out loud.

"What this is," he said for Bradley's benefit, "Is a list Pretorius made of who he knew—and thought—he was working for. Says 'the Plan' in retraced letters. Then, 'the Club.' Then it says: *CERTAIN: al Fahd. LIKELY: Blake/ Lee/Heidigger. ADDITIONAL: eleven. MORE: ??* with two question marks. Seems to me, half of those would be enough—too much, in fact."

And Bradley looked him straight in the eye and murmured, "I told you that Taylor thought you might be out of your depth when you found the instigators. What do you want me to do?"

"*Nothin', fer Chrissake!*" blurted Yesilkov. "Y've done enough."

Bradley's gaze didn't even flicker, but held steady in his. Yates said, "Well, guess we've got to check this out, some-how—check if they're all going somewhere. If I was them, I'd get the hell off Earth before that virus is released—and they probably planned for it. For all we know, they still think the Plan's operational. Or there could be a whole redundant crew of flunkies—another Spenser, another de Kuyper, another Pretorius, another lab, and another batch of virus."

"Jesus," breathed Yesilkov, aghast.

"I agree," said Bradley. "Let's find out if any or all of them have booked extraterrestrial vacations. After all, there's the UN anniversary celebration coming up. . . ."

Yates stared back at the woman who ought not to be this calm, this clever, or this connected, and wondered how he'd ever thought anything involving Ella Bradley could be sim-ple. He flashed that night in her apartment for an instant, and closed his eyes.

When he opened them, she was again watching her own hands fiddle with the mess on his desktop.

Damn good idea, to check the lunar dignitary list for the upcoming bash. And then he asked himself not just why he hadn't thought of it himself, but how come Bradley had beat him to it.

He'd have given anything he owned, right then, to have

had a copy of the message that Taylor McLeod had left on Ella Bradley's answering machine.

When he folded the paper he was holding and looked up, Yesilkov was already striding over to the desk, telling Bradley to "Move, honey. We gotta call in the data pulls for here: who's comin' to the party's definitely a question for Entry Division."

Chapter 32

CLUB OUTING

Mahavishtu called Sakai and the two of them conference-called Heidigger, who in turn phoned Madame Pleyal, the Undersecretary: "The twentieth anniversary commemoration at United Nations Headquarters on Luna demands a prefestivities dinner, Madame. Just the fifteen of us, of course. Al-Fahd suggests that we have that dinner—at his expense, of course—in the best French restaurant on the Moon . . . Le Moulin Rouge. There aren't many vacancies suitable for fifteen people, especially on such short notice. Do you agree and accept?"

Everyone on the conference line held his breath. Then Madame Pleyal's modulated chuckle sounded. "A fine idea, Heidigger. Apt, even. Do thank al-Fahd in my behalf. Say eightish on Monday night?" She rang off.

Over the conference line expelled breaths mingled into a communal sigh of relief. They couldn't have booked a meeting earlier—they were too cautious. Something impromptu, something that seemed like a last-minute proposition, was what was called for. They had much to discuss, the fifteen of them.

And everyone repaired to his own boudoir, in fifteen different earthly nations, to pack for the Club meeting they'd hold at Le Moulin Rouge on the very evening that the virus was to be released on Earth.

All was prepared, or their agent Pretorius would have called. All was in readiness. They packed extensively and for protracted stays.

Some took jewelry, some took gold coinage, some took bearer bonds. All took whatever they might need to ride out any unforseen repercussions, sure in the knowledge that the Earth they were leaving was a very different place from the Earth to which they'd return in two weeks—after the virus had done its work.

"I don't *believe* the nerve of these fuckers," Sonya Yesilkov said, sprawled over both the chairs opposite Yates' desk, gnawing on a stylus and holding the flimsy that had been sent from her office.

The big man was watching her closely; Bradley had gone home to "take a shower." Yesilkov was acutely aware both of her physical position, legs spread, and of Yates, behind his desk.

She'd felt better in her life, but sometimes a little hair of the dog was just the thing. And she needed some warmth, some human touch to chase away the chill that the message she was holding exuded as if it were vacuum frozen. She slid her fingernail down the closure of her blouse, opening it to mid-chest before she continued, "Says here that the Honorable Undersecretary, Madame Pleyal, and her party of *fourteen*, wants the Moulin Rouge freed from its Security seal." She winked at Yates and stretched provocatively, lacing her hands behind her head.

"And since you're the investigating officer," Yates guessed, "they're asking you to vet and free the room."

"That's right, buddy," Yesilkov said, hooking one booted foot on the edge of a chair. *Come on, fella. Take the hint. Or do I have to come to you?* "Want me to let 'em have the room? Strong stomachs, this bunch, if they're who we think—wantin' to have dinner there where they tested the virus in the first place."

"Proves to me that they're the right jokers—anybody else would pick someplace else. And Madame Pleyal can pick anyplace she wants. Only somebody who knew there wasn't any contamination at Le Moulin Rouge would ask for it to be opened up special. . . . "

"Ain't many places'll hold fifteen hotshots up here . . . could be just coincidence." *End my career, and yours, buddy boy, if we jump wrong on this one. Only Bradley'll walk out of it no-fault.* "Excuse me, Madame Undersecre-

tary, but you're under arrest for conspiracy . . ."

If Yates was going to get her killed, or worse—demoted—
the least he could do was fuck her again first. Prove it meant
something, beyond line-of-duty. Because they were both
way beyond the line of duty. If it hadn't been for Bradley's
friend Smith (though Sonya Yesilkov wouldn't admit it on
her deathbed), she might have come home from Sky Devon
in a body bag. Or still be in jail there, in the hands of the
"proper authorities." Of whom, if you wanted to crane
your neck hard enough and squint into the sun to boot,
Undersecretary Pleyal and her playmates were members in
good standing. The Club.

You fucking bet your balls, Yates, they named it right.
Come persuade me I'm not as scared as I ought to be.

But Yates just stared off into space, thinking, his face
grim. He wasn't a bit cute when he looked like that. His
hard face got positively mean looking, what with all those
channels there deepening. He must've been hell on wheels
when he was younger, before he got all broke down, all
right. He was one bad sucker still. . . .

Yesilkov got tired of waiting for Yates to take her hint,
and slid down in her chair. She could get with somebody
else, no sweat, she could. She didn't need Yates, playing
her off against that bubble-bath bimbo. She'd go see what
the guy from—

Yates got up and strode purposefully toward her.

She didn't move to straighten up.

When he stood over her, he didn't reach for her. He said,
"I want you to give them their clearance, Sonya—clear the
room for them, break the Security seal. Then you and I are
going to make sure that they get just the reception they
deserve."

"Oh yeah?"

"Yeah. One that Taylor McLeod's boys aren't going to
be able to use against us, or anybody else. One that's going
to be so hush-hush that any file Bradley got us into is going
to disappear like it never existed."

Pique forgotten, Yesilkov sat upright. "Okay, smart guy,
tell me how."

Sam Yates smiled and his face softened marginally. "You

know, not that I don't trust my own office, but what Bradley said about takin' a shower's left me with a real urge to see how you look wet. And then we can say anything we want, what with the water running, and we'll be sure beyond doubt that nobody's takin' a transcript.''

Oh boy! "You've convinced me, Supervisor." Yesilkov chuckled. "Purely on security grounds, y' understand. What'll it be, your shower or mine?"

Yates laughed. "Last time I looked," he said, "*my* wife was back on Earth. Let's go t' my place, okay?" He held out his hand. She took it and he helped her up. She didn't really need the help, but she appreciated the gentlemanly aspects of Sam Yates.

Appreciated them so much that she said coyly as he let his hand drift to her waist, "Since y'er bein' so nice an' egalitarian an' all, I'm gonna give you this little souvenir I picked up at Sky Devon. Nothin' heavy, y' see, but somethin' I thought I'd hold on to in case old Pecker-Smith got any ideas of usin' what happened to muscle me inta somethin' I'd rather not do. So we'll share it, all right? And what we do with it?"

Yates' hand fell away. He stepped a pace back and regarded her narrowly, the corners of his mouth tight. "What you got, Sonya?"

"I got," she said, reaching beneath the loosened placket of her blouse, "this piece a' jewelry Spenser had on—the one de Kuyper was talkin' about, I'm bettin'. Y' know, the one with the virus inside?"

And she pulled out the crystal phial that hung from her neck on Spenser's gold chain.

Chapter 33

PARTY FAVOR

When he finally got the maintenance supervisor on the phone, Sam Yates' mouth went dry. Guilt by association wasn't good investigative technique. This maintenance supervisor was an Afrikaner, all right; but it didn't necessarily follow that, because of van Zell and de Kuyper and van Rooyan and Malan, every Afrikaner on the Moon had to be involved in the Plan.

Still, it was worth a shot. And Yates had to get this work done by somebody. So he said to the Afrikaner from maintenance, "Supervisor, I'm speaking for Karel Pretorius."

The voice on the other end of the line didn't say "For who?" or "Whozzat?" or even "Who're you?"

The man said, "I see," very cautiously. And waited.

Yates was prayerfully glad he'd decided to do this on the phone rather than in person. He hadn't any idea how these men had communicated their orders, but he couldn't risk being recognized as a hostile player by this one—if the man *was* part of the Plan.

He couldn't risk it because not only was he Sam Yates from Entry, he was the guy who'd been in that firefight on MM corridor. If the man on the other end of the line happened to have been privy to the kidnapping attempt, he might recognize Yates if he saw him. And then the shit would really hit the fan.

The Afrikaner from Maintenance cleared his throat, a cautious prompt.

Yates said, "Yes. You must pick up a package in the transit lounge—in locker three-niner-niner. The contents must be wired into Le Moulin Rouge's circuitry. There's a diagram and a schematic. The Plan requires this. Van Rooyan was supposed to do it, but . . ." he let his voice trail off, hoping the other man couldn't hear his heart pound.

If he wasn't talking to a principle, he was going to hang up on lots of unanswerable questions.

But the man said, "By when must this be done? And how dangerous is it? The Moulin Rouge, she is unsealed? I want double, yes? Delivered in the usual way, after twenty-four hours?"

Those questions, Yates was prepared to handle. All except the last, which wasn't really a question as much as a bargaining position. He didn't barter with the maintenance supervisor. And he didn't sweat the amount he'd agreed to pay or the method of delivery. Within twenty minutes after the job was done, the man would be picked up by Yesilkov's patrols on some trumped-up charge. He told the maintenance supervisor what the Afrikaner needed to know and rang off before he blew it with some slip or other.

Then he put his head in his hands and listened to his heart beat. So far, so good. The maintenance supervisor wasn't a problem. In fact he was, as far as Yates and Yesilkov were concerned, a weapon of sorts. They were going to hold the guy incommunicado, on a drunk & disorderly if they had to, until everything was over. They needed a hole card, somebody alive who knew something about what had happened, in case Taylor McLeod's office decided that anybody who knew about the Plan was too dangerous to stay alive.

He'd tried to explain that to Bradley—that she couldn't trust somebody like McLeod just because he was her friend, when international security was at stake.

She'd laughed in his face.

Well, there was always Yesilkov.

Chapter 34

LE MOULIN ROUGE
REDUX

Dressed in the unifrom of one of Yesilkov's patrol officers, Ella Bradley stood stiffly by the security lieutenant and Sam Yates at the head of the corridor leading to Le Moulin Rouge.

Hide in plain sight. Well, Yates could have been right; it just might work. Among the lunar security detail and private bodyguards here to protect the Undersecretary and her guests, the trio was unremarkable. Part of the status quo. Yesilkov's office had been asked to provide "supplementary" coverage.

At the time the request came in, Yates had wanted to know what they were supplementing.

Now, watching the dignitaries arrive, Yesilkov's answering quip seemed prophetic: "Buncha Saudi hirelings with gold-plated needle stunners—Brits and Frogs and such."

There were plenty of English and French speakers among the plainclothed security men coming and going down the hall. Some had come very early, to "check out" the preparations and the room in which Pleyal and her guests would meet—check it for bugs, check it for unfriendlies, check it for the right silverware and the right sort of help.

Terrorism was what the bodyguards were looking for. Yesilkov had gone to some pains to make sure they wouldn't find anything even mildly troubling. The last thing the trio needed was some overzealous private security chief deciding he had to get into the switching panels.

So they were standing there, before the door marked MAINTENANCE: AUTHORIZED PERSONNEL ONLY. They'd co-opted the room behind that door and thrown together an improvised security headquarters.

But the men in the corridor didn't know that. Only Yesilkov, Yates, and Ella knew that they had monitors in there and virtually undetectable bugging equipment—undetectable because it wasn't powered up, wouldn't be until all the Club members had entered Le Moulin Rouge and the bodyguards were safely locked outside.

For now and for some time to come, it was Yesilkov's show. In her lieutenant's uniform she was the ranking officer in the corridor. The private muscle was trained to interface with people like Yesilkov.

They came up to her and whispered in her ear. They shook her hand. They showed their weapons and their documentation, because they didn't want any trouble with the locals.

Nobody wanted any trouble, Yesilkov included. Yates had approached Ella five minutes earlier and said, "Relax. You look like you're expecting the roof to fall in on you any minute. Think of it as an OPEC or UAR staff meeting—all these guys you see are going to disappear as soon as the pit bulls show up."

"Pit bulls?" she'd asked.

"The regular personal bodyguards. These are just low-level staffers. Once it's clear the place isn't going to blow up and these technical types have vetted the room, all of them will disappear—at least as far as the next corridor, where we've set up a hospitality suite for them. Then the real security types will show up . . . the ones who sleep at the foot of Pleyal's bed, and the like."

"But what's all this for, then? If they'll be vulner—"

"Don't say that. Don't even think it." Yates was very severe today, in his Entry blues. "Watch and see if I'm right."

So she'd been watching, and she was beginning to realize that Yates and Yesilkov knew their business: the crowd in the hallway was starting to disperse.

And through it, like Moses parting the waters, came the first of the alleged club members, a NATO general named Heidigger. Flanking him were two men with whom Ella would not want to tangle, men in impeccable suits with knife-sharp creases in their pants and heavy arms no amount of tailoring could disguise.

Heidigger passed with only a nod to Yesilkov. As he approached Le Moulin Rouge's curtained glass door, the two personal bodyguards peeled off, standing at attention beside three men Ella hadn't noticed before, men holding plasma dischargers.

Yates touched her arm and whispered, "Here comes the dragon lady."

She turned in time to see Madame Pleyal herself, with a complement of guards trailing behind. When the woman with the high-piled hair pinned with jewels had swept by her, Ella caught a whiff of lilac perfume. At the doorway Madame Pleyal's guards executed the same maneuver as the first pair had, waiting with their fellows.

Then came Sakai, recognizable at first by his nut-brown tan and diminutive stature; then, if one knew how to look for it, by his glass eye. Then Lee, full of Oriental stealth, in a magnificent embroidered robe.

There was a hiatus during which Yates brought her attention to the thinning guards in the corridor, saying, "See, off to the hospitality room," with a satisfied smirk, as if he'd just planned a flawless cocktail party.

Then more dignitaries—more Club members—arrived: Perilla, the Portuguese-bred Brazilian; Mahavishtu, whose lips were purple as the circles under his eyes; Blake, blond and Anglo-Saxon, another of the military men; and yet another general among men she didn't recognize, until fourteen guests had arrived.

Down near the door to Le Moulin Rouge, the picked elite guards stood at parade rest, all but the three with the plasma dischargers, who were flanking the door.

These three were ever watchful and didn't even blink when the rest of the guards, in what amounted to loose formation, headed up the corridor, past the waiting trio, on their way to the hospitality suite that the lunar colony had provided.

"Jesus," said Yates, looking at his watch, "what about al-Fahd? He's not here, and by the way those guards stampeded for their feed troughs, he's not coming.''

"That can't be," Ella said with an awful tightness in her throat. The Saudi, al-Fahd, was the only *certain* Club member on the list they'd taken from Pretorius' corpse. Without al-Fahd here, everything they'd planned was then baseless, precipitate action taken on a flimsy basis of supposition and . . . "Well, what do we do?"

"Do?" Yesilkov whispered without moving her lips. "We do just what we was gonna do before. What you think this is, the Cotillion?"

"I think," said Ella, edging closer to Yesilkov as the last of the bodyguards passed her, "that perhaps we should reconsider. It might be that al-Fahd just can't bring himself to have dinner where the virus was first released . . . after all, it's his bloodline that virus was tailored for. But it could be something more—"

"Ella," Sam Yates broke in, "don't have second thoughts, okay? We're committed to this. We're going to record it for posterity starting in"—again he consulted his watch—"three minutes, if Sonya will kindly get her butt in gear. There's no use worrying now."

Ella met Yates' eyes, and they were as flat and shiny as armored panels. She shivered. Beside her, Yesilkov nodded and fished out her key.

The security lieutenant opened the MAINTENANCE door and slipped inside. When she came out, she said, "Okay. We're go. Let's—"

"Look, Sonya," Yates said, "maybe Ella's right, maybe we ought to wait. If al-Fahd's just late—"

"We'll worry about al-Fahd later, Sam." Yesilkov's chest was rising and falling rapidly. Ella could almost see the pulse beating in the other woman's throat.

"We can't risk," Yesilkov continued, "this meeting breaking up—because they're spooked by al-Fahd's no-show or fer any other reason. Y'er just afraid t' take additional action—y' wanta be able to pretend it's all one event that happened and you just were sorta on the scene. Y'er afraid of gettin' al-Fahd on a one-ta-one basis, that's fine. I'm not. But we can't lose these—or else we'll be pickin' 'em off till we're old and gray. We gotta go *now* if we're gonna. Fourteen outa fifteen ain't half bad.''

"Yeah, I guess," said Yates. But his arms were crossed over his chest.

Ella didn't blame Yates for hesitating: they'd conceived this as one fell swoop, a chance to take out the entire Club. Or the two security officers had. Ella was here primarily because they didn't trust what she might do if she weren't a party to this murderous scheme.

The only thing they needed her for was protection—protection from the aftermath of what all three of them were about to do.

Now that they were on the verge of taking this action, Ella staggered under an avalanche of doubts. But Yates didn't.

He said, "Okay, Sonya. If you're all enabled in there, I'm going to push this thing and see what happens."

"Goddamn, Sam, just *do* it, okay?"

Sam Yates reached down to touch what seemed to be a transceiver in a holster on his hip and depressed a red button there.

Nothing happened. Not in the hallway, not visibly. But behind the closed and curtained glass door of Le Moulin Rouge, the phial that the Afrikaner maintenance man had wired into the lighting system above the inside door burst. Burst in a vacuum-sealed chamber that couldn't be opened until Yates pushed another button, a chamber that had been "reconstructed" to order by Sonya Yesilkov's compromised maintenance man, who left the Security seal mechanisms operational—controlled by the remote on Yates' hip.

Ella bit her lip, envisioning in her mind's eye what was—or soon would be—going on behind the pretty pink curtains of Le Moulin Rouge.

Yates shook Ella's arm. "Okay, let's move."

She'd been drilled in the scheme; she knew what she had to do. She resented terribly how Yates had involved her in this. He'd done it because she'd involved them with Taylor, he'd explained gently. Now that she was an accessory to imminent murder, she hated Sam Yates and Sonya Yesilkov and everything they stood for, hated them more than she'd thought it possible to hate.

With wooden steps she paced Yates down the hall, toward the remaining guards.

The trio faced the three men with plasma guns who were guarding the Club while it celebrated; Ella was certain that the hard eyes of the men facing them could see right through to her guilt. She began to sweat.

Yesilkov said, "Okay, fellas. We're showing you ours; you show us yours." Both Yesilkov and Yates had their ID folios out and open.

One guard said, "Go, 'way, lady, we been through all this before." Another elbowed the first and muttered in what Ella thought was German. The third peered over Ella's head as if there might be someone hostile approaching behind her.

Then the first man sighed, "Okay, okay, officers, just hold on a minute," and Ella realized that the fellow was not only jumpy, but having a hard time in the Moon's lower gravity: his motions were awkward, exaggerated.

As he and his German compatriot got out their identification, the third guard was still watching the corridor down which Ella had come, watching warily; watching through narrowed eyes whose pupils were pinned.

One false move, Ella realized, and that man's gun was going to go off. He already had his finger on its trigger, something she'd learned from Yates one wasn't supposed to do until one wanted to shoot something. Or someone.

"You, too, cowboy," said Yesilkov to the third guard as, down at the corridor's end, a carload of uniformed patrolmen pulled up and came racing toward them on foot.

From behind the glass door of Le Moulin Rouge, muffled screams began.

Ella could hear them, so the guards could too. She was just backing away from the Club guards when the one who'd never shown his ID raised his plasma discharger in one quick motion and fired.

Over the heads of the patrolmen in the hall, the ball of heat and flame hissed, blackening ceiling panels. Beneath it the security patrol hit the deck.

Closer to hand, everyone but the shooter froze: Yesilkov, Yates, the other two Club guards. All but Bradley, who threw herself against the corridor's far wall in uncontrollable terror.

She didn't even know she crumpled down it, her knuckles jammed against her teeth. Her eyes were on the Club guards, and everything was happening in slow motion.

The guard who had cleared his plasma discharger turned, stared at Ella for an instant, his eyes like shattered glass. Then he reached for the door, and Sonya Yesilkov put a needle from her stunner into the back of his neck.

Beyond the shooter, as he fell forward, something moved in Le Moulin Rouge. A bloody hand clutched the pink curtain, tearing it away as the owner of that hand, staring blankly, fell against the glass and slowly down it in a smear of gore.

After that everything moved at twice normal speed. Yesilkov was yelling at the two remaining guards to surrender their weapons and live to tell about it. Yates was reaching for those weapons and patting the men down for others they might be hiding. The English-speaking guard was protesting that they'd never get away with this, whatever the hell it was they thought they were doing.

And Ella Bradley was sitting on the floor of the corridor, slumped against the wall, her knuckles still pressed against her teeth, trying to watch it all through her tears.

Chapter 35

SECURITY MEASURES

The single remaining member of the Club was in his hotel suite when the lieutenant from Security came to call.

For al-Fahd, who had had the good sense to miss the dinner party he'd paid for, the upcoming interview held no threat. He assumed, and rightly, that he'd be asked why he wasn't at his own celebration.

So when Sonya Yesilkov, Lieutenant, UN Directorate of Security, Patrol Division, Company Four, strode in, a briefcase in hand, and introduced herself, al-Fahd could afford to be polite. Even accommodating.

There was nothing this female Russian in jackboots could do or say that would threaten him. If she came close to implying anything, or intuiting anything, or deciding to launch some investigation, al-Fahd would simply have her summarily demoted and dismissed from her post on the Moon. On Earth, dealing with people of her sort was something requiring minimal effort.

"Sit down, Lieutenant," he offered, and gestured to a gilded chair. This was the Presidential suite, but it was fit for a man of nobler blood than presidents, a man such as al-Fahd. "This is my chief security officer," he added, nodding to the silent man who stood in a corner, not bothering to introduce one flunky to the other. The names of these people were unimportant. "What can I do for you, Lieutenant?"

"Well, sir, y' see, I got some questions about what happened at Le Moulin Rouge—"

"We all do, Lieutenant, I assure you. We all do." Best to let the meaning sink in. This woman might be stupid. Stupid people could be troublesome. Revising his estimate of the situation, al-Fahd continued: "What sort of questions could there be that I might answer?''

"Well, sir, y' weren't there, and y'er on their guest list. Which is lucky for you an' all, but I gotta check everything out. Didya have some reason for skippin' that party? A threat y' took seriously and the others didn't? Some intelligence or other? Anything at all?''

"A bad stomach, Lieutenant, was what I had. As a matter of fact, I called the hotel doctor to attend me. Some side-effect of your one-sixth gravity, he assured me. And, as you said, it was lucky that I was feeling unwell.''

"Yeah, real lucky," the lieutenant muttered as she took furious longhand notes. "D'ya think y' could gimme any leads—who'da done such a thing? Why? Enemies that group had in common? Somebody who—''

"Lieutenant Yesilkova," said al-Fahd with the sharp and yet gentle tone he used on his racehorses, "this is none of your affair, such questions. This is a matter for the intelligence agencies of the various nations who have lost luminaries. Surely you realize you have neither the rank nor the connections to embark upon this sort of investigation?''
Translation: your career is on the line, and if you offend me I will see you in a work camp in North Yemen.

"Yeah, well, I guess that's right. Turn it over to the big guys.'' Yesilkov closed her notebook, stuffed it in a breast pocket already stressed by her bustline, and stood up. "Thanks for yer time, sir. I'll be going now.''

"You're welcome, Lieutenant. I hope your trip here was worthwhile. And I'm sorry I couldn't give you more time, but I'm very busy. This horrible tragedy has put a strain on all of us.''

"Yeah, I bet," said Yesilkov, walking backward toward the hotel room's door. "I'll just see myself out. Sorry t' bother ya, sir.''

The security lieutenant retreated hurriedly, fumbling for the door latch, then slipping out the door with a final, nervous wave.

Five minutes later al-Fahd's British bodyguard said, "Excuse me, sir, but that woman from Security left her bleedin' briefcase—'' and reached for it. . . .

The ensuing explosion rocked the entire floor of al-Fahd's hotel.

EPILOGUE

Sam Yates was exhausted. He'd spent four days covering his ass, and he'd done a good enough job of it. But his temper was real short.

So when Yesilkov came by to see if he was ready to break for dinner, he left without a word to Echeverria, the third-shift receptionist, about where he'd be if anybody needed him.

But Ella Bradley found him, eating pizza with Yesilkov on the Strip.

She pulled up in a big, six-place car with USG plates that idled by the curb, and got out, flashing some leg as she did so. Right behind her came a guy nearly Yates' height but softer in build, a dark-haired man in loose clothing, which gave Yates a hint as to who the stranger might be.

The fact that the car was chauffeured and didn't move from the curb, just sat there forcing traffic out and around it, was a good enough hint anyhow.

Yates leaned over the table to Yesilkov, who was catching strings of pizza cheese with her tongue, and said, "Don't look now, but if that's not Peck Smith who's with Ella, lay you odds it's Taylor McLeod himself."

Yesilkov craned her neck and said around the mouthful she was chewing, " 'S not Peck Smith."

"That's what I figured," Yates said, and stretched with more insouciance than he felt as Ella and the man with the briefcase came toward their table.

Bradley waved like she was at some embassy staff picnic, smiling broadly. The man beside her had perfectly cut dark, straight hair, a level gray-eyed gaze, and features that had probably reached the New World on the Mayflower.

Yates detested him at first sight.

"Hiya, Ella, what's shakin'?" he said, without getting up the way the big guy obviously thought he should. Beside Yates, Yesilkov nodded primly and slid down in her chair, hunching over the table as if she could make herself a smaller target.

"Samuel Yates, Sonya Yesilkov, I'd like you meet Taylor McLeod. May we join you?" Ella said.

Dusting off your best manners for him, huh? Okay, any number can play. "Be our guests," said Yates, waving openhandedly to the plastic chairs around the small, street-café tables.

McLeod somehow met that hand with his and shook Yates' firmly. "I've been looking forward to this meeting, Supervisor," McLeod's voice was low and devoid of r's, so Yates' rank sounded like "supahvisah." "Both Ella and Peck Smith have told me some tall tales about you."

You mean you don't trust me either? Well, we've got our cards on the table, then. "I bet. As far as Sonya and I are concerned, that's all they are—tales, rumors, baseless stories . . . kinda thing happens sometimes when people are jammed together like this with not a helluva lot to do. . . . "

"Good." McLeod nodded approvingly, as if Yates had just ridden his first bike with no training wheels. "Let's keep it that way, shall we?"

"You don't have ta worry 'bout us, sir," Yesilkov put in, nervously picking at pizza cheese going rubbery on the plastic plate between them. "Pizza?" she said brightly, shoving the half-eaten pie toward the two newcomers with one finger.

"Ah, thanks no," said McLeod, unbuttoning the single button on his suit jacket before leaning back in his chair. Ella, beside him, was peering at Yates with an imploring look.

For the life of him, Sam Yates couldn't figure out what it was that Ella Bradley wanted him to say or do. But McLeod's fiddling with his suitcoat jogged Yates' memory. "You know, I owe you a suit, I guess."

"Think nothing of it," said McLeod with a decrecatory

wave. "You may well have saved Ella's life. A decent suit is the least you deserve."

A decent suit? In any other circumstances I'd find a way to let you know what a clown outfit that is you're wearing, you overranked butler. . . . Easy, Sam: she wants you to be nice.

"Whatever," Yates said aloud. "I ordered you one—same Savile Row tailor, same material, close as the guy could come, anyhow. Said he didn't have just the same bolt, but he had something you'd liked that was similar. I had him ship it up here, since I knew where your office was."

McLeod smiled politely, this time meeting Yates' eyes. Sam Yates sat up straight. You didn't mess with somebody who looked at you like that, not unless you had a damned good reason.

And Ella wasn't saying a word, just sitting there watching her hands in her lap.

McLeod replied, though, in a confidentially low tone of voice: "Nice detection on your part, Supervisor Yates—finding my tailor. But really, you needn't have bothered. Returning the one Ella loaned you will do—"

"One she loaned me's got blood and serum stains that aren't going to come out of merino wool, I've been told by experts. Let's cut the small talk. What do you want with me—us?" He shot a look at Yesilkov.

Ella put her folded hands on the table, and Sam Yates noticed a ring she hadn't worn before. Then he knew what they wanted here—or hoped he did.

Before Taylor could comment about the bloodstains, Ella said, "Sam, Ting—Taylor and I—are announcing our engagement next week. We wanted you to be the first to know." She smiled wanly.

Sam Yates wanted to ask if it was his fault if she wanted this guy, or was just paying off for everybody's mess: Yates', Yesilkov's, her own. But he couldn't do that.

"That's great. Congratulations. I guess that means you'll be leaving the Moon for greener pastures."

In the awkward silence only Yesilkov laughed, an explosive little burst.

"It means nothing of the sort," Ella Bradley said archly,

with a glint in her eye. "We'll be working here, both of us, until the wedding next year. And probably thereafter."

"So," said Yates, nodding his head. "I don't know if you want or need any assurances from me, McLeod, about how closely held the truth is—"

"I don't need any such thing, *Yates*," said Taylor McLeod, stressing a form of address he obviously considered inappropriate. "But Ella wanted you two to know in no uncertain terms that we've got matters well in hand. There's no need to be concerned or to follow up in any way. I suppose, although it's irregular, it's our thank-you gift to you two. You just go about your business as usual, and there will *be* no repercussions. You have my word on it." Taylor McLeod stood up and again offered Yates his hand.

The USIA man's grasp was as firm and dry now as it had been previously. Ella's, when she offered it, was moist and cold.

He looked hard at her and said very softly, "You okay, babe?"

She nodded, and again he caught the twinkle in her eye. She said good-bye to Yesilkov politely, and she and McLeod walked back to their car.

Yates waited until he'd seen McLeod take her hand and help her decorously into its rear seat before he took another breath. The car door slammed and the big machine moved off into traffic.

"Chrissake," muttered Yesilkov, "I feel like I just been interrogated."

"Vetted, more like," Sam Yates murmured, easing down in his own chair to prod his greasy pizza. "But it's nice to know they aren't going to try and hang this mess on us—not soon, not someday, not ever."

"Oh yeah," said Sonya Yesilkov with laughter in her voice. "And it's nice to know that your girlfriend's plannin' on seein' y' now and again, even though she's landed her an upscale husband."

"Nah, that's not why she came. You're wrong. That one gets married, she'll *be* married . . . like you and me don't know how to—"

Yesilkov cocked her head at him and made a derisive

noise that caused Yates to recall the odd look Ella had given him. Promise or apology, surely. But he was damned if he knew which.

Then Yesilkov started to laugh teasingly, and he found himself joining in, protesting, ''Look, get off my back, Sonya. Knowing the McLeods 'socially' has got to be better than Leavenworth. Not only did we come out of this alive, but we've still got our jobs and each other. And friends in high places . . .''

You couldn't get much higher than the Moon.